HALF A DOZEN GIRLS

ANNA CHAPIN RAY

1st WORLD
LIBRARY
Literary Society

Half a Dozen Girls

Anna Chapin Ray

© 1st World Library, 2008
PO Box 2211
Fairfield, IA 52556
www.1stworldlibrary.com
First Edition

LCCN: 2007935354

Softcover ISBN: 978-1-4218-9306-8
Hardcover ISBN: 978-1-4218-9406-5
eBook ISBN: 978-1-4218-9206-1

Purchase *"Half a Dozen Girls"*
as a traditional bound book at:
www.1stWorldLibrary.com/purchase.asp?ISBN=978-1-4218-9306-8

1st World Library is a literary, educational organization
dedicated to:

- Creating a free internet library of downloadable ebooks

- Hosting writing competitions and offering book publishing
  scholarships.

Interested in more 1st World Library books? contact:
literacy@1stworldlibrary.com
Check us out at: www.1stworldlibrary.com

1st World Library Literary Society

Giving Back to the World

"If you want to work on the core problem, it's early school literacy."

- James Barksdale, former CEO of Netscape

"No skill is more crucial to the future of a child, or to a democratic and prosperous society, than literacy."

- Los Angeles Times

"Literacy... means far more than learning how to read and write... The aim is to transmit... knowledge and promote social participation."

- UNESCO

"Literacy is not a luxury, it is a right and a responsibility. If our world is to meet the challenges of the twenty-first century we must harness the energy and creativity of all our citizens."

- President Bill Clinton

"Parents should be encouraged to read to their children, and teachers should be equipped with all available techniques for teaching literacy, so the varying needs and capacities of individual kids can be taken into account."

- Hugh Mackay

TO MY PARENTS

I OFFER THESE MEMORIES OF A HAPPY,
NAUGHTY CHILDHOOD.

My fairest child, I have no song to give you;
No lark could pipe to skies so dull and gray:
Yet, ere we part, one lesson I can leave you
For every day.

"Be good, sweet maid, and let who will be clever;
Do noble things, not dream them, all day long:
And so make life, death, and that vast forever
One grand, sweet song."

CHARLES KINGSLEY.

CONTENTS

CHAPTER I

THE ADAMS FAMILY

"'There was a little girl,
And she had a little curl,
And it hung right down over her forehead;
And when she was good,
She was very, very good,
And when she was bad, *she was horrid*!'"

"And that's you!" chanted Polly Adams in a vigorous crescendo, as she watched the retreating figure of her guest. Then climbing down from her perch on the front gate, she added to herself, "Mean old thing! I s'pose she thinks I care because she's gone home; but I'm glad of it, so there!" And with an emphatic shake of her curly head, she ran into the house.

Up-stairs, in the large front room, sat her mother and her aunt, busy with their sewing. The blinds were closed, to keep out the warm sun of a sultry July day, and only an occasional breath of air found its way in between their tightly turned slats. The whir of the locust outside, and the regular creak, creak of Aunt Jane's tall rocking-chair were the only sounds to break the stillness. This peaceful scene was ruthlessly disturbed by Polly, who came flying into the room and dropped into a chair at her mother's side.

"Oh, how warm you are here!" she exclaimed, as she pushed back the short red-gold hair that curled in little, soft rings about her forehead.

"Little girls that will run on such a day as this must expect to be warm," remarked Aunt Jane sedately, while she measured a hem with a bit of paper notched to show the proper width. "Now if you and Molly would bring your patchwork up here, and sew quietly with your mother and me, you would be quite cool and comfortable."

"Patchwork!" echoed Polly, with a scornful little laugh. "Girls don't sew patchwork nowadays, Aunt Jane."

"It would be better for them if they did, then," returned Aunt Jane severely. "It is a much more useful way of spending one's time, than embroidering nonsensical red wheels and flowers and birds on your aprons, as you have been doing. Your grandmother used to make us sew patchwork; and before I was your age, I had pieced up three bedquilts,—one rising-sun, one fox-chase, and the other just plain boxes."

"I don't care," Polly interrupted saucily; "I never could see the use of cutting up yards and yards of calico, just for the sake of sewing it together again. Wouldn't you rather have me make you a pretty apron, Jerusalem?" And she leaned over to pat her mother's cheek affectionately, as she added, "And besides, Molly's gone home."

"Has she?" asked Mrs. Adams, in some surprise. "I thought she was going to spend the day."

Polly blushed a little.

"So she was," she admitted at length; "but she changed her mind."

Mrs. Adams looked at her little daughter inquiringly for a moment, and seemed about to speak, but catching the eye of Aunt Jane, who was watching them sharply, she only said,—

"I am sorry; for I wanted to send a pattern to Mrs. Hapgood, when she went home, and now I shall have to wait."

"I'll take it over now, mamma; I'd just as soon." And Polly jumped up and caught her sailor hat from the table where she had tossed it.

"I should like to have you, if you will, Polly. It is in my room, and I'll get it for you."

She put down her work and went out into the hall, followed by Polly.

"Have you and Molly been quarrelling again?" she asked, when the door had closed between them and Aunt Jane.

"Only a little bit, mamma," confessed Polly. "Molly was teasing me all the time, and at last I was mad, so I said I wished she'd go home, and she went right straight off."

"I am sorry my daughter should be so rude to her company," began Mrs. Adams soberly.

"So'm I," interrupted Polly; "I don't mean to; but she makes me cross, and before I know it I flare up. I wish she hadn't gone, too; for we promised to go over to see Florence this afternoon, and she'll think it is queer if we don't."

"I wish you would try to be a little more patient, Polly," said her mother. "You mustn't be cross every time that Molly laughs at you; and you answered Aunt Jane very rudely just now. You need to watch that tongue of yours, my dear, and not let it run away with you. And now take this to Mrs. Hapgood, and tell her she will need to allow a good large seam when she cuts it, for Molly is taller than you."

"Yes'm," said Polly meekly, as she held up her face for the kiss, without which she never left the house.

Then she slowly went down the stairs, and out at the door, thinking over what her mother had just said to her, and resolving, as she did at least twice every day, that she would never, never quarrel with Molly again. But not in vain had Mrs. Adams devoted the past thirteen years to watching her only child, and she understood Polly's present mood well enough to call to her from the window,—

"You'd better bring Molly back to lunch, I think. We're going to have raspberry shortcake, and you know she likes that."

And Polly looked up, with a brightening face, to answer,—

"All right."

Then, in spite of the warm day, she went hurrying off down the street, while her mother stood by the window, watching until the bright curls under the blue sailor hat had passed out of sight. Then she turned away with a half-smile, saying to herself,—

"Poor Polly! She has hard times fighting her temper; but Molly does tease her unmercifully. After all, she comes naturally by it, for she's very much as I was, at her age."

"What's the matter?" queried Aunt Jane, as her sister came

Anna Chapin Ray

back and took up her work once more. "Have Molly and Polly been having another fuss?"

"Nothing serious, I think," said Mrs. Adams lightly.

Aunt Jane's thin lips straightened out into an ominous line as she answered,—

"Strange those two children can't get on together! I think it is largely Polly's fault, for Molly is a sweet, quiet girl. You are spoiling Polly, Isabel, as I keep telling you. Some day you'll come to realize it, and be sorry."

Mrs. Adams bit her lip for an instant, and a clear, bright color came into her cheeks; but after a moment she replied quietly,—

"You must allow me to be the judge of that, Jane."

"Of course you can do as you like with your own child," retorted Aunt Jane stiffly; "but I can't shut my eyes to what is going on around me, and let a naturally good child be spoiled for want of a firm hand, without saying a word to stop it. Your mother didn't bring you up in that way, Isabel, though she did indulge you a great deal more than she did us older children."

As Aunt Jane paused, Mrs. Adams rose abruptly and left the room, saying something about a letter which she must write in time for the next mail.

Aunt Jane could be exasperating at times, as even her younger sister was forced to admit, and occasionally she was driven to the necessity of running away from her, rather than yield to the temptation of answering sharp words with sharper. Mrs. Adams could and did bear patiently with unasked advice in all matters but one; but in regard to the discipline of her little daughter she stood firm, for she and her husband had agreed that here Aunt Jane was not to be allowed to interfere. Yet, though Aunt Jane soon found that her sister left her and went away whenever the subject was mentioned, the worthy woman was not to be turned aside, but returned to the charge with unfailing persistency.

The intimacy between mother and daughter was a peculiar one, and at times seemed far more like that between two sisters. Mrs. Adams was one of the women whose highest ambition was of the rather old-fashioned kind,—to make a pleasant, homelike home, and to be an intelligent, helpful wife and mother. From her quiet corner she looked out at her friends who had "careers," with curiosity rather than envy, and, for herself, was content to have her world bounded by the interests of her husband and Polly. It might be a narrow life, but it was a busy and a happy one. With all her household cares, she still found time to look into the books which were interesting her husband, and intelligently discuss their contents with him; she read aloud with Polly, played games with her, and watched over her with a quick under-standing of this warm-hearted, impetuous little daughter, in whom she saw herself so closely reflected that she knew, from the memory of her own childhood, just how to deal with all of Polly's freaks and whims. And her endless patience and devotion were well rewarded, for Polly adored her pretty, bright little mother with all the fervor of her being. There were times, it is true, when Polly rebelled against all restraint; but such moments were of short duration, and, for the most part, she yielded easily to the pleasant, firm discipline which made duty enjoyable, and punishment the necessary result of wrong-doing, a result as hard for the mother to inflict as for the child to bear. In her gentler moods, Polly realized that nowhere else could she find so good a friend, so interested and sympathetic in all that concerned her, and the two spent long hours together, now talking quite seriously, now chattering and laughing like children, with a perfect good-fellowship which appeared very disrespectful to Aunt Jane, who believed in the old-time rule, that children should be seen, not heard. However, Polly never minded Aunt Jane's frown in the least, but went on playing with her mother and petting her, confiding to her her joys and sorrows, her friendships and her quarrels, and calling her by an endless succession of endearing names, of which her latest was Jerusalem, an epithet taken from her favorite, "Oh, Mother dear, Jerusalem," and adapted to its present use, to the great mystification of her aunt, to whom Polly refused to explain its derivation.

Between his office hours and his patients, Polly saw but little of her father; for Dr. Adams was the popular physician of the large, quiet, old New England town where they lived. A man who had grown up among books, and among thinking, wide-awake people, he was a worthy descendant of the two presidents with whom he claimed kinship. He was a strong, fine-looking man, so full of quiet energy that his very presence in the sick-room was encouraging to the invalid; and he had come to be at once the friend, physician, and adviser of every family in town, whether rich or poor. If his patients could afford to pay him for his visits, very well; if not, it was just as well, for neither Dr. Adams nor his wife desired to be rich. To live comfortably themselves, to lay up a little for the future, and to be able to help their poorer neighbors, now and then,—this was all they wished, and this was easily accomplished. In past years, two or three other doctors had settled in the town; but after a few months of trial they had closed their offices and gone away, because not one of Dr. Adams's patients could be tempted to leave him, and his lively black horse and shabby buggy were seen flying about the streets, while their shiny new carriages either stood idle in their stables, or were taken out for an occasional pleasure drive.

If Polly had been asked what was her greatest trial, her answer, truthful and emphatic, would have been: "Aunt Jane." It was a mystery to her as, indeed, it was to every one else, how two sisters could be so unlike. Mrs. Adams was a pretty, graceful little woman, with a dainty charm about her, and a winning, off-hand manner, which made her a favorite with both young and old. Aunt Jane Roberts was tall and thin, with a cast-iron sort of countenance, surmounted by a row of little, tight, gray frizzles of such remarkable durability that, though evidently the result of art rather than nature, neither wind nor storm, appeared to have any effect upon them. On festal occasions it was her habit to adorn herself with a symmetrical little blue satin bow, placed above these curls and slightly to one side; but there was nothing in the least flippant or coquettish about this decoration, for it was as precise and unvarying as the gray frizz below it, and only seemed to intensify the hard, unyielding lines of her face.

Miss Roberts was fifteen years older than her sister, and she appeared to have been stamped with the seal of single blessedness while she still lay in her cradle and played with her rattle;—that is, if she ever had unbent so far as to play with anything. Even her walk was not like that of most women; she moved along with a slow, deliberate stride which was at times almost spectral, and reminded one of the resistless, onward march of the fates. Aunt Jane was serious-minded and progressive, and, worst of all, she was conscientious. However great a blessing a conscience must be considered, there are some consciences that make their owners extremely unpleasant. Whenever Aunt Jane was particularly trying, her friends brought forward the singular excuse: "Jane is *so* conscientious; she means to do just right." And she certainly did. So far as she could distinguish its direction, Aunt Jane trod the path of duty, but she trod it

Anna Chapin Ray

as a martyr, not like one who finds it a pleasant, sunshiny road, with bright, interesting spots scattered all along its way. She had advanced ideas about women and pronounced theories as to the rearing of children; she was a member of countless clubs, and served on all the committees to talk about reform; she visited the jail periodically, and marched through the wards of the hospital with a stony air of sympathy highly gratifying to the inmates, who tried to be polite to her because of her relationship to the doctor, whom they all adored. The demands of her public duties left Miss Roberts little time for home life; but in the few rare intervals, she sewed for her sister, refusing the more attractive work, and devoting herself to sheets, pillow-cases, and kitchen towels, in the penitential, self-sacrificing way which is so trying to the person receiving the favor. She appeared to regard these labors as an offset to the frank criticisms of her sister's housekeeping, which she never hesitated to make when the opportunity offered. Aunt Jane had come to live with her sister soon after Mrs. Adams was married; and the doctor's happy, even temper enabled him to make the best of the situation, though he had at once given Miss Roberts to understand that she was in no way to interfere with him or his concerns.

No introduction to the Adams family would be complete which failed to mention Job Trotter, for Job was a faithful servant who had done good service for many a long day. He was the old family horse whom the doctor had driven for years, but who, owing to age and infirmity, had been put on the retired list as a veteran, and given over to the tender mercies of Mrs. Adams. She changed his youthful nickname of Trot to the more fitting one of Job, and stoutly maintained his superiority to the lively colt that succeeded him between the thills of the doctor's buggy. Job, too, appeared to share her opinion, and never failed to give a vicious snap at his rival, whenever they came in contact. There was a family legend that Job had been a fast animal in his day, and Mrs. Adams often told the story of the doctor's first ride after him: how, at the end of a mile, he had turned his pale face to the horse-dealer who was driving, and piteously besought him: "In mercy's name, man, let me get out; I've had enough of this!" But all this was enveloped in the haze of the remote past, and now Job was neither a dangerous nor exhilarating steed, but rather, a restful one, who allowed his driver to contemplate the landscape and impress its charms upon his memory. Job had been twenty-three years old when the doctor handed him over to his wife; and, as if to prove his relationship to the family, and to Aunt Jane in particular, he had never advanced a year in age since then, but, long, long afterwards, his headstone bore the legend:

IN MEMORY OF
JOB TROTTER,
A FAITHFUL FRIEND,
WHO DIED AT THE AGE OF TWENTY-THREE.

A rear view of Job still showed him a fine-looking horse, for his delicate skin, slightly dappled here and there, his long, thick tail and proudly arching neck plainly betokened his aristocracy. But unfortunately, reckless driving in his youth had bent his fore legs to a decided angle, and turned in his toes in an absurdly deprecating fashion, until Mrs. Adams declared that she would put a skirt on him to cover these defects, unless people stopped turning to look after him and laugh.

But it was when he was in motion that Job exhibited his peculiarities to the best advantage. His ordinary gait was a slow, dignified walk, varied, at times, by a trot of which the direction was of the up-and-down species, and made his progress even slower than usual. But now and then the old fellow would seem to be inspired with a little of his former

Anna Chapin Ray

spirit, and, after a skittish little kick, he would straighten his body with a suddenness which brought Mrs. Adams to her feet, and rush off at a mad pace that soon faltered and failed, when the old brown head would turn, and the gentle eyes seem to say pleadingly,—

"I did try, but I can't."

In reality, the cause of Job's slowness lay, not so much in his age as in his afflicted knees; and they kept his driver in a constant state of anxiety as to which pair would give out next. Now his hind legs would suddenly fail him, and he would apparently attempt to seat himself in the dust; then, just as he had recovered from that shock, his front knees would collapse, and Job would plunge madly forward on his venerable nose.

But, after all, they had many a pleasant drive up and down the country roads, where the old horse plodded onwards, apparently enjoying the scenery as much as his mistress did, now stopping to graze by the roadside, now suddenly turning aside and, before his driver was aware of his intention, landing her in the dooryard of some farmhouse where the doctor had visited a patient years before. For Job had a retentive memory, and was never known to forget a road or a house where he had once been. During the last of the time that the doctor had driven him, he had lent him to do occasional service at funerals, where Job was never known to disgrace himself by breaking into an indecorous trot. Something in the ceremony of these melancholy journeys had struck Job's fancy and impressed the circumstances on his memory to such an extent that, ever after, he was reluctant to pass the cemetery gate, but tugged hard at the lines to show his desire to enter. It was not so bad when Mrs. Adams and Polly were by themselves; but Mrs. Adams often invited some convalescing patient of the doctor to go for a quiet little drive, and it was mortifying to have Job, taking advantage of the moment when his mistress was deep in conversation, stalk solemnly under the arching gateway and bring his invalid passenger to a halt beside some new-made grave. There seemed to be no apology that could fitly meet the occasion and do away with the gloomy suggestiveness of the situation.

Aunt Jane rarely had time to drive with Job, for an ordinarily fast walker could pass him by; but Polly and her mother enjoyed him to the utmost, and spoiled him as much as they enjoyed him, letting him stroll along as he chose, stopping whenever and wherever he wished. To avoid being dependent on the man, who was often away driving the doctor upon his rounds, Mrs. Adams had learned to harness Job herself, and nearly every pleasant day she could be seen buckling the straps and fastening him into the carriage, while the old creature stood quiet, rubbing his head against her shoulder, now and then, with a gentle, caressing motion, or turning suddenly to pretend to snap at Polly, who was much in awe of him, and then throwing up his head and showing his teeth, in a scornful laugh at her fear.

This was the family circle in which Polly Adams had spent the thirteen happy years of her life, respecting and loving her father, adoring her mother, and continually coming in conflict with Aunt Jane. And Polly herself? Like countless other girls, she was good and bad, naughty and lovable by turns, now yielding to violent fits of temper, now going into the depths of penitence for them; but always, in the inmost recesses of her childish soul, possessed with a firm resolve to be as good a woman as her mother was before her. She knew no higher ambition.

CHAPTER II

THE V

Everybody in town knew the Hapgood house. It stood close to the street, under a row of huge elms, and surrounded with clumps of purple and white lilac bushes whose topmost blossoms peeped curiously in at the chamber windows. Such houses are only found in New England, but there they abound with their broad front "stoops," the long slant of their rear roofs, where a ladder is firmly fixed, to serve in case of fire, and the great, low rooms grouped around the immense chimney in the middle. The Hapgood house had been in the family for generations, and was kept in such an excellent state of repair that it bade fair to outlast many of the more recent houses of the town. A wing had been built out at the side; but even with this modern addition, no one needed to glance up at the date on the chimney—sixteen hundred and no-matter-what—to assure himself of the great age of the stately old house before him.

Up in the Hapgood attic a serious consultation was going on.

"Now, girls," Polly Adams began solemnly, "'most half of our vacation has gone, and I think we ought to do something before it's over."

"Aren't we doing something this very minute, I should like to know?" inquired Molly Hapgood, who had felt privileged, in her capacity as hostess, to throw herself down on the old bed which occupied one corner of the garret.

Polly frowned on such levity.

"I don't mean that, Molly, and you know it. What I think is, that we should get together regularly every two or three days and do something special. Aunt Jane is in lots of clubs and things, and—"

"I've heard it said," interrupted Jean Dwight solemnly, "that Aunt Jane spent so much time doing good outside that she never had a chance to be good at home." "Now, Jean, that isn't fair," said Polly laughing. "You know I'd be the very last one to hold up Aunt Jane as an example, only she has such good times with her everlasting old people that I thought we might do something like it."

"Which do you propose to do," asked Molly disrespectfully, "start a society for the improvement of the jail or open a mission at the poor-house to teach Miss Bean some manners?"

"Let's have a dramatic club, and get up a play," suggested the fourth member of the group, who was seated on a dilapidated hair-covered trunk under the open window, regardless of the strong east wind which now and then lifted a stray lock of her long yellow hair and blew it forward across her cheek.

"What a splendid idea, Florence!" said Jean, rapturously bouncing about in her seat on the foot of the bed. "How does that suit you, Polly?"

"We might do that, for one thing," assented Polly cautiously;

Anna Chapin Ray

"but oughtn't we to try something a little—well, a little improving, too." "I'd like to know if that wouldn't be improving?" asked Molly. "It would teach us to act, and then, if we wanted, we could charge an admission fee and raise some money."

"I think it would be splendid, girls," said Polly, in spite of herself carried away by the prospect, and forgetting her own plan. "What shall we take?"

"Let's take 'Uncle Tom's Cabin,'" said Jean. "We could make it over into a play easily enough, and Florence would be just the one for Eva. Alan could be Uncle Tom, you know."

"I think we could get something better than that," remarked Florence, in some disgust. "If I'm Eva, I'll have to die, and I don't know the first thing about that."

"Oh, that's easy enough," answered Molly, with the air of one who had experience; "just stiffen yourself out and fall over. But I don't believe you could ever get Alan to act."

"Why not take a ready-made play?" asked Polly. "It would save ever so much work."

"What is there?" said Molly, sitting up to discuss the matter.

"We don't want any Shakespeare," added Jean; "that's all killing, and Florence doesn't want to go dead, you know."

"I'll tell you what, girls," said Molly, as if struck with a sudden idea, "we'll have an original play, and Jean shall write it."

Florence and Polly applauded the suggestion, while Jean groaned,—

"I can't, girls. I never could in this world."

"Yes, you can," returned Molly, who had firm faith in her friend's ability. "You go right to work on it, and you ought to get it all done in a week or two, so we can give it before school opens."

"And we want just five people in it," said Polly. "I know I can get Alan to act, if Molly can't."

Molly shrugged her shoulders incredulously, while Jean inquired, with the calmness of desperation,—

"What shall it be about?"

"John Smith and Pocahontas," replied Polly promptly. "He almost gets killed, and doesn't quite; so that will get the audience all stirred up, but save the trouble of dying."

"But that only needs three," observed Florence thoughtfully, "and there are five of us."

"Doesn't he take her home to England, I'd like to know? There's a picture in the history where he shows Pocahontas to the queen. One of us can be king, and the other queen."

"But at court there are always lots of people round," remonstrated Florence, with an eye to the truth of the situation.

"Never mind; we can make believe that the queen has sent them off, so as not to scare Pocahontas; that's what they call poetical license," said Polly. "Jean can see about that. There are lots of splendid things to wear, right here in this garret. Don't you suppose your mother would let us take them, Molly?"

Anna Chapin Ray

"Yes, I know she will," replied Molly.

There was silence for a moment, while the girls considered the matter. Then Polly returned to her first charge.

"But it will take a good while to get ready to start this, so I'd like to suggest our doing something else, while we wait."

"Polly has something in her head," said Jean. "Tell us what 'tis, Poll,"

"Well, I'll tell you," said Polly, as she rose and began to walk up and down the floor. "Aunt Jane was scolding, the other day, because I hadn't read 'Pilgrim's Progress.' She said it was a living disgrace to me, and that I must do it, right off. Now, what if we have a reading club and do it together? Have any of you read it? I don't believe you ever have."

The girls admitted that they had not.

"That's just what I thought," said Polly triumphantly. "It's so stupid that I can't do it alone, for I read the first page yesterday, and I know. But we don't any of us want to be 'a living disgrace'; so what if we read aloud an hour every other afternoon? 'T wouldn't take us so very long, and," here she laughed frankly, "I don't suppose it would hurt us any."

"I don't know but we ought to," remarked Molly virtuously, while Jean added,—

"I've heard people say it was like measles. You'd better take it young, if you did at all."

"When shall we begin?" demanded Polly, fired with enthusiasm at the prospect.

"To-morrow," said Molly; "and you'd better come here to read, for we can be nice and quiet up here. Come to-morrow at three, and we'll read till four."

"Oh!" exclaimed Florence, suddenly springing up, as a small, dark body came flying in at the open window above her head, and went tumbling across the floor and down the stairs.

"What was that?" asked Molly, rolling off the bed.

"A green apple. I think," replied Polly, as she ran after it and seized it. "Yes; here it is."

"That's Alan's doing," said Molly sternly, "I do wish he'd ever let us alone."

"I don't," said Polly, coming to his defence; "he's ever so much fun. I get tired of all girls."

"Thank you, ma'am," said Jean quickly, bowing low, in answer to the compliment.

But Polly missed the bow, for her curly head was out of the window, and she was laughing down at a slender, light-haired lad who was just taking fresh aim at the open window.

"Come up here, Alan!" she called.

"Oh, don't, Polly!" remonstrated Molly from within. "He'll laugh at us, and spoil all our fun."

"No, he won't," answered Polly valiantly; then, more loudly, "What did you say, Alan?"

"What are you girls about up there?" he inquired.

"Come up and see." And she drew in her head just in time to escape a second missile.

"All right; I'll come if you'll promise to play something, and not spend all your time gabbling." And Alan vanished through the side door. A minute or two afterwards, his shoes were heard clattering up the attic stairs.

The four girls, whom he found sitting in a row on the edge of the bed, were such good friends of him and of each other, that the five were commonly spoken of as "the V," or, sometimes, as "the quintette." Alan Hapgood, who was regarded as the point of the V, was a wide-awake, irrepressible youth of twelve, who had a large share in the doings of his older sister and her friends. They did their best to spoil him by their unlimited admiration; but, to be sure, the temptation to do so was a strong one, for Alan was a lovable fellow, always merry and good-natured, generous and accommodating to his friends, and quick to plan and execute the pranks which added the spice of mischief to the doings of the V. In person he was tall for his age, and slight, with thick, yellow hair, that lay in a smooth, soft line across his forehead, large gray eyes, and a generous mouth, full of strong, white teeth which were usually in sight, for Alan was nearly always laughing,—not a handsome boy, exactly, for his features were quite irregular, but a splendid one, whom one would instinctively select as a gentleman's son, and an intelligent, manly lad.

His sister Molly, two years older, was an attractive, bright girl, whose only beauty lay in her smooth, heavy braids of brown hair. She and Polly had been constant companions from their babyhood, had quarrelled and "made up," had quarrelled and made up again, three hundred and sixty-five days a year for the last thirteen years, and at the end of that time they were closer friends than ever. Two girls more unlike it would have been hard to find, for Molly was as quiet and deliberate as Polly was impetuous; but nevertheless, in spite of their continual disagreements, they were inseparable. They were in the same class in school and in Sunday-school, they had the same friends, and read the same books, and had a share in the same mischief. They even carried this trait so far as to both come down with mumps on the same day, when their unwonted absence from school was the source of much speculation among their friends, who fondly pictured them as indulging in some frolic, until the melancholy truth was known.

Next to Alan, Jean Dwight was the boy of the V, a strong, hearty, happy young woman of fourteen, who succeeded in getting a great deal of enjoyment out of this humdrum, work-a-day world. Her rosy cheeks glowed and her brown eyes shone with health; for Jean was as full of life as a young colt, and vented her superfluous energy in climbing trees, walking fences, and running races, until Aunt Jane and her followers raised their hands and eyes in well-bred horror. But Jean's unselfish devotion to her mother, her real refinement, her quick understanding, and her sound common sense did much to atone for her hoydenish ways, and gave promise of the fine womanhood which lay before her. At first it had been a matter of some surprise, in the aristocratic old town, that Mrs. Adams and Mrs. Hapgood, representatives of "our first families," as they were universally acknowledged to be, could allow their children to be so intimate with Jean Dwight, whose father was only a carpenter, and whose mother took in sewing. However, any comments were promptly silenced when Mrs. Adams had been heard to say, one day, that she was always glad to have Polly with such a womanly girl as Jean Dwight, so free from any nonsensical, grown-up airs. From that time onward Jean's position was an established fact.

Florence Lang was the acknowledged beauty of the V, a dainty maiden of thirteen, with fluffy, yellow hair, great blue eyes, and a pink and white skin which might have made a French doll sigh with envy. The only daughter of a luxurious home, she was always beautifully dressed, always quiet in her manners. No matter how excited and demoralized the rest of the V might become, Florence never failed to come out of the frolic as gentle and unspotted as she went in, greatly to the disgust and envy of Polly, whose clothes had a tendency to get mysteriously torn, whose shoes appeared to go in search of dust, and whose short, curly hair had a perfect genius for getting into a state of wild disorder. It was not that Florence seemed to take any more care of herself than the others, but she was naturally one of those favored beings to whom no particle of dust could cling, who could use none but the choicest language. Such gentle children have admirers enough; it is the luckless, quick-tempered Pollies, the warm-hearted, harum-scarum Jeans, who need a champion.

If Molly and Polly had never disagreed, the quintette would have been only a trio; for, when they were at peace, they were all in all to each other. But in times of strife Molly was devoted to Florence Lang, while Polly took refuge with Jean Dwight. In this way the V was formed; and though the closest intimacy was between Molly and Polly, the four girls were firm friends, and there were few days when they were not to be found together, usually either at the Hapgood house, or at Polly's, where their visit was never quite satisfactory unless Mrs. Adams was in the midst of the group. Alan, too, was often with them, for a tendency to rheumatism, which occasionally developed into a severe attack of the disease, kept him in rather delicate health, and prevented his entering into the athletic sports which are the usual amusement for lads of his age. But though he was thus, of necessity, thrown much with his sister and her girl friends,

Alan was far from belonging to that uninteresting species of humanity, the girl-boy; instead of that, he was a genuine, rollicking boy, with never a trace of the prig about him.

"Well, what was it you wanted of me?" Alan asked, as soon as his head reached the level of the attic floor.

"We didn't want you; you came," retorted Molly, with the frankness of a sister.

"No such thing; you called me,—at least, Polly did." And Alan marched across the floor to seat himself beside his champion, sure that there he would find a welcome.

He was not mistaken, for Polly remarked protectingly,—

"I did call you, Alan, for we want to have some fun, this horrid day, and we need you to stir us up."

"All right; how shall I go to work?" inquired Alan cheerfully. "Shall I dance a breakdown, or will you play tag?"

"Let's play hide-and-seek," suggested Jean; "it's so nice and dark up here, to-day."

"Wait a minute," interposed Florence. "Alan, we may as well tell you now: Jean is going to write a play for us to act, and you are going to be John Smith and have your head cut off."

"The mischief, I am!" with a prolonged whistle of surprise and disgust. "It strikes me I have something to say about what shall be done with my head."

"Stop using such dreadful expressions, Alan," said Molly primly. "You know mamma doesn't like to hear you say 'the mischief.'"

"Well, she didn't, 'cause she isn't here," returned Alan, in nowise abashed by his reproof. "And I don't believe she'd like to hear you girls planning to cut my head off, either."

"Oh, Alan, you goose!" said Polly. "John Smith's head wasn't cut off, for Pocahontas saved him, you know. All you'll have to do will be to lie down with your head on a stone, and have one of us girls get ready to hit you with a club."

"If you girls are going to manage the club," remarked the boy, with masculine scorn, "I'd much rather have you try to hit me, for then I'd be safe."

"That's a very old joke, Alan," said Jean, with disgust; "and besides, it isn't polite. You ought to be proud to be asked to have a part in our grand play."

"Will you act, or won't you?" demanded Polly sternly, as she seized him by his short, thick hair.

"Oh, anything to get peace," groaned Alan.

"Say yes, then."

"Yes."

"Very well. Now, you are to be ready whenever we want you; you are to do just what we want, and do it in just the way we want. Do you promise?"

"Yes, yes! But do hurry up and play something, or it will be dark before you begin."

"There!" said Polly, nodding triumphantly to the girls as she released him. "Didn't I tell you I'd get him to act?"

"You couldn't bribe him to keep out of it," said Jean, as they sprang up for their game.

The old attic was a favorite meeting-place for the V, who held high carnival there, now racing up and down the great floor and hiding in dark corners behind aged chests and spinning-wheels, now robing themselves in the time-honored garments which had done duty for various ancestors of the Hapgood family, and exchanging visits of mock ceremony, or inviting Mrs. Hapgood up to witness a remarkable tableau or an impromptu charade. Piles of illustrated papers filled one corner, and, when all else failed, the children used to pore over the sensational pictures of the Civil War, dwelling with an especial interest on the scenes of death and carnage. In another corner was arranged a long row of old andirons, warming-pans, and candlesticks, flanked by an ancient wooden cradle with a projecting cover above the head. Rows of dilapidated chairs there were, of every date and every degree of shabbiness,—those old friends which start in the parlor and slowly descend in rank, first to the sitting-room or library, then up-stairs, and so, by easy stages, to the hospital asylum of the garret. And up through the very midst of it all, midway between the two small windows which lighted the opposite ends of the attic, rose the huge gray stone chimney, like a massive backbone to the body of the house. What stories of the past the old chimney could have told! What descriptions of Hapgoods, long dead, who had warmed themselves about it! What secret papers had been burned in its wide throat! What sweet and tender home scenes had been enacted on the old settles ranged before its glowing hearths, which put to shame our tiny modern fireplaces and insignificant grates! But the old chimney kept its own counsel, and did not whisper a word, even to the swallows that built their nests in the crannies of its sides. If it had spoken, there would be no need for any one else to write of the doings of the V; for the chimney had silently watched the children day by day, and knew, better than any one besides, the simple story of their young lives.

"Now," Polly reminded them, as they were running down the stairs an hour later; "remember to come to-morrow at just three, all of you."

"What's up?" inquired Alan curiously.

"'Pilgrim's Progress,'" said Jean, as she leaped down from the fourth stair, and landed in an ignominious pile on her knees; "we're going to read it aloud together."

"I'm sorry for you, then," responded Alan. "Mother read it to me when I had scarlet fever, ever so long ago, and it's no end stupid."

"We're going to try it, anyway," said Polly, with an air of determination. "Come on, Jean; it's time I was at home. I'll see you to-morrow, girls."

CHAPTER III

THE GIRLS TRY TO IMPROVE THEIR MINDS

Polly's reading-club started off valiantly the next afternoon, and for an hour the girls read aloud industriously, while the rain pattered on the shingles above their heads. The experiment had all the charm of novelty, and the weather was in their favor, since there was little temptation to be out of doors; so, at the close of the first day, the reading was voted a great success. However, the next time there was a slight decrease in the interest, and Jean's suggestion as they sat down, that they should read for half an hour and play games the rest of the time, was hailed with delight by all but Polly, who was haunted by the possibility of being that "living disgrace" which Aunt Jane had pronounced her. Still, Polly was in the minority, and the change of programme was adopted. At the third meeting, Molly was the one to propose an adjournment at the end of the first quarter of an hour, and the girls were not slow to take advantage of the suggestion, and go rushing down-stairs, and out into the bright afternoon sunshine, to join Alan who was lazily swinging in the hammock, with his eyes fixed on the bits of white cloud that went drifting across the blue above him.

It was with an air of great decision that Polly marched up the attic stairs, two days later. She had purposely delayed her

Anna Chapin Ray

coming, and the others were anxiously awaiting her. The warm sun streamed in at the western window, and threw a golden light over the dainty summer gowns of the three girls who were in a row on the slippery haircloth seat of an old mahogany sofa, which had an empty starch-box substituted for its missing leg. Alan sat in front of them, placidly rocking to and fro, astride the cradle that he had dragged out into the middle of the floor, to serve as an easy-chair.

"Hurry up, Polyanthus," he remarked encouragingly. "These girls are scolding me like everything, and I want you to come and fight for me."

"Do help us to send him off, Polly," his sister begged. "He insisted on coming up here with us, even after I told him we didn't want him."

"Why don't you go out and play ball with the other boys, Alan?" urged Jean.

"Now, Jean, that's too bad!" said Polly, filled with righteous indignation. "It's not fair to twit Alan because there are some things he can't do."

"Let him be," said Florence; "he'll get so tired of it at the end of ten minutes, that nothing would tempt him to stay here."

"Good for you, Florence; you're a trump," returned Alan. "I promise you, I won't so much as speak, if you'll let me stay; but it's awfully dull doing nothing, and mother's bound I shan't play ball. You wouldn't catch me here, if I could."

"Ungrateful wretch!" exclaimed Polly, while Jean added,—

"No danger of your saying anything! You'll be sound asleep before we've read a page."

"What's the use of reading it, then?" was Alan's pertinent question.

"I'm sure I don't know," answered Florence. "It's one of Polly's ideas, or rather, Aunt Jane's."

"Aunt Jane ought to be ganched!" remarked Alan, with calm disrespect; for Polly made no secret of Aunt Jane's eccentricities, and they were a common subject of discussion among the V.

"I know it," confessed Polly, filled with shame at the thought of having such a relative.

"Come, Polly, what is the use of reading this poky old book?" urged Molly. "'T isn't doing any of us the least bit of good. I've listened just as hard as I could, and I'm sure I haven't any idea what it's all about, it's told in such a queer way."

Molly's use of the word "queer" said more than a dozen lesser adjectives. She had a singularly expressive manner of drawing it out, that threw untold meaning into its simple form. Alan used to declare that, if Molly once pronounced anything queer, its reputation was spoiled, as far as her hearers were concerned. This time Jean upheld her.

"It is very poky," she announced, as she pulled a bit of hair out from one of the holes in the cushion, and fell to picking it to pieces. "I think it's too warm weather for it, Polly. I don't care what Aunt Jane says; I'm not going to waste these glorious summer days over such stuff." And she pointed disdainfully at the book, a square, clumsy volume, bound in dingy black cloth covers.

Polly looked rather hurt.

"I know all that, girls," she began; "but an hour a day, and only every other day, too, isn't very much to spend on it."

"It's an hour too much, though, Polly," said Molly decisively. "This garret is so warm; wait till cooler weather, and then we'll try again. We shouldn't have time to finish it, anyway, before Jean had the play ready for us. How is it getting along, Jean?"

"Awfully!" confessed Jean. "Whenever I sit down to write, my head is as empty as an egg is, after you've blown it."

"Now, you girls let me plan for you," said Alan, moved to pity by Polly's downcast face. "You let your old book go till fall, and then start again, but only read half an hour a day. That's all your brains can take in, and I'll try to be on hand to explain it to you. How does that suit, Poll?"

"I suppose it will have to do," sighed Polly. "I hate to give up, now we've started; but if you won't read, you won't."

"Very true," remarked Jean, while Florence added,—

"Now, tell us truly, Polly, do you know what the man is talking about half the time?"

"No, I don't know as I do," admitted Polly.

"Then what do you want to read it for?" pursued Florence, determined to come to an understanding.

"Oh, it sounds sort of good, you know," said Polly vaguely; "just as if we ought to like it. 'Most everybody does read it, and I didn't know but, if we kept at it long enough, it might teach us a little something."

"Who wants to be taught? And besides, I'd rather have something a little fresher than this," said Jean, making no secret of her heresy.

"Polly! Polly!" called a voice from below.

Polly sprang up from the floor, where she had seated herself.

"That's mamma; what can she want?" she exclaimed, running to the window and putting her head out.

Down in the street sat Mrs. Adams in their low, two-seated carriage, while Job stood nodding sleepily in the sun, as he waited for the signal to proceed.

"Don't you girls want to go for a little drive?" she called, as her daughter's head came in sight.

In an instant three other heads appeared, and she was saluted with three voices,—

"How lovely!"

"What fun!"

"We'll be down in a minute."

The minute was a short one; for the girls snatched their hats in passing through the hall, and quickly surrounded the carriage, in a gay, laughing group. Alan came sauntering down the stairs after them, and stood leaning in the doorway, watching them settle themselves preparatory to starting. Something in the lad's position struck Mrs. Adams, and she beckoned to him.

"Come too, Alan; that is, if you can stand it with so many girls."

"May I? Is there room?"

He ran out to the carriage, then stopped, hesitating, as he saw Polly touch her mother's arm, and shake her head silently.

"I don't believe I'll go," he said, drawing back.

"Why not?" asked Mrs. Adams, in surprise.

"I don't think Polly wants me to," answered the boy frankly. "I don't want to be in the way." And he turned back to the house.

"'Tisn't that, mamma," said Polly, blushing at being caught. "I'd like to have Alan go, well enough, only I was afraid it would be too much for Job to take so many of us."

"In that case, you might have offered to be the one to give up," said her mother, in a low tone, which, though very gentle, still brought a deeper flush to Polly's face. Then she added to Alan, "Nonsense, my boy! You are thin as a rail, and don't weigh anything to speak of. Get in here this minute, and if Job gets tired, I'll make you all walk home."

Alan mounted to the front seat, where he made himself comfortable, with a boyish disregard of Florence's fresh pink gingham gown; Mrs. Adams shook the lines persuasively; Job waked and began to trudge along with an air of sombre patience which would have done credit to the scriptural original of his name.

"I am glad you are all of you used to Job," said Mrs. Adams smilingly, as they moved slowly down the main street and across the railroad track. "He really has been a valuable horse in his day, and there was a time when nothing could go by him,—why, what is the matter?" And she looked around at the girls on the back seat, as they burst into an irreverent laugh.

"Nothing, mamma," said Polly, leaning forward with her elbows on the back of the seat in front of her; "only we thought we'd heard you say something about it before."

"Let's drop them out, if they're so saucy," suggested Alan. "Don't you want me to drive, Mrs. Adams?"

"Thank you, Alan; but I don't dare trust you, when you are no more used to him, for he stumbles so. Go on, Job!" she added, with an inviting chirrup, as she leaned forward and rattled the whip up and down in its socket, to remind Job of its existence.

But Job was familiar with that operation, and from long experience he had learned its lack of significance. Accordingly, he only tilted one ear back towards his mistress, and went on at his former jog.

It was one of the finest days of the summer, one of the days when the season seems to have reached its height and appears to be standing still, for a moment, in the full enjoyment of its own beauty. A shower early in the day had washed away the dust, and every leaf and blossom by the roadside stood up in all the glad pride of its clean face, and turned its eyes disdainfully upward, away from the brown earth below. The girls chattered and laughed while they rode through the town, past the cemetery, where Mrs. Adams had some difficulty in overcoming Job's desire to turn in, across the long white bridge over the river, and through the quiet little village on its eastern bank. Then they turned southward, where the road lay over the level meadows, now past a great corn-field, now by the side of a piece of grass land dotted thickly with large yellow daisies. At their right was the broad

Anna Chapin Ray

blue river, shining like metal in the sun; before them rose the two mountains that watch over the old town, one beautiful in its irregular outlines, the other impressive in its bold dignity. No one who has lived near these hills can ever forget their spell. Though long years may have passed before his return, yet his first glance is always towards the bare, rugged cliffs, the wooded sides, and the white summit houses of these twin guardians of the quiet valley town.

"I believe I am perfectly happy," said Florence, with a sigh of content, as she leaned back and surveyed the meadows.

"I should be, if I could have some of those daisies," said Polly, pointing to a great bunch of them close by.

"Want 'em? All right, here goes!" And before Mrs. Adams could bring Job to a halt, Alan was out over the wheel.

"Don't stop; I can catch up with you," he called. "It's too hard work to get Job under way again."

He was as good as his word; for he hastily pulled up the flowers by the roots, came running after the carriage, and tossed them into Polly's lap.

"There! Now aren't you glad you brought me?" he exclaimed triumphantly, as he scrambled up the back of the carriage, like a monkey, and worked his way along to the front seat again. "You're a daisy, yourself, Alan," answered Polly, leaning out over the wheel to break off the roots. "These are lovely. Want some, girls?"

"It's going to rain to-morrow, I just know," said Molly, disregarding the daisies. "If it does, it will spoil our picnic, and that will be a shame."

"Oh, it won't rain," said Jean. "What makes you think so, Molly?"

"It always does," said Molly wisely, "when the hills look such a lovely dark blue. I heard somebody say so, ever so long ago, and I never knew it to fail."

"I don't believe in signs," remarked Polly vindictively, with her mouth full of daisy stems. "It's all just as it happens, only some people have a sign for everything. For my part, I'll wait till I see the rain coming, before I believe in it."

"That's Polly all over," said Alan. "She won't take anything on trust; she has to see it first."

"How did the reading come on to-day?" inquired Mrs. Adams, leaning back in her seat, and letting Job ramble from side to side of the road, at his will.

"Not very well," said Florence, seeing that none of the others started to reply.

"I hope I didn't break it up," Mrs. Adams answered, as she took out the whip, to brush a fly from Job's plump side.

Alan giggled.

"You needn't be afraid, Mrs. Adams; the girls are glad to get off on any terms."

"I'll tell you how 'tis, Mrs. Adams," said Jean, coming to the rescue, rather to Polly's relief. "You see, it's such warm weather, and the book wasn't real interesting, so we decided to let it go till by and by. Do you think we're very dreadful?" And she laughed up into Mrs. Adams's face, with perfect confidence in her approval.

Mrs. Adams laughed too.

"I didn't really think you would carry out your plan for very long," she said. "Polly takes Aunt Jane's words too seriously. In old times, everybody read 'Pilgrim's Progress,' but it's going out of fashion now, and—Whoa, Job! What are you doing?" she exclaimed, as the carriage tilted to one side so unexpectedly that Florence and Molly screamed a little.

Job, grieved at finding himself ignored and left out of the conversation, had apparently determined to amuse himself in his own way. He had meandered back and forth across the road, as was shown by the serpentine character of his tracks; now, catching sight of a tempting stalk of mullein by the fence, he had walked across the gutter and was just stretching his head forward to seize the coveted morsel, when Mrs. Adams interrupted him. Her first impulse was to draw him back, but kinder feelings prevailed, and she bent forward to give him the full length of the lines, saying indulgently,—

"The mischief is done already, Job, so you may as well have your lunch, for you can't tip us up any farther." And she sat there quite patiently, in spite of her strained position, until Job had devoured the mullein in a leisurely fashion. Then she reined him back into the road, remarking, "It isn't fair for poor Job to do all the work and not have any of the fun, is it?"

"I'll tell you, Mrs. Adams," suggested Alan; "let's all get out and put Job into the carriage, and draw him a mile or two, just to rest him."

"You shan't make fun of Job!" said Polly indignantly. "You didn't like what Jean said to you, and now you go and say, Job is o-l-d and s-l-o-w."

"What in the world do you spell the words for, Poll?" asked Jean. "I never have been able to make out."

"Why, Job knows what you are saying, as well as anybody, and may be he is sensitive about it," replied Polly, to the great amusement of the girls.

"We might read 'Pilgrim's Progress' to him, then," said Jean wickedly. "Perhaps it would teach him to go ahead, if he knows so much."

"Poor old Job! his going days are nearly over, aren't they, Joby?" said Mrs. Adams caressingly, as she rubbed the whip up and down over his glossy side. "Well, he's a poor, tired old fellow with a heavy load, so perhaps we'd better turn here and go home."

This proceeding met with Job's full approval. He had been walking more and more slowly, as if overcome by the effort which he had been forced to make, and seemed scarcely able to totter onward, stumbling at every stone. But with the change of direction, his life came back to him, and with a whisk of his tail and an ungainly flourish of his hind legs, he started off at a trot, turning neither to the right nor the left, but only intent on reaching home and supper.

"There!" said Mrs. Adams in a tone of disgust; "when Job does that I just want to whip him. He has played that trick on me over and over again, and still I am always deceived by it. It isn't more than two weeks since Polly and I were driving to the Glen, one very warm day. It was a strange road, and all at once Job was taken ill in such a queer way; he staggered and almost fell. Polly and I were so frightened, for we thought he was going to die, right then and there. We jumped out and walked along beside him, leading him and petting him. The road was so narrow that we couldn't turn him around,

Anna Chapin Ray

without going on ever so far; nobody was in sight, and we were both of us just ready to cry from sheer nervousness. At last we came to where we could turn him, and backed him around as carefully as could be. What did the old goose do but put down his head and give it the funniest sideways toss, and then trot off towards home, leaving us standing there in the road."

"What did you do? did you walk home?" asked Alan, while the girls laughed.

"No, indeed! We made him stop for us, and he had to trot the rest of the way, you may be sure. Go on, Job!" urged Mrs. Adams, shaking the lines violently.

But Job settled that matter by whisking his tail over the lines and holding them firmly, in spite of the attempts his mistress made to free them once more. Finding her labors of no avail, she turned her attention to the girls again.

"What if you take another plan for your reading?" she asked, pulling off one of her long gloves and turning slightly, as she rested her elbow on the back of the seat. "If you care to come to our house one or two mornings a week, through the rest of the vacation, and read aloud with me some good book,—I don't mean goody,—I should be delighted to have you. You could do the reading and amuse me while I sew."

"That's elegant!" exclaimed Jean rapturously. "What shall we read, girls?"

"But are you sure that you want us?" asked Florence doubtfully, for her mother was not particularly hospitable to the members of the V, and it seemed impossible to her that Mrs. Adams could be in earnest in her proposition.

"Indeed I do," responded Mrs. Adams heartily. "I can take that time for darning the doctor's stockings, and Polly's too, for that matter, for her toes are always coming through. I don't like to do it, but I shall be so well entertained that I probably shan't mind it at all."

"See here," said the practical Jean; "let's all bring our stockings to darn. There can't but one of us read at a time, and I just hate to do nothing but sit and twirl my thumbs."

"But I don't know how to darn stockings," said Florence helplessly.

"Time you did, then," said Jean. "If you had as many small brothers as I do, you'd have plenty of practice. Besides, I think any girl as old as we are ought to know how to mend her own stockings, whether she's rich or poor."

"So do I, Jean," said Mrs. Adams approvingly; "and yet I am ashamed to say that I have never taught Polly. But I think I'll add your plan to mine, and tell the girls to bring their darning-bags with them; and I will give you all lessons in a duty and necessity that can be made almost a fine art."

"I hate to sew," said Molly disconsolately.

"So do I," responded Jean calmly, "but I have to just the same; and that's the reason I thought I'd like to take the time when we read to do some of the worst things."

"I say," remarked Alan meditatively, as he plunged his hands into his pockets, "where's my share in this coming in?"

"Why, nowhere; you're nothing but a boy, you know," replied his sister, with an air of conscious superiority.

"One boy is as good as a dozen girls, though, ma'am," retorted Alan.

"Do you want to come too?" asked Polly. "He can, can't he, mamma?"

"I don't know as I want to, all the time," said Alan. "I'd like it when I can't do anything else; but when the boys are round, I'd rather be with them, of course."

"That settles it," said Polly, leaning forward to tickle his ear with a long-stemmed daisy. "Take us or leave us; but we don't want any half-way friends that like us when they can't get anything any better."

"Don't you mind her, Alan," said Mrs. Adams. "You can come, if you want to, and I'll protect you myself."

"If you come, though," added Polly, determined to have the last word, "you'll have to bring some stockings to darn. We shan't let in any lazy people."

CHAPTER IV

MISS BEAN COMES TO LUNCH

"Oh, dear me, Jean!" sighed Polly. "I do believe there's Miss Deborah Bean coming down the street."

"What of her?" inquired Jean indifferently.

"Why, if 'tis, she's coming here to lunch. She says all the hateful things she can think of; and you don't know how queer she is. I can't help laughing at her; and that makes mamma cross, for she wants me to be polite to her, because she's old as Methuselah and poor as Job's turkey."

"I didn't suppose your mother was ever cross," said Jean.

"Oh, she isn't cross, exactly; but sometimes she doesn't like things as well as others."

"Most people don't," remarked Jean sagely.

Miss Bean's present home was in the poorhouse, from which place of retreat she made expeditions into the town, at intervals, to visit her old acquaintances, and among them was Mrs. Adams, for whose mother she had sewed, during her younger, stronger days. On these great occasions, she was wont to cast aside the plain gown which she ordinarily wore, and bring out to the light of day the one that had for years served as her best when she went into the institution. Accordingly, it was a strange figure that turned in at the doctor's gate, and came to a halt before the two girls who were sitting on the grass under one of the tall elms on the lawn. Her gown was of some black woollen stuff, figured with green, and its short, full skirt fell in voluminous folds over her large hoops. A white muslin cape covered her shoulders; and her head was adorned with a yellow straw shaker bonnet, in the depths of which her wrinkled face, with its pointed chin and bright eyes, looked like the face of some mammoth specimen of the cat tribe, an effect that was increased by her high, shrill voice. Black lace mitts covered her hands; and she carried, point upward, a venerable brown umbrella, loosely rolled up, and held in place with two rubber bands.

"Is your ma at home?" she asked Polly abruptly.

"She's in the house," answered Polly, rising with some reluctance. "I'll go and call her. You stay here, Jean."

"Jean who?" inquired Miss Bean, bringing her spectacles to bear on Jean's blooming face.

"Jean Dwight, ma'am," said Jean demurely, in spite of a strong desire to laugh.

"Bill Dwight's daughter?"

Jean nodded, while her color rose at the rough abbreviation of her father's name.

"I want to know! He was a son of old Enos Dwight and Melissy Pettigrew; and I can remember the time, and not so very long ago, either, when the Adamses wouldn't have had anything to do with such folks," remarked Miss Bean, who Avas not only a firm believer in the aristocracy of the old town, but regarded it as her right to utter all the disagreeable truths that came into her brain.

To-day she had spoken rashly, for Polly, angry at the insult to her friend, faced her with blazing eyes, while every little curl on her head was dancing with indignation.

"It doesn't make any difference what you think about it, Miss Bean. My mother has charge of me, not you; and she's glad to have Jean come here."

"Dear sakes! Red hair does show in the temper," sighed Miss Bean, unconsciously touching another sore spot, for Polly's hair was one of her trials.

"I'd rather have red hair and a temper, than meddle with what doesn't—" Polly was beginning hotly; but remembering that the old woman, though uninvited, was yet a guest, she added hastily, "Come into the house."

When she came out under the trees again, she found Jean still sitting on the grass, with a little suspicious moisture around her eyes. Polly dropped down by her side, and impulsively pulling Jean's head over into her lap, she bent down and kissed her.

"It's a shame, Jean!" said she. "Don't you mind a word the old thing says. I don't care anything about your grandpa and grandma; they might have been brought up in jail, for all I care. It's you that I like. She's a horrid old woman."

"I don't mean to care," said Jean disconsolately; "but some people always have to tell me I'm a nobody."

"No, you aren't, you're somebody," contradicted Polly. "And as long as you're splendid yourself, I don't see what difference it makes whether you have forty cents or forty million dollars, and whether you carpenter for a living or doctor for it,—or beg for it, the way she does."

They were silent for a minute, and then Polly added, with a laugh,—

"There's one thing about it, we'll have some fun out of her, for she's going to stay to lunch, and she's so funny at the table. She minces so, and she never refuses anything to eat without telling just why she doesn't like it. One time, mamma offered her some pie, and she said, 'Oh, my, no! I never eat it. Pie-crust is grease packed in flour.' I'm so glad you are here to-day."

When the girls went into the house at lunch time, Miss Bean was in the midst of a stream of gossip. Her usual surroundings gave rise to no more varied subjects than the personal appearance of her companions, and the routine of the housework, in which they all had a share. Doubtless it was partly for this reason that the worthy woman made the most of her brief outings, to gather up any bits of information which might serve to enliven the days to come, and render her an object of admiration in the community where she was passing her time. In spite of Aunt Jane's frowns, and the efforts of Mrs. Adams to turn the conversation, she was running on and on, helped by an occasional word from the doctor, who derived much amusement from the old woman's visits. As Polly and Jean seated themselves across the table from her, she glanced up to eye them with little favor, and then went on,—

"As I was saying, I stopped in to Miss Hapgood's on my way up, and she'd just got a letter from Kate. You remember Kate

Harvey, her sister that married Henry Shepard and went out to Omaha to live, don't you? He's made a lot of money, but people always said he was a miserable sort of fellow."

"Let the doctor give you some of the oysters, Miss Bean," interrupted Mrs. Adams desperately. "No, I don't eat oysters now; there's no R in August," replied Miss Bean frankly.

"Unless you spell it O-r-gust," whispered Jean, in an aside which made Polly choke over her glass of water.

"Well," resumed Miss Bean tranquilly, "Kate's got two daughters of her own, about Molly's age, and she wants 'em to come there and board, and go to school at Miss Webster's. I don't know's I wonder, for I don't suppose there's any schools in them little western towns; but Mis' Hapgood's all upset about it. I told her she'd better take 'em, and charge a good, round price for 'em; but she says she hasn't much room, and then she don't know how they'd get along with Molly."

"Do you think they'll come?" inquired Polly eagerly.

"I don't know," answered Miss Bean coldly. "Mis' Hapgood hasn't made up her mind. She sets great store by Kate, being her only sister," she went on, turning back to the doctor; "and so I shouldn't much wonder if she took 'em, after all. They say his father shot himself, and—"

"Have some of these preserved plums, Miss Bean," said Mrs. Adams, lifting the spoon persuasively.

"No, thank you. Preserves isn't very hulsome, and I don't go much on them, excepting pie-plant and molasses," answered Miss Bean, as she poured out her coffee into her saucer.

At this somewhat unexpected response, Jean pinched Polly's hand under the table, and they both giggled.

"Some folks," continued Miss Bean reflectively, "say it's a coward that commits suicide; but, my soul and body! I think it's just the other way; I never should get up spunk enough." Then, with an abrupt change of subject, she added: "Speaking of folks dying, I see Mr. Solomon Baxter as I was coming along. He's aged a good deal since his wife died, and no wonder, poor man! with all his six children to look out for. He shook hands with me, and he seemed so all cut up when I told him how lonesome he looked, that I says to him: 'Mr. Baxter, why don't you get married again? There's lots of good women left, as many as there ever was. Why don't you take Miss Roberts, now? She'd manage your children for you, I'll warrant.'"

This was too much for the doctor and the girls, and they burst out laughing, while Aunt Jane remarked stiffly,—

"Thank you, Miss Bean; but I have no present desire to be married."

"Well, I didn't know but what you might think 'twas a case of duty," responded Miss Bean grimly.

As soon as the meal was over, Polly and Jean adjourned to the lawn again, and sat down to discuss the situation, for they were both much excited over the possible coming of Molly's cousins.

"I saw some pictures of them, once," said Polly, as she settled herself in the hammock. "They were pretty, and they were just elegantly dressed, with piles of lace and things, and gold chains round their necks."

"Miss Bean said they had lots of money," said Jean thoughtfully.

"Yes," answered Polly; "and they looked as if they had it all on.. Mamma says 'tisn't a good idea for young girls to wear jewelry, and she won't let me have any at all, but just these." As she spoke, Polly touched the string of gold beads that lay closely about her throat. They had been her great-grandmother's beads, and Polly had received them for her name.

"I shouldn't wonder if they did that more out West," said Jean. "How old are they, Polly?"

"One is older than Molly," answered Polly "and the other is about Alan's age. Molly hasn't ever seen them, for they've always lived out there I hope they won't come, though," she added emphatically.

"Why not?" inquired Jean. "If they're nice I think it would be fun to have them here."

"I don't," said Polly. "There are just enough of us, as it is; and if they were here, we shouldn't get any good of Molly."

"It won't make any difference, if they don't go to the same school with us. And besides, you said this morning that you couldn't bear Molly," said Jean a little maliciously.

"You know I never meant any such thing, Jean," said Polly impatiently. "I like Molly Hapgood better than any other girl in this town, and you know that just as well as I do."

"What about me?" inquired Jean, laughing, for she was accustomed to Polly's moods, and was by no means angry at the alarming frankness of her reply, as she said tragically,—

"I like you ever so much, Jean; but, honestly, I like Molly better, when she's nice, for we've always been together; and I don't want these dreadful girls to come in between us."

"I don't believe they will, any more than Florence and I do," said Jean soothingly.

At the mention of Florence's name, Polly straightened up, and looked right into Jean's eyes.

"Jean Dwight," said she, "if you'll never, never tell, I am going to say something to you that I never told anybody before."

"What is it?" asked Jean curiously.

"You promise not to tell?"

"Why, of course, if you don't want me to."

"Well," said Polly, in a whisper, "I think Florence is a perfect little flat. There! I suppose mamma would say I was as bad as Miss Bean, with all her gossip, but I can't help it, it's true. But don't let's talk about it any more, it makes me so cross. Perhaps they won't come, anyway."

"Here comes Alan," said Jean, glancing up as the boy turned in at the gate; "maybe he can tell us something about them." In fact, the lad had come to see Polly for no other purpose than to talk the matter over with her, for Polly was his truest friend in the V, and the two children exchanged confidences with the same simple good-fellowship they might have shown, had they both been girls. Polly never snubbed Alan because he was younger, as Molly did, but invariably stood as his champion when the other girls scolded him, and tried to send him away; and Alan, on his side, never rubbed Polly the wrong way, but respected her quick temper. Of course he teased her, as every natural boy teases the girls with whom he is thrown; but it was a gay, good-natured sort of teasing that never irritated Polly in the least. During his long, rheumatic fever of the winter before, she had been a most devoted friend, dropping in to see him at all sorts of odd hours, to amuse him with her merry nonsense, and had greatly disgusted the girls by frankly announcing her preference for his society over their own. And Alan returned the compliment with interest, declaring that he would "rather have Poll in one of her tantrums than the rest of them with all their best manners."

He came deliberately across the lawn, with his black and white striped cap cocked on the very back of his head, and his hands in the side pockets of his gray coat, and calmly disregarding the curiosity of the girls, he made no attempt to speak until he had comfortably settled himself on the grass at their feet.

"Well," he inquired at length, after he had arranged himself to his liking, with his hands clasped under his yellow head; "what is it you want to know?"

"Everything," demanded Polly, comprehensively.

"All right," he answered, lazily shutting his eyes. "The earth is the planet on which we live, and is about twenty-five thousand miles round; a decimal fraction is one whose denominator is ten, one hundred, one thousand, or and so forth; America was discovered in—"

"Oh, Alan, do be sensible if you can," said Jean. "We know all that stuff. What we want is to hear about these cousins of yours that are coming."

"How did you know anything about them?" asked the boy, in surprise.

"Miss Bean is here," answered Polly. "She went to see your mother on the way, and heard about it." "Oh."

There was a world of disgust in Alan's tone. Presently he went on,—

"Well, everybody will have to hear of it now. I came over to tell you, Poll, but it seems that old woman is in ahead."

"Are they really coming, then?" asked Polly anxiously.

"Hope not," said Alan, rolling over on his face and pulling up a handful of grass; "girls enough round already."

"That's not polite," returned Polly; "but go on."

"There isn't any on," said Alan. "All there is about it is that they want to come, and I'm afraid mother is going to let them. Molly likes it, but I don't want them round in the way. I know they'll be prim and fussy, without any fun in them. I believe I'll come over here and live."

"Come on," said Polly hospitably; then she proceeded in a moral tone, "But, Alan, you ought not to talk so about them, for they're your cousins, and you ought to like your relations, you know."

"Do you like Aunt Jane?" inquired Alan, suddenly rolling over to face her once more.

But Polly was spared the necessity of making any reply, by a sudden voice behind her.

"And so this is your garden, Mrs. Adams! It's a likely place for petunias and sweet williams, but I don't think much of those new-fangled things," pointing to a brilliant bed of dwarf nasturtiums near by. Then she went on in a sing-song tone,—

"'So I've come out to view the land
Where I must shortly lie.'"

"Needn't think I expect to lie in your garden, though," she hastily added, evidently fearful of being misunderstood.

"Hush, Alan! you must not laugh at her," said Polly, stifling her own merriment as best she could.

But Miss Bean, absorbed in her eloquence, had passed on out of hearing, and Jean returned to the charge.

"Come, Alan, there's a dear boy," she began persuasively, "tell us about the girls."

"I don't know much about them," answered Alan. "Katharine is the older one, about fifteen, and Jessie is just my age. Her birthday is the third and mine the seventh. I suppose they're well enough, but their pictures look a little toploftical, and I'm not over fond of that kind. They are going to bring their pony, if they come, and that will be fun, if mother will only let me ride him."

"You'll get your neck broken," predicted Polly. "Do you remember the day we tried to ride Job, and he lay down and rolled us off?"

"That was your fault," returned Alan; "if you hadn't gripped his mane so, he'd have been all right. Well," he added, sitting up and stretching himself, "mother sent me to the market, and I s'pose I must go, but I thought I'd just stop in a minute."

"Oh, dear! how I wish I had a brother!" sighed Polly, watching his boyish figure, as he sauntered away across the grass.

"Yes," said Jean slowly, as she thought of the four little brothers at home, "it is nice, but it has its drawbacks, Polly. When they all want to do the same thing at the same time, and can't wait a minute, why, then it doesn't seem quite so agreeable."

In the warm twilight, Mrs. Adams and Polly sat on the broad piazza. Miss Bean had taken her departure, long before, and Jean had gone home to help her mother get supper and put the younger children to bed. The birds were twittering their last sleepy good nights, and two or three little stars were faintly showing in the blue sky above the dark mountain, while scores of tiny fireflies were dotting the air below.

"There, Jerusalem!" Polly was saying triumphantly, as she perched herself on the broad arm of her mother's piazza chair; "now everybody is out of the way, and I can have you all to myself."

"What is it to-night?" inquired Mrs. Adams, laughing, as she pulled her light shawl over her shoulders to keep out the evening air.

"Lots of things, mamma," answered Polly, with a sudden thoughtfulness; "there's been a good deal to-day."

"About Molly's cousins, for instance?" asked Mrs. Adams.

"Yes," replied Polly; "I don't think we want them, mamma. I

know they won't fit in a bit. And Alan says he doesn't want them."

"That's not quite fair of Alan," said her mother: "he oughtn't to say so without knowing anything more about them. But, Polly, you may find them pleasant friends, and like them better than you do Molly."

Polly shook her head with decision.

"I'm sure I shan't. But I'm afraid Molly will like them better than she does us."

"Jealous, Polly?" And there was a tone of regret in her mother's voice as she went on: "I am a little disappointed in my daughter. Of course, Polly, Molly will be thrown with them a great deal, much more than with you; and, so long as they are her cousins, she will probably be fond of them. But, after all these years, can't you trust Molly's friendship enough to believe that it won't make any difference in her feeling to you, but that she can love and care for you all, at the same time?"

"Sometimes I think she can, and sometimes I think she can't,'" said Polly slowly. "Once in a while, when we have had a 'scrap,' as Alan calls it, I think she doesn't care a bit about me."

"Whose fault is it, when you quarrel?" asked Mrs. Adams, smoothing the short curls. "I don't think it is all Molly's fault, any more than it is all yours. If my small daughter wants her friends to care for her, she must govern that temper and study self-control."

"I know that, mamma," broke in Polly impetuously; "but you don't have any idea how hard 'tis, nor how sorry I am after it is over."

"It is just because I do know it so well, my dear, that I keep saying this to you; for I hope I can save you from a part, at least, of the pain I have suffered in just this same way. I have been through it all, Polly, and I know that every time you give up to your temper, it is just so much easier to do it again; and if you were to go on long enough, in time you would get to where it would be impossible to stop yourself, and you would do something that might be a sorrow to you, through all your life. It is just so with every habit; the more you give way to it, the more it becomes a part of your nature. That is the reason I am trying to help you form the habit of a quiet, even temper. And now," added Mrs. Adams, changing the subject, "what else was there that we wanted to talk over?"

"'Twas Jean," said Polly, as she slipped down on the floor at her mother's feet. "Miss Bean was twitting her to-day because she wasn't rich." And Polly repeated the little conversation which had taken place under the trees.

Mrs. Adams listened thoughtfully. When Polly had finished, she said decidedly,—

"That was rather uncalled for, I think, Polly. Whatever Jean's parents may be, they are really refined people, and Jean is at heart a lady."

"What difference does it make, anyway?" asked Polly impatiently.

"Not so much as most people think," said Mrs. Adams. "If your parents are cultivated people, it helps you to make something of yourself; and whatever teaching you get from them is so much stock in trade, just as money would be, if you were starting in business. If, when you have this start, you don't make the most of it, it shows that you are unworthy of it; and if you become a grand woman without it, then you deserve ever so much more credit than the people who have had everything in their favor. Do you understand me, Polly?"

"Yes, I think I do," said Polly. "And it doesn't make any difference whether we are rich or poor, does it?"

Her mother paused for a moment, as if the question were a hard one to answer. Polly had a way of asking deeper questions than she realized. Mrs. Adams rocked back and forth in silence two or three times; then she said,—

"Yes and no, Polly. Money in itself doesn't make the least bit of difference; but people that have it can make more of themselves,—I don't say that they do, remember. If Jean didn't have to wash so many dishes nor mend so many stockings, she could give more time to study and reading every year. But, after all, I don't believe she would be half so fine, unselfish a girl as she is now, when she has to give up doing what she likes, to help her mother. It is just the same whether it is money, or family, or a fine mind, or beauty; the more that is given you, the more you are expected to make of it, and the more the shame to you if you neglect it. But we're getting into very deep subjects for so near bed-time. What did Alan come for?"

"Just to tell me about the girls," said Polly. "He says they're going to have a pony, and everything."

"How well Alan has been, all summer," remarked her mother.

There was a sudden click of the gate-latch, and a tall figure came up the walk.

Anna Chapin Ray

"Sitting here in the damp, Isabel, and catching your death of cold! I can't afford time to sit around in the dark doing nothing, when I think of all the good that can be done around us." And Aunt Jane stalked past them into the house, and sat down to cut the leaves of the last scientific magazine.

However, though Mrs. Adams did not reply, she had made up her mind that her usual goodnight talk with Polly was far more important than all the clubs in the world, and no words from Aunt Jane could induce her to give up her nightly habit.

CHAPTER V

TWO MORE GIRLS

"It does seem as if to-morrow afternoon never would come," Molly was saying, as she and Polly stood leaning on the fence in the early twilight.

"What time will they get here?" Polly asked her.

"Three o'clock, and I just feel as if I couldn't wait, when I think how every minute is bringing them along. It's going to be splendid to have them here. You must come over to see them the very first thing, Polly, for I want them to know my best friend right away."

"I do hope they'll be nice," said Polly thoughtfully.

"Nice!" echoed Molly. "Of course they are. I'll tell you what, Polly, Alan has been running them down to you. He is so queer about it; I should think he'd like to have them come. They're just as pretty as they can be, and boys always like pretty girls."

"Oh, dear," sighed Polly; "how nice it would be to be pretty!"

Anna Chapin Ray

"Why, you aren't so bad, Polly." And Molly surveyed her with frank criticism. "If only your nose wasn't quite so puggy, and you didn't have quite so many freckles, you'd be real good-looking. Besides, Alan says he likes your looks better than he does Florence's."

"Does he?" And Polly flushed with pleasure.

"Yes, he told mamma so the other day; you know boys have queer tastes," answered Molly flatteringly.

"But I wish I did know of something to take off freckles and tan," said Polly, rubbing her cheeks with a vicious force. "Aunt Jane wants me to wear a veil and keep white; but I'd rather be black and speckled all over, than make a mummy of myself. I think fresh air and sunshine were made to be enjoyed, and not to be peeked out at through a rag."

"It must be horrid to freckle," said Molly sympathetically. "Did you ever try anything for it, Poll?"

"No, only lemon juice once, and it all ran into my eyes and made them smart; but it didn't touch the freckles any."

"They say buttermilk is good," suggested Molly. "Why not try that?"

"That's a good idea," said Polly. "We have some, and I don't believe it would hurt. How do you use it, Molly? I'll do it to-night, and then I could start white with your cousins, anyway; and so much depends on first impressions, you know."

"I'm not just sure about it," answered Molly; "but I think they put it on over night, and rub it in well. You'd better not do it, if you are afraid it can do any harm."

"Oh, it can't," said Polly, with assurance; "and even if it does, anything is better than looking like a fright."

"But you aren't a fright," said Molly loyally; then added, "What does keep Alan so? His errand wasn't going to take two minutes, and your mother will be tired of him."

"No, she won't," said Polly; "she likes Alan. Don't be in a hurry, Molly; this is the last chance we shall have to talk for a year."

In spite of herself, Polly's voice failed a little on the last words. She loved her friend dearly, and the coming of the cousins, with the probability of its causing a separation between them, had been her first real sorrow. For Molly's sake she tried to be eager and interested about them, but when she was alone with Jean or Alan, she was disconsolate enough over the prospect. The three or four weeks had flown past, every day bringing the change nearer, and the last evening had come. Arm in arm, the two girls had been pacing up and down the walk, while they waited for Alan, and that half-hour had made Polly realize more than ever how fond she was of this companion with whom she had spent so many contented hours. The memory of their frequent quarrels seemed to sink away into the past, and only the thought of their good times was before them then. But Alan's whistle was heard, as he came out of the house; and he and Molly went away down the street, leaving Polly standing alone at the gate. She looked after them until they disappeared in the gathering darkness; then her curly head dropped on her folded arms, and she began to sob with all the fervor of her impetuous, affectionate nature. It was over in a minute or two, and no one was the wiser for it but the birds in the tall elm trees above her head. Then she turned forlornly, and started to walk to the house; but, with Polly, the reaction always came quickly, and by the time she reached the steps, she was humming the air which Alan had just whistled, as she planned about the gown she would wear when she went to see the cousins, and pictured to herself the details of their first meeting. It was all so like Polly, to be in the depths of grief at one moment, and to be singing the next. Her sorrows were just as sincere as Molly's, while they lasted, but the very intensity of them made it impossible for them to continue long at a time. Polly's life was one of superlatives: when she was happy, she was radiant; when she was unhappy, she was miserable. There was no middle ground for her.

But to-night Polly was bent on beautifying herself. For Molly's sake, as well as for her own, she was anxious to make a good appearance in the eyes of the two girls whom she was to meet on the morrow. The last thing before she went to her room, she secretly visited the kitchen and helped herself to a generous bowl of buttermilk, which she carried up stairs. She set it down on the table and, lamp in hand, went to the mirror. In the main, Polly was not a conceited girl, nor a vain one. On the contrary, she thought little about her personal appearance, except to give an occasional sigh over her hair and freckles. But, just now, it seemed to her that beauty was the one thing to be desired, and holding up the lamp, she gazed at herself steadily, unconscious of the picture she made, with the light falling full upon her bright hair and eager young face. Then she set down the lamp with a suddenness which threatened to shatter it.

"Oh, you fright!" she said to herself, in a tone of disgusted sincerity.

She turned away and took up the bowl from the table, sniffed at it daintily, and wrinkled her nose in disgust. The strong, sour odor of the buttermilk was not pleasant, certainly, but what mattered that, if it removed the obnoxious freckles?

She shut her teeth, held her breath, and resolutely applied it to her face, putting it on freely, and rubbing it in until her arms ached and her cheeks burned under their unwonted treatment. The next morning she repeated the operation with even greater zeal, and ended by a vigorous application of soap and water, and a rough towel. Then she drew near the glass once more, to see and admire her soft, white skin, where no freckle would be found. As she gazed, her eyes grew round with wonder, and she stood as if transfixed at the sight before her. To say the least, it was striking. The freckles had not disappeared, but still the buttermilk had done its work, and Polly's face presented every appearance of having been varnished, for, thanks to the polishing which it had undergone, it shone like a new copper tea-kettle. For an instant, tears of mortification stood in the gray eyes; then Polly's sense of the ridiculous had its way, and, dropping into a chair, she laughed till her cheeks were crimson under their metallic surface, and her lashes were damp with hysterical tears.

"What in the world are you laughing at, Polly?" asked Aunt Jane's voice at her door. "The breakfast bell has rung, and it's time you were down-stairs."

"Yes'm," replied Polly, suddenly becoming sober again, as she remembered that she must present herself to the family in this plight, and would probably be well laughed at for her pains.

She delayed in her room as long as she dared, but her mother had always insisted on perfect regularity at meal times, and Polly knew that she must appear. With one last, despairing glance at the mirror, a glance which was by no means reassuring, she turned away and silently went down the stairs and into the dining-room, hoping to take her place at the table so quietly that she could escape notice. It was not her mother whom she dreaded, but she shrank from her father's teasing and Aunt Jane's merciless comments. As she drew her chair up to the table, Aunt Jane glanced up from her oatmeal.

"Late again, Polly! Why, what have you been putting on your face, child?"

Polly's cheeks grew scarlet, but she answered, with an attempt at carelessness,—

"Oh, nothing but a little buttermilk. Why?"

"Why?" responded Aunt Jane, with needless emphasis, "I should think you'd better ask why! Have you looked in the glass this morning?"

"Yes," answered Polly faintly, for they were all staring at her, and she saw a mischievous twinkle come into her father's blue eyes.

"Well, I'd like to know what fresh piece of nonsense this is," Aunt Jane was beginning severely, when the doctor interposed,—

"Wait a minute, Jane; don't be in such a hurry to scold. Come, Polly, tell us what you have been doing to make yourself look like a South Sea Islander or a Pawnee?"

Polly dropped her eyes and played with her fork for a minute; but sulkiness was not in her nature, and after a pause, she confessed.

"Molly said buttermilk was good for freckles, so I put some on mine, but they didn't come off. You see," she added, turning to her mother with the certainty that she would find sympathy in that quarter, if in no other, "the Shepard girls are coming to-day, and Molly wanted me to go over to see them right away, and I wanted to look as well as I can."

Polly was interrupted by a hearty laugh from the doctor, who laid down his knife and fork and leaned back in his chair, to enjoy his merriment to the utmost.

"I think there's no doubt of their being struck by your looks, Polly," he said at length. Then, as he saw her bite her lips to steady them, he added kindly, "Shall I tell my little girl what I really think about it? I don't consider the freckles themselves beautiful; but I would rather see her with enough of them to prove that she lives out of doors in the sunshine, as every healthy child should, than be one of the little, pale-faced beauties brought up in the house, or under veils and broad hats. If I can't have but one, I want my Polly to have health rather than beauty, for health is beauty, especially in children."

"Better have a freckled face than a freckled soul," added Aunt Jane, feeling that here was the opportunity to make a fine moral point.

"There's more connection there than you think, Jane," responded Dr. Adams quickly. "A child is much more likely to have an unfreckled, unspotted soul, when her body has the health which comes with plenty of exposure to the air and sun. Show me a healthy child, and a small amount of care will make her a good one; I'm not so sure of the sickly ones. It's my opinion that more can be made of a healthy sinner than a feeble saint. Isn't it so, Poll?" And he leaned over to pass his broad hand caressingly down the shining face, as he added gaily, "There's one good thing about it, my dear; we shan't have to waste any gas to-night. The light of your countenance will be quite enough."

They were still sitting lingering over their meal, when Alan came in to bring a note from Molly. At sight of Polly, he started back in mock dismay, exclaiming,—

"Great Scott, Polly! What's the matter?"

"Don't tell Molly, Alan," she begged; "but I tried to get rid of my freckles, that's all."

Alan gave a low, expressive whistle.

"I'm glad it's nothing worse. We had a girl once, that told Molly if she let the moon shine on her while she was asleep, she'd all swell up and turn black, and I didn't know but you were beginning to do that."

"I thought you had given up slang, Alan," remarked Mrs. Adams, as she motioned him to a chair beside her.

"So I have, mostly. Mother didn't want me to use much, and I couldn't get along without any; so we split the difference and agreed that I could have one. I chose 'great Scott,' but it doesn't always fit the case. I say, Polly, you'll be over to-night, won't you?"

Polly looked doubtfully at her mother.

"Isn't it rather soon, Alan?" Mrs. Adams asked.

"Not a bit of it," answered the boy. "Mother will be busy with Uncle Henry, because he'll only be here one night, and we'll have to see to the girls. Molly can't manage them both, and I'm no use at all, so we need Polly to help us out. Mother said you'd better come over about five, Poll, and stay to supper."

"I don't know whether I can get bleached in time," answered Polly, laughing, as she followed him to the door; "but I'll come if I can. And don't you dare tell Molly."

"Catch me telling tales!" returned Alan, with some dignity. "That's not in my line, Poll; and not on you, anyway."

With an appearance of great carelessness, Polly strolled out to the hammock soon after two o'clock that afternoon, and settled herself, book in hand. But for the next hour, there was little reading done, for Polly's gray eyes often wandered from the pages before her, and fixed themselves on the distant corner around which the Shepard family must come. It was a long hour of waiting, and Polly had begun to think that the train must have been wrecked by the way, when the distant, shrill whistle was heard. At the sound, she drew herself into a more dignified position, settled her skirts about her and fell to reading with a will. But though her eyes went down the left-hand page and up again to the top of the right-hand one, she could not have told so much as the title of the book, so absorbed was she in listening for the wheels that would pass the house. She heard them drawing near, but continued to be lost in her reading until just as the carriage was in front of her. Then she glanced up, as if by accident, and was filled with confusion to see Alan leaning down from his seat on the box and pointing at her, while two broad hats and two girl faces were bent forward to survey her curiously. Alan waved his cap; she answered his salute, and the carriage went swiftly on, leaving Polly to stare at the pile of trunks strapped on behind it, with a vague feeling that her intended effect had been a little marred by Alan's demonstration.

"Served me right, though!" she remarked philosophically to herself, as she curled herself up to read in earnest, now that her excitement was over. "I needn't have tried to pose for them; that sort of thing doesn't suit me; I'd better leave it to Florence."

It was with some misgiving, that Polly, two hours later, started to take the familiar walk to the Hapgood house. Every riotous curl was brushed until it lay close to her small head, but already the golden ends were doing their best to break loose once more; thanks to her mother's efforts, her burnished skin had lost a little of its coppery lustre; and her fresh blue and white gingham gown was as dainty and trim as loving hands could make it. But Polly, as she looked in the glass before starting, only saw that her hair was red, and that her freckles would insist on showing. However, Alan's compliment came to her relief, and she dismissed the question of her looks with a smile, as something not worth a thought, and ran off down-stairs to say good by to her mother.

Alan saw her coming, and started to meet her.

"What's the matter, Alan?" she said, noticing his frown, as she joined him.

"Nothing but a crick in my knee," he explained cheerfully; "I think I took cold last night, perhaps. They're up-stairs with Molly," he added vaguely. "I'll call them down, or will you go up?"

"I'll wait here," said Polly, seating herself on the broad stone step. "What are they like, Alan?"

"Stunning beauties, both of them," responded Alan, with some enthusiasm. "Katharine knows it, that's the worst of it. I do hate a girl that thinks she's pretty. I'd rather they'd be homely as Miss Bean, and not think about themselves, all the time. But I'll go call them." And he departed, leaving Polly to meditate on his words.

The girls soon came down the old stairway behind her, and as Polly shyly rose to meet them, she felt at once the truth of Alan's description of Katharine. There was a strong family resemblance between the sisters, both were dark, and they had the same bright, brown eyes and smooth, dark brown hair; but Katharine was by far the more beautiful, with her pink cheeks, small regular teeth, full lips, and long straight nose with just a suggestion of sauciness in the slant of its tip. It was this nose that captivated Polly, and, indeed, Katharine was like a beautiful picture, in figure and feature, while her rapidly changing expressions and her brilliant health added a charm which no picture could ever have. She seemed years older than the other girls, and this effect was increased by the elegance of her dress and by her quiet, settled manners, which made Polly feel very young and shabby in her spotless gingham. Katharine shook hands with a dignity that quite overawed Polly, who turned to look at Jessie with a conscious feeling of relief. Jessie was a plump, lively young woman of twelve, with less, perhaps, of her sister's delicate beauty; but the lack was more than made good by her perfect unconsciousness of self, and her frank, winning manner, which led Polly to forget her formal greeting, and seize her hand, saying impulsively,—

"I'm so glad you've come to live here!"

Jessie laughed, showing a pair of deep dimples in her dark skin, as she answered, with a cordiality equal to Polly's own,—

"And I'm so glad Molly has such nice friends,"

That settled the matter between them, and, arm in arm, they strolled out to the tennis court, chatting like old friends, while Molly and Alan followed with Katharine, who looked about her indifferently, nodding slightly, from time to time, in answer to some question.

"I do think these old houses are splendid," Jessie was saying eagerly. "I never saw one before. Out in Omaha we call a house old that has been built twenty years."

"Haven't you ever been East before?" asked Polly, with a feeling of pity for any girl who had never known the delights of life in an old New England town.

"Never since I was a year old, so I don't remember much about it," answered Jessie. "I think I am going to like it, though, for the place is lovely, and Aunt Ruth is so sweet."

"I hope you won't be homesick, I'm sure," said Polly encouragingly.

Jessie laughed outright at the idea.

"Why should I be homesick?" she inquired, rather to Polly's surprise.

"Why, I don't know exactly, only I should think you'd be lonely without your father and mother," she began.

"That's what Aunt Ruth seemed to think," interrupted Jessie; "but I shan't be, a bit. You see, mamma is off travelling with papa ever so much of the time, and when she's at home, even, we don't see much of her, for we are in school days, and she goes out, or else has company 'most every evening."

"Is that the way people do out there?" inquired Polly, with perfect innocence.

The others were standing near and, at the question, Alan shot a sly glance at Molly, as Katharine answered, with an air of patronage,—

"Not all people, you know; but mamma is in society, and is very gay, so of course she can't be expected to have much time for us."

"Oh!" said Polly, as if a new light had dawned on her. The simple life of the old town and her own mother's devotion to her had not taught her to know that, when the question arises between them, home life must give place to social.

But Molly saw they were treading on dangerous ground, so, to ward off a possible skirmish, she suggested,—

"Let's have a game of tennis. You girls play, don't you?"

It proved that they did, and Alan was sent off to get the net and rackets, followed by Polly, who went racing after him, to help him bring out his load.

"Why, do girls run here?" asked Katharine, with an air of surprise.

"Yes, of course we do; run and play tag, and do all sorts of dreadful things," answered Molly, with some spirit. "What do you do, I'd like to know?"

"Of course it's different in a city," replied her cousin sedately. "We play tennis and skate; but we never run, all for nothing. Only little girls do that."

"What nonsense!" was Molly's comment. "I'd call myself a little girl, then, if I couldn't have any fun without. I hope you don't consider yourself a young lady—Excuse me, Katharine," she added hastily. "I didn't mean to be rude; but you'll have to take us as you find us, I'm afraid."

But Alan and Polly had reappeared, and the game began, watched by Alan, who refused all the girls' entreaties to play.

"I can't to-night, Poll," he answered to her glance; "I'm too stiff in the joints, but I'll act as umpire."

By the time the game was over, they were excellent friends, even Katharine's reserve having yielded to admiration for the playing of these two girls, who returned her swiftest balls with the precision born of long practice. As the bell rang for dinner, she dropped her racket and held out a hand to each, saying, with the winning grace she knew how to assume at her pleasure,—

"I never saw better players in my life. We shall have to try a series of match games this fall, West against the East."

"They do play pretty well, don't they?" inquired Alan from the rear, with a tone of conscious pride. "I've coached them both, and they can play every bit as well as I can."

"That's modesty," said Polly, laughing. "Alan wouldn't play, just because he was afraid you'd beat him. We play five here, quite often."

"How do you arrange it?" asked Katharine.

"Put in an extra one on the weak side," answered Polly, stooping to pick up a ball she had dropped. "It isn't quite as much fun, but there are just five of us, and it gives us all a chance," she added, as they entered the dining-room and she took her place between Alan and Jessie.

"How do you like it, Kit?" asked Jessie, when they were in their room that night.

"Like what?" inquired Katharine, with a sleepy yawn.

"Oh, auntie and Molly and all?"

"Auntie is rather nice, only she is a little bit countrified," returned Katharine critically; "and Molly is well enough; but what a funny little thing that Polly Adams is! She acts more like a boy, the way she goes rushing around with Alan."

"I like her, though," said Jessie.

"She isn't so bad," answered Katharine thoughtfully; "she's a good-hearted little thing, even if she isn't like the Omaha girls. I do like Alan, though, Jessie; don't you? He is a splendid-looking fellow, and has ever so much fun in him. He seems ever so much older than he really is."

"Perhaps it's because he has been sick a good deal," suggested Jessie.

"It may be that is it," assented Katharine, pulling off the silver bangles that clanked like a criminal's fetters at every motion of her hand; "but he doesn't look as if he'd been ill a day in his life. I'm so glad there's a boy in the family; for they always keep things going. I wonder what our school will be like."

The two girls speculated on the future until they heard Alan, in the next room, kick off his shoes and let them drop, with a thud, on the floor. Then, tired with their journey, they fell asleep.

Anna Chapin Ray

CHAPTER VI

POLLY ENCOUNTERS THE SERVANT QUESTION

As time went on, Polly's first impression of the sisters was unchanged. In fact, the girls all agreed in pronouncing Jessie "a dear," and she was at once made to feel at home with the V, which hospitably extended its arms to take her in. But with Katharine it was a different matter. Critical of others, and constantly studying the effect of all that she herself said or did, she was rather a damper on the good times of the girls. Fortunately, she usually scorned them as children, and spent much of her time with her mates in the fashionable boarding-school at which she and her sister were day pupils. And yet, she was not to blame for this artificial side of her nature. At heart she was as true and sweet a girl as Molly herself; but, bred up in the atmosphere of her western city home where there was but one end in view, to struggle up to the top of the social scale, if need be, over the bodies of one's dearest friends, what wonder was it that her growth towards womanhood was cramped by being forced out of its natural beauty into the artificial lines of fashionable society. But it was not yet too late to undo the harm, for a generous, warm heart lay under her affected indifference and ambition; and her parents had been wiser than they realized, when they sent their daughters East to be educated, and left them in the care of the motherly woman whose social position was too assured to have her feel the need for striving, and who, like Mrs. Adams, believed that a woman's highest life lay in her home and children, and that society was incidental, rather than the main end in view.

There were times, and they were by no means rare, when Katharine's native sweetness showed itself, and then the girls welcomed her to their circle. Florence was her favorite among them, while she openly courted Alan's favor, to the amusement of the boy's mother, who smiled quietly to herself over his unconsciousness of her attempts and his continued, unswerving devotion to Polly.

"But what I don't understand," she said to Florence, one day, when they were out for a walk together, "is how you girls ever happened to pick up Jean Dwight."

"Pick her up? What do you mean?" asked Florence, meeting her friend's look with a glance which was almost defiant, for she was too loyal to Jean to fail to notice the scorn in Katharine's tone and manner.

"You know what I mean, Florence, so don't pretend to be as absurd as Polly Adams and Molly are. Of course you and I both know that you three girls could have the pick of the town, if you chose; and I don't see why you take up with the daughter of a carpenter."

Polly had called Florence "a flat," but there was no suggestion of weakness in her reply now. On the contrary, she drew up her small figure to its full height, and spoke with a simple, childish dignity which might have put to shame her companion.

"You needn't say any more about it, Katharine. It is just because we do have the pick of the town that we have taken up with Jean Dwight. At least, she is too much of a lady to slander her friends behind their backs, even if she is only a carpenter's daughter."

"Don't be so crushing, Florence. I only wanted to know what was the reason you were with her so much," answered Katharine, trying to pass off the matter lightly, although she was privately resolving to cultivate the acquaintance of this girl, of whom her friends were so fond.

One bright day in early October, the V had walked up from school together as far as Molly's, where they settled themselves on the piazza to talk over the doings of the day. Katharine and Jessie had joined them, and they sat there chatting till the clock struck five. At the sound, Polly sprang up.

"Oh, dear! I ought to have gone home long ago," she said regretfully. "Is anybody else coming?"

"I'm going to stay a little longer," answered Jean. "Wait just a few minutes, Poll."

"I can't, Jean; mamma will be expecting me." And Polly picked up her hat and started for home, followed by Alan who escorted her to the gate.

She was surprised, when she entered the house, to find the lower rooms deserted and in some confusion. Her astonishment was increased when, on going up-stairs, she saw her mother with her bonnet on, busy in packing her small satchel. Mrs. Adams's red eyes and white face told her daughter that something was amiss.

"So you have come, at last!" she exclaimed, with an air of relief, as she caught sight of Polly in the door; "I was just thinking that I should have to send Mary after you."

"What's the matter, mamma; are you going away?" Polly asked anxiously.

"For a little while, dear. We have had a telegram that Uncle Charlie is very, very ill. And Aunt Jane and I are going to New York to-night."

So Aunt Jane was going too! Polly was relieved at that. Uncle Charlie she scarcely knew, so her main anxiety was for her mother, of whose devotion to this only brother she was well aware. "Is he going to die, mamma?" she asked slowly.

The tears were falling on the toilet-case in Mrs. Adams's hand, but she answered steadily,—

"I hope not, dear; but they are very anxious about him. I am sorry to leave you all alone here with papa, and he is away so much of the time, too."

"Don't you worry about me, Jerusalem," answered Polly courageously, though her heart sank, a little, as she thought of the lonely evenings.

"I presume I shan't be gone long," said Mrs. Adams thoughtfully; "but it is so uncertain. If only Aunt Jane could be here, it would be a comfort to you."

But Polly shook her head violently.

"I'd rather be alone, mamma. I shall get along beautifully, and you've no idea what good care I'll take of papa."

Mrs. Adams was crossing the room to get her slippers. As she passed Polly, she stooped to kiss her.

Anna Chapin Ray

"And you have no idea," she said, "what a comfort it is to me that you take it so bravely. I know it will be forlorn for you, but there isn't any help for it. Papa is getting ready, now, to drive us to the station, for it is almost time for the train."

As she spoke, the doctor's voice was heard from below, calling to them to hurry; Aunt Jane swept out from her room; Mrs. Adams snapped the fastener of her bag and turned to say good by to her daughter. Polly went down-stairs behind her and stood in the door, looking after them with rather a long face, though she waved her hand bravely until they were around the corner.

Then she went back up-stairs, feeling as if, all at once, an earthquake had struck their quiet home. She and her mother had rarely been separated, and the suddenness and sadness of the present summons only added to the loneliness. The house was in that state of disorder which always follows a hurried packing, and Polly went mechanically up and down, putting the rooms in order while, in imagination, she followed the travellers to the train. Then, when, all was done, she went into her own room and sat down to consider the situation. Taken all in all, it was not an encouraging picture that the next few days presented. Her father was liable to be called away at any hour of the night, leaving her alone with Mary who slept at the far end of the house; there would be the lonely hours when she was out of school; the next day was Saturday—what should she do with herself? The prospect was too much for poor Polly and, throwing herself down on her bed, she gave herself up to the luxury of a hearty cry.

"I wish I were dead now,
Or else in my bed now,
I'd cover my head now,
And have a good cry."

"Is this what you call a hospitable welcome?" asked a sudden voice.

Polly raised her head in surprise, and saw Molly standing in the doorway, with a smile on her face and a great bundle in her hand. Polly sprang up and threw her arms around her friend excitedly.

"Oh, Molly Hapgood! where did you come from? I never, never was so glad to see anybody in all my life."

"If that's a fact," said Molly coolly, "why didn't you come down-stairs to meet me, and not make me hunt for you, all over the house?"

"How could I meet you, when I didn't know you were coming?" demanded Polly.

"Didn't you?" asked Molly, surprised in her turn. "Why, your mother just stopped at our house and told me that she had to go away for a few days, and you wanted me to come and stay with you till she came back. She said you'd tell me all about it."

"Isn't that just like her!" exclaimed Polly rapturously. "And you're going to stay here all the time? How perfectly splendid!"

"Where's she gone?" asked Molly, as she unpacked her brown paper Saratoga.

"Uncle Charlie, in New York, is so ill they've sent for mamma and Aunt Jane," answered Polly, with sudden seriousness, "and they don't know anything more than that. It said—the telegram, I mean—'Charles very ill, come at once,' and mamma is dreadfully worried. Of course she doesn't know how long she'll be gone. Oh, I am so glad you've come!" And Polly, with the tears still damp upon her cheeks, pranced excitedly up and down the room.

"You don't know how lonesome it was going to be," she went on, when she had quieted down a little. "Now, if only Uncle Charlie will get well, I don't care much how long they're gone. We'll just have an elegant time."

"I don't think Katharine liked my coming very well," remarked Molly, with a giggle, as she pulled out an extra gown and hung it over the foot of Polly's dainty white and gold bed. "She seems to think I can't stir, now they are at the house; but I'm not going to give up all my fun for them. They're nothing but boarders; 'tisn't as if they were on a visit; and Alan can see to them once in a while. He can't bear Katharine," she continued, after a pause; "he heard her say to Florence, once, that he was distangy looking, and he never has forgiven her since. We don't either of us know just what it means, but he thinks it has something to do with his nose."

Polly threw herself into a chair and burst out laughing.

"Oh, Molly, Molly! What will you say next? That means distinguished; it's French, you know." "I don't know anything about French, Poll; and you needn't laugh at me, for you don't know much yourself," returned Molly, with some dignity.

"I don't believe Katharine does, either," answered Polly. "The way I happened to know about that was because she said so to me once, and I asked mamma what it meant. She says she doesn't think it's nice for girls to keep putting French and German words into what they say, for it looks as if they did it to show off. Come on, let's go down and see what we're going to have for dinner."

Soon after dinner, the doctor went away to his office, and the girls decided to settle themselves for a quiet visit in front of the open fire in the parlor. This was their first evening alone together since Jessie and Katharine had come, and there was much to be talked over.

"Don't let's have any light but just the fire," Molly suggested. "Then we'll sit on the rug and have it all to ourselves."

"I can't help feeling as if Aunt Jane were likely to drop in at any minute, though," Polly remarked. "She doesn't approve of people's sitting in the dark; she thinks it is lazy."

"She's half way to New York by this time," said Molly; "but I do wish your mother was here."

"So do I," groaned Polly fervently, as she caught sight of the empty fire-place, for there was not one single stick on the andirons.

Now, to lay an open fire ready for the lighting is at once a science and a fine art, and Polly was by no means versed in the operation. Why, of all days in the year, this happened to be the one on which Mrs. Adams had neglected to arrange her usual pile of round sticks and kindlings and shavings, it would be hard to say. Some little unexpected call on her time had made her forget this regular duty, and had left her daughter as hostess to preside over a cheerless hearthstone.

"What's the trouble?" asked Molly, as she detected the discouraged ring to her friend's tone. "Don't you know how to lay a fire?"

"I never have laid one, all alone," admitted Polly, whose share in the matter, it must be confessed, had been to tuck a handful of soft, light shavings under the andirons and apply

Anna Chapin Ray

the match. "But," she added valiantly; "I've watched mamma often enough, and I know I can do it. We must have a fire; the furnace one is 'most out, for Mary forgot to put in any coal, and it's just freezing here. You sit down, and I'll go get some wood."

She came back in a few moments, tugging a great basket of wood, which she arranged in an orderly, solid pile across the andirons, much as she might have placed it, had she been packing it in a woodshed. Then she added a generous handful of shavings, and touched it off with a match.

"There!" said she, with a prolonged accent of contentment; "you see it's easy enough. It will all be going, in a minute."

"Don't you be too sure," returned Molly, doubtfully eyeing the shavings which flashed into flame and quickly died away, leaving the wood unscorched.

"What do you suppose is the matter?" said Polly, rather annoyed at her lack of success.

"Seems to me you've put the wood in too tight," said Molly, arming herself with the shovel, and trying to pry the sticks apart.

"Perhaps I have," said Polly meekly.

Regardless of soot and ashes, she pulled the wood out on the rug, and began again. This time she arranged it cris-crossing as regularly as the walls of a log-house, and, having exhausted her supply of shavings, she lighted a newspaper and thrust it into the middle opening. The girls watched it with eager eyes. It blazed up like the shavings and, like them, burned out, leaving only the blackened cinders, with here and there a line of red, to show where an edge had been.

This was discouraging; the room was uncomfortably cool, and they were wasting their entire evening in preparing for their talk.

"The third time conquers," said Molly, laughing, as she saw Polly tearing down her log cabin. "What are you going to do next, Poll?"

"Lay it yourself, if you want to," retorted Polly, showing more heat than the fire had done.

"I never did such a thing in my life," Molly assured her. "Can't Mary do it?"

"I don't know," said Polly, dropping back from her knees until she sat on her heels; "anyway, she's so cross I don't dare ask her."

"What makes your mother keep her if she's so cross?" inquired Molly, leaning forward to blow the last spark which still lingered on the newspaper.

"Because she can't get anything else," answered Polly, unconsciously touching the key-note of the whole servant question.

"Well," remarked Molly, after a pause, while Polly again wrestled with the fire, "we shall catch our deaths of cold here, Polly; we may as well go to bed, for this isn't going to burn to-night."

"I'm sorry, Molly," her hostess said penitently, as they went up-stairs after leaving a note on the table addressed to the doctor, and containing the simple but alarming statement: "Good night; we've gone to bed to keep from freezing."

Anna Chapin Ray

"I don't care a bit," said Molly. "I like to talk after I'm in bed, and we shall have ever and ever so long before we get sleepy."

At breakfast, the next morning, the girls had to bear with much teasing from the doctor on the subject of their struggles, the evening before; and, as he rose from the table, he suggested that they should ask Alan to give them a few lessons in making bonfires.

"I shan't be back to lunch," he added, as he put his head through the dining-room door again; "but I'd like dinner on time to-night, surely, for I must go down to the hospital before my evening hour."

"I'll tell Mary," said Polly, jumping up to follow him to the front door, as was her mother's custom.

"Now," she continued, as she went back to the table, "what let's do all day?"

Their plans were soon formed: a drive with Job in the morning, for, of late, after many cautions, Polly had been allowed to drive the old creature; and in the afternoon they would go to see Jean.

"I wonder if Alan wouldn't go with us, this morning," said Polly.

"I think he'd like to," answered Molly. "He caught cold a week ago, and since then he's been so stiff that he hasn't been anywhere but just to school and back; and I should think he would be glad to get away from Katharine. He says he gets so tired of her."

"We'll ask him, then," said Polly. "I think 'twould be a good idea to start early, so I'll go out to tell Mary about lunch, and have John harness right away."

She was gone for some time, and when she came back to Molly in the sitting-room, her face was flushed and her eyes were shining with an angry gleam.

"Why, Polly?" said Molly, raising her eyebrows inquiringly.

"It's that horrid Mary!" responded Polly, casting herself down on the sofa with unnecessary vigor. "I don't see what we are going to do, Molly Hapgood; I've a good mind to send you right straight off home."

"You've done it before now," Molly began teasingly, but seeing the real trouble in her friend's face, she relented and asked, "What's gone wrong, Polly?"

"It hasn't gone, it's only going," answered Polly lugubriously. "It's Mary. She says mamma has been promising her a vacation for a long time, and that she's going to take it now, for it's such a good time when part of the family are away. I told her she mustn't; but she says she's going to, or else she'll go for good. I don't dare let her do that, but whatever am I going to do, Molly? She's going right off now, and you'd better go home to stay." And Polly rose and stalked tragically up and down the room, with her fingers buried in her curls.

Molly surveyed her in pity; then she rose to meet the emergency like a heroine.

"I'm not going to go home one single step, Polly," she declared. "I'll stay here and help you through with it."

"But you'll starve, Molly," remonstrated her hostess tearfully.

"Nonsense!" responded Molly. "Now you just sit down and don't go rushing round like this, and we'll talk the matter over, and take an account of stock."

This was encouraging, and Polly felt her spirits coming up again.

"Well?" she asked, as she seated herself on the sofa once more.

"In the first place," said Molly, with a calmness born of inexperience, "we'll tell her to go. I have heard mamma say, often and often, that it's easier to do the work yourself than to have a girl around that's restless and wanting to be off all the time."

There was something so impressive in Molly's manner, as she delivered herself of this sentiment, that Polly gazed at her with a new respect. She had never dreamed that her friend knew so much about housekeeping.

"And so," Molly went on, "we'll just get rid of her and do the work ourselves. I've always been dying to try it, and this is a splendid chance. We won't do much sweeping and dusting, for it will only be for a day or two—How long was she going to be gone, Polly?"

"A week," answered Polly briefly.

"A whole week!" Molly's face fell. Then she resumed, "Well, we shall get on, in some way or other."

"We needn't do much but get the meals and wash the dishes," said Polly, with renewed courage.

"We shouldn't have time, if we wanted to," returned Molly.

"Now, Polly, the question is: how much do you know about cooking?"

"Not very much," Polly confessed. "I can boil eggs and make toast, and I have made coffee, once or twice, just for fun."

"That's good," said Molly enthusiastically; "you're a treasure, Polly. I can do codfish and milk, and make molasses candy, and fry griddle-cakes. We shan't have such a bad time, after all."

"We have ever so many cook-books," suggested Polly. "Can't we do something with them?"

"I'm afraid they'd be tough, unless we boiled them a good while," giggled Molly. "But really, Poll, we can work out of them; try lots of new things, you know, to astonish your father. What does he like?"

"Welsh rarebit," responded Polly promptly; "and baked macaroni, and lemon pudding, and—"

"Not too much, Polly; we can't do all that at once. We'll try something new every meal. Oh, say! don't let's tell your father Mary has gone. We'll have dinner all ready when he comes, and not let him know that we cooked it ourselves, until he's eaten it. Then we'll tell him and surprise him."

"Well," assented Polly, with a vague misgiving that her father might discover the change of cook; "I think it will be fun, Molly; and then, if we get hard up, there are plenty of crackers and preserves to fall back on."

"We shan't want them," said Molly scornfully. "I know we shall have a great deal better things to eat than if Mary stayed. Servant girls are so unreliable!" she added, with a whimsical imitation of Aunt Jane's manner.

"I'll tell you one thing," said Polly, with decision, "we must not tell the girls or Alan, for if they knew about it, they would invite themselves to meals. If we cook for us three, that is all we can do."

"What if they come here to see us?" asked Molly.

"We'll lock the door and hide," replied Polly inhospitably. "There are times when company is a nuisance,—I don't mean you, Molly, for you are head housekeeper, and I couldn't get along without you. But come, we'll go up and put our room in order, while we are waiting for her to get out of the way."

At this very moment Mrs. Adams, one hundred and fifty miles away, was congratulating herself that she had left her little daughter with such a competent servant who, though far from amiable, yet was quite capable of taking the entire charge of the house during her absence. Perhaps it was just as well that she was not within hearing of the conversation which the girls had just been holding.

CHAPTER VII

POLLY'S HOUSEKEEPING

"I'm going now, miss," remarked Mary's voice at the foot of the front stairs.

"Go on, then," said Polly, with dignity, turning to Molly to add, "She wouldn't dare do that if mamma were here. Then she never thinks of calling to us, like this."

Peeping stealthily out at the front window, the girls watched her as she walked off, dressed in her state and festival suit. Then they descended to the kitchen to survey their field of operations.

"She's left it in splendid order, and there's a hot fire; that's one good thing," said Polly, lifting the stove lid to look in.

"With a fire and a cook-book, we can work wonders," said Molly. "Now, Polly, let's plan."

"All right." And Polly sat down on the wood-box. "What shall we have for lunch? That comes first."

"I'll tell you," suggested Molly suddenly, as if struck with a brilliant idea; "let's not have much for lunch. Your father won't be here, so we can eat up whatever was left over from breakfast, and have all our time for the dinner."

"But 'tisn't time to get dinner now; it's only eleven o'clock," said Polly.

"Yes, it is time," returned Molly. "I want to try a lemon pudding for dessert, if he likes them, and it takes ever so much time, I know. We must feed him up well, so he won't look thin to your mother when, she gets back."

"Let's see how the oven is," said Polly, pulling open the door and peering in. "It feels nice and warm, so perhaps we'd better go to work."

"Where are your cook-books?" demanded Molly.

"Here." And Polly brought out a number of books and pamphlets. "We ought to find a rule in some of these."

Molly possessed herself of the largest.

"'Marion Holland'—no, 'Harland,'" she read. "Oh, I've heard of her! I'll look in this, and you take another. Let's see, where's the index? 'Soups—fish—poultry—meats—company.' Oh, where is it? 'Eggs—cake.' That sounds like it. 'Servants—puddings.' At last! 'Apple—cottage—cracker—lemon.' Here are two lemon puddings, Polly." And Molly glanced up to see Polly, with an anxious frown, reading intently from her own small book. She looked up, in her turn, to answer,—

"Here's another, so you read yours and then I'll read mine, and we'll see which we like best."

"'One cup of sugar, four eggs, two tablespoons cornstarch, two lemons, one pint milk, one tablespoon butter,'" read

Molly. "You get your milk hot and put in the starch and boil five minutes—Oh, there's a lot more to do! Just see here."

Both heads were bent over the book. Then Polly exclaimed,—

"Mine is easier, I know. Listen: 'A quarter of a pound of suet, half a pound of bread crumbs, four ounces of sugar, the juice of two lemons, the grated rind of one, and one egg. Boil it well in an *Agate* pot, and serve with sauce.'"

There was an expressive pause.

"Yours is better, after all," said Polly. "I don't know what suet is, but I don't believe we have any; and besides, it's ever so much easier to measure cups than pounds."

The girls enveloped themselves in gingham aprons and set to work. Polly rummaged in store-room and pantry, and brought out the necessary materials for the pudding, while Molly measured and mixed.

"Polly," she called suddenly, in a tone of distress. Polly put her head out from the pantry. Her face was decorated with coal-dust from the stove and flour from the barrel, but she was too intent upon her work to care for that.

"Well," she asked, "what's the matter?"

"There isn't enough cornstarch," said Molly, showing the empty paper.

"How much more do you need?" asked Polly, looking rather blank.

"Another spoonful," replied Molly; "and the milk is all

Anna Chapin Ray

boiling now, ready for it."

"I wish we had Alan here, to send for some," sighed Polly.

"There isn't time. Don't you suppose your mother has another package?" asked Molly, stirring the boiling milk in an excited fashion that sent occasional drops spattering and hissing over the stove.

"Perhaps she has." And Polly hurried away to the store-room, jingling her keys with a comical air of consequence.

She came flying back, in a moment, with a small package in her hand.

"I wonder if this won't do just as well," she said. "It's marked elastic starch, instead of cornstarch, but it looks ever so much like the other, and it's all there is, anyway."

Molly eyed it with little favor.

"It isn't just the same," she said thoughtfully; "but if we can't get anything else, we may as well use it. Here goes, anyway." And she added a heaping spoonful.

The pudding was mixed, poured into a baking dish and set into the oven.

"There," said Molly, with an air of relief, "that's done, all but watching to see that it doesn't burn."

"And clearing up the table," sighed Polly. "It doesn't seem as if we could have used so many dishes, just for one little pudding; does it, Molly?"

"Never mind," said Molly consolingly; "when it's done, we

shall feel paid for it all. I don't mind washing dishes. You put the sugar and stuff away, while I do them. I wish I felt sure about this other starch," she added, taking up the paper and glancing at it.

Polly's back was turned, when she heard an exclamation of horror. Looking around, she saw Molly who, with the package still in her hand, had dropped into a chair.

"What is it?" she asked anxiously.

"See here!" And Molly pointed solemnly to the label, then burst into another fit of merriment, as she watched Polly's face grow blank while she road aloud,—

"'Elastic Starch: Prepared for Laundry Purposes, only.'"

"Whatever do you suppose it will do to us?" asked Molly, struggling to regain her self-control, and then laughing harder than ever.

"I'm sure I don't know," answered Polly. "It can't kill us, but it may stiffen us up some. I wonder if we'd better try to eat it, Molly." "I'm not going to have all my work wasted," said Molly decidedly, as she opened the oven door and peeped in. "It's browning just beautifully, and looks all right. We won't say or think anything about it, and I don't believe it will hurt us any. Even if it does, we have a doctor right in the house."

"Unless it kills him, first of all," added Polly gloomily. "But I'm tired now, Molly; we'll have lunch while that is baking, and then we can rest till time to get dinner. I never supposed it was so much work to keep house."

"What are you going to have for dinner?" asked Molly, ignoring the last remark.

"Beefsteak and potatoes and pudding," said Polly. "That's enough. We don't want to begin better than we can keep up."

Their lunch was over, and the dishes piled up, to be washed later, when they should feel more like it; the girls had made themselves presentable again after their labors, and were sunning themselves like two young turtles, on the front steps, when they saw Alan coming towards the house.

"Now, Molly," Polly cautioned her; "remember we aren't going to tell that we are housekeeping."

"What have you been doing with yourselves?" inquired Alan, as he sat down on the step below them and pulled his soft hat forward, to keep the dazzling sun out of his eyes. "I came here just before noon, but I couldn't start up anybody. Where were you?"

"How strange we didn't hear you!" said Molly innocently. "We were here all the morning. Are you sure the bell rang?"

"I should say it did," said Alan. "I pulled it till I was tired. You must have been deaf, or asleep."

"We weren't either; we were only just busy," answered Polly, with, an air of importance which would have roused Alan's suspicions, had not Molly come to the rescue by asking about her cousins.

"They're off driving, this afternoon," answered Alan. "They tried to make me go, but I told them flatly I didn't want to, so they took Florence instead. I had to play casino with Kit all last evening, and that was all I could stand. I say, I'm going to stay to dinner over here, if you ask me to." The girls exchanged glances of consternation which, happily, passed over the top of Alan's head, and were unseen.

"Well," assented Polly, with some reluctance; "you can stay, I suppose, but you won't get much to be thankful for, I warn you."

"As long as you tease so hard," responded Alan, disregarding the coolness of her tone; "I'll stay, then. I told mother I knew you'd be in a fight, by this time, and need me to make peace, so she'd better not expect me till I came. Now, honestly, aren't you glad to see me?" And he beamed up at the girls with such goodwill that they relaxed their severity, and took the lad into their confidence.

"Now, Alan," Molly began solemnly; "if you stay here, you mustn't ever tell the other girls, but Mary has gone, and Polly and I are doing the cooking ourselves."

Alan whistled; but not even his whistle was as disrespectful as was his following remark,—

"Anything left over from yesterday that I can have?"

"You must behave, if you stay, Alan," said Polly firmly. "You can go home, or else you can go to work with us, when it's time. I've told you before now that we won't have any lazy people around this house."

"All right; what shall I do first?" And Alan pulled off his cuffs and folded back the bottoms of his sleeves. "Hullo! who's this coming?" he exclaimed, as a figure turned in at the gate.

"Why, it's Mr. Solomon Baxter," said Polly, in some surprise. "How queer! He never comes here." "Perhaps he's after your father," suggested Molly, in an undertone.

"He must be," answered Polly, as she rose to meet him; "but

I should think he would know that papa's at his office, not here." Mr. Baxter was a widower of fifty, whose wife had recently died, leaving him with six children under ten years old. Whatever may have been the motives leading to the match, surely Mrs. Baxter could never have married her husband either for his personal beauty or for his repose of manner; for Mr. Baxter's bald head was covered with a smooth yellow wig, and his figure presented every appearance of having its joints so tightly wired together that they could not play freely in their places, while it was a matter of common report that his nervous, excitable manner had worried his wife until she was glad to be at rest.

"How do you do? Is your aunt at home?" he answered Polly's greeting.

This was unexpected, but Polly reflected that they might be on some committee together.

"I am sorry, but she and mamma were sent for to go to New York," she explained courteously. "Their brother is ill. Won't you come in, sir?"

"Just for a little while, perhaps," said Mr. Baxter, following her into the parlor. "If they're away, who's keeping house?"

"We are, Molly Hapgood and I," answered Polly, a little surprised at the question.

"A good girl?"

Polly looked up in astonishment, thinking that he had taken that way of praising her. On the contrary, she discovered that this was intended as a question.

"What was it you said," she asked.

"Have you a good girl?"

"We haven't any," replied Polly meekly; "ours went away this morning."

"Just like them! They're the greatest plague in the world!" said Mr. Baxter explosively, and so rapidly that his words appeared to be tumbling over each other, in their haste to escape from his lips. "They haven't any honor; mine went off yesterday, and I haven't any to-day. She was a splendid girl with a great trunk full of real nice clothes, and such refined tastes, she always drank English breakfast tea. But she wouldn't stay, because I would not let her have all the soap she wanted. Extravagant things!" Mr. Baxter suddenly reined in his tongue; then added abruptly, "Who's housekeeper generally, your mother or your aunt?"

"Mamma is," replied Polly.

"Oh!" Mr. Baxter's tone was rather annoyed. There was a prolonged pause, while Polly watched the clock and reflected that it was time to put on the potatoes.

"Are your children well?" inquired Molly politely, feeling that it was her duty to say something.

"Quite well, only the baby has the croup almost every night. They have a great many colds, but I tell them that it's good enough for them, and perhaps it may teach them to be a little more careful," answered their fond parent sympathetically.

"I had a cold last winter," remarked Alan, launching himself into the conversation with this bit of personal reminiscence.

"Oh," said Mr. Baxter again.

There was another pause, a long one this time. Polly broke it, for she saw that both Molly and Alan were on the point of laughing.

"It is a beautiful day," she began. "We were going to ride this morning with Job, but—" She paused abruptly. Job had done conspicuous duty in Mrs. Baxter's funeral procession, in fact, he had helped to bear the disconsolate widower and his children to her grave. Polly felt that further mention of him would be ill-timed. Mr. Baxter appeared to be pursuing his own train of thought. "Is Miss Roberts well?" he asked, after another interval.

"Very," answered Polly.

"Not given to being sick much?"

"No, she is very strong."

"Well," said Mr. Baxter, rising with an air of relief, "I must be going. Just tell your aunt, sissy, that I called on her. Where's my hat?"

He had mislaid it somewhere, and while he charged up and down the parlor looking for it, Alan and Molly prudently withdrew, to laugh unseen. At length he discovered it in the hall, and went away, leaving the children to speculate vainly on the cause of his visit.

"Sissy!" exclaimed Polly violently. "Sissy! I wonder how he'd like me to call him bubby! I'll try it, the next time he comes. But he stayed so forever that we shan't have time to cook any potatoes for dinner."

They surely would not, for the fire was out and the stove was cold.

"Your poor father!" groaned Molly. "And we weren't going to let him know that anything was wrong."

"Never mind," said Polly; "we'll give him just meat and pudding. That's enough for any man."

They cheered up at that, and, with Alan's help, they went to work to build a fire, making many discoveries during the operation about dampers and grates and their uses. But time, always unaccommodating, refused to wait for them, and six o'clock came far too soon, and brought the doctor in its train.

Dr. Adams was rather perplexed when he went into the house and was met by no one at the door. Polly and her mother usually greeted him, but to-night the front of the house was deserted.

"The girls must be off somewhere," he said to himself. "Well, I'll go out and tell Mary to give me my dinner now, without waiting for them."

He made his way to the kitchen, noting to his surprise, as he passed through the dining-room, that the table was only half set for the meal, and that the few articles on it had a little the appearance of having been thrown at it from a distance. Dr. Adams was an orderly, methodical man, and his wife's careful housekeeping was quite to his liking. However, he reflected that, during her absence, there must and would be irregularities, and passed on to the kitchen. As he opened the door, he was met by a cloud of dense, bluish white smoke which brought the quick tears to his eyes. Through the thick air he could see, not the ample proportions of his usual cook, but three small figures that were hurrying to and fro with a purposeless, ineffectual bustle which yet accomplished nothing. One of the figures hailed him in disconsolate tones,—

"Oh, papa! are you home so soon?"

"So soon?" he answered, as well as he could for coughing; "it's six o'clock now. Is dinner ready? What are you doing out here?"

It took but a moment to explain the matter, and then the doctor showed that it was not without reason that Polly called him the best father in the world. He was just back from a long drive out into the country with a fellow doctor, to pass judgment upon a critical case; he must visit a man in the hospital before his evening office hour; he was tired, hungry, and in a hurry, and there was no immediate prospect of dinner. But the three weary, heated, crocky faces before him moved him to pity, and he threw open the outer door, saying briskly,—

"Let's have a little air here, and see what's the matter."

"The fire won't seem to burn," said Alan. "It just smokes and goes out."

"So I see," said the doctor laughing. "Perhaps it would go better, my boy, if the dampers were not shut up tight. All it needs is a little draught,—see?" And in a moment there was a comfortable crackling sound going on inside the stove.

Before his marriage, the doctor had been in the habit of camping out every summer, and his old experiences came to his aid in the present crisis. While the girls flew in to set the table, he quickly brought the fire into order, and cooked the meat as handily as a woman. Thanks to him, the supper proved a merry one in spite of the smoky dining-room, the meagre bill of fare, and the great white blister on the side of Alan's hand, which the lad was doing his best to keep out of the doctor's sight. Molly raised her eyebrows and darted a comical glance at Polly when the doctor asked for a second plate of the pudding, and it was not until long afterwards that the girls knew of the manful effort he had made to swallow the sticky compound.

"Can I do anything more to help you?" he asked, stopping behind Alan's chair as he was going away.

"You've done enough already, I should think," answered Molly gratefully.

"It was too bad for Mary to leave you in the lurch," he replied. Then, as his eyes fell on Alan's hand, he added, "That's a hard burn, my boy! Why in the world didn't you say something about it?"

"What was the use?" inquired Alan calmly. "Grumbling about it wouldn't do it any good."

"No; but I could," responded the doctor. "I like your pluck, but there's no use making a martyr of yourself for nothing. Come into my den and let me put something on it." And after a moment's delay, he went striding away down the street, looking at his watch as he walked.

"How do people ever manage to keep house?" sighed Molly, an hour later.

The dishes were washed, the rooms in order, and the two girls were luxuriously settled on the sofa, which they had drawn up in front of Alan's blazing fire on the hearth. Alan himself was stretched out on the rug, with his yellow head resting against the seat of the sofa, beside Polly's hand. Too tired to talk, the children had sat there quietly watching the fire until Molly broke the silence.

"I don't see, I'm sure," returned Polly. "It never seems as if mamma did much, even when we haven't any girl; and I'm tired almost to death, with what little we've done."

"I'm slowly getting to think," said Molly reflectively; "that our mothers are wonderful women. If it takes three of us to spoil one dinner, how do they get along, to do all the housekeeping and look out for us and sew and all?"

"Perhaps they know more to start with," suggested Alan, ducking his head out of reach of Polly's threatening fingers.

"If you hadn't been and gone and burned yourself in our service, Alan," she said, laughing, "I would turn you out of the house."

But Molly was too much in earnest to heed this by-play.

"I believe I'll learn to cook," she went on. "I don't mean fancy cooking, but good, plain things that one could live on."

"Why not go to cooking school?" asked Polly.

"Yes," rejoined Molly scornfully; "and learn to make chicken salad and angel cake and chocolate creams. That's all very well, but I want to know how to do something that will help along, when we get in a tight place. Hark! what's that?" she added, as a sudden flurry of rain swept against the windows.

"That's cheerful!" said Alan, starting up. "I don't care about getting a ducking. I wish I'd gone home before this."

"No matter," urged Polly. "Stay till papa comes; he'll be in at nine, and then we'll give you an umbrella and things."

"Well." And Alan threw more wood on the fire and then

settled back into his former position; "I may as well, for I don't believe it will rain any harder than it does now, and maybe it will stop. I say, Polly," he went on; "tell us a story, there's a good fellow."

"I'm too tired to-night, Alan," Polly began; "I haven't an idea in my head and—Is that you, papa?" she called, as the front door opened and shut.

"No, it's mamma," and Mrs. Adams walked into the parlor.

"Jerusalem!" and Polly sprang up with a glad cry. "Wherever did you come from?"

She was surrounded and dragged forward to the sofa, where Alan took her cloak, Molly her bonnet, and Polly pulled off her gloves.

"This is delightful to be so waited on," said Mrs. Adams. "It is worth while going away, to have the pleasure of coming back to my three children. Now come and sit down, and tell me all about it." And with a girl at each side and a boy at her feet, she prepared to hear the story of their doings.

"First, how is Uncle Charlie?" asked Polly, sure from her mother's bright face that there was no bad news.

"It was a sudden attack of indigestion, and he was much better before we reached him; but for a little while they thought there was no chance for him. Aunt Jane is going to stay for a week or two, but I was in a hurry to come back to my baby. And that reminds me, I stopped at your house, Alan, to tell your mother I had come and that Molly would stay here till Monday; and when I found that you were here, I said I should keep you, too, till morning. But now you must tell me how you've been amusing yourselves."

"With cooking," said Polly, with a tragic groan. "Mary's gone off for a week, and the fire went out, and Alan burned himself, and we nearly starved. I'm glad you've come back; oh, you can't guess how glad!"

By degrees they told the tale of their woes, not omitting the slightest detail, while Mrs. Adams leaned back on the sofa and laughed till the tears came.

"But there's one good thing about it all," observed Molly, in conclusion. "We've had a perfectly dreadful time, but it will teach us to appreciate our mothers and know a little what they are doing, the whole time."

CHAPTER VIII

HALLOWE'EN

"You have such a different way of looking at things from what mamma did," said Katharine.

"Perhaps it is because we have lived so differently," Mrs. Hapgood answered her.

It was a cold, gray day in late October, a day which showed that November was close at hand. The other girls were off for some frolic, Alan was reading and dozing on the sofa in the next room, so Mrs. Hapgood and Katharine had the parlor to themselves, and were snugly settled in two willow chairs drawn up in front of the fire, Katharine busy on a dainty bit of embroidery, Mrs. Hapgood putting a new sleeve into a gown which had yielded before Molly's energetic elbows.

"I wonder if that is it." And Katharine laid down her work and fell to pondering on the matter. After a time, she resumed, "After all, auntie, I don't know but I like your way better. I thought at first it was going to be slow here. At home, there's never any time for quiet talks like this; it's just nothing but a hurry and a scrabble, and when we get through, we've nothing to show for it. I've only been here six weeks, but I really feel as if I know you now better than I do mamma." And Katharine rested her head against the back of her chair, while the dark eyes fixed on the fire grew a little dim.

Mrs. Hapgood leaned over and rested her hand on the girl's, as it lay on the arm of her chair.

"I'm glad to have you say so, Katharine," said she. "For this year, I am to stand in place of a mother to you, you know, and I like to have you feel at home here."

"I know all that," answered Katharine; "and I'm glad they sent me here, only it mixes me all up. When I was at home and kept hearing little bits about it, the parties and the flowers and the pretty gowns, I felt as if I couldn't wait to be old enough to be in it all. When I came away, mamma said I was to be here a year, and then, go home to come out, so I could be ready to be married at eighteen, as she did. A year is such a little while to wait that I thought I was almost there. But when I came here, I found the girls of my age acting like children, and having splendid times doing what I had always thought was silly, and not caring the least bit about society and all that. I shall just get used to this and like it, and then go back into the other once more."

"But not in just the same way, I hope."

"I suppose not, auntie; but it won't make so very much difference, after all."

"Perhaps not," her aunt answered; "but it may make a little. If you hadn't come to us, you would never have seen the other side, that there are a few good times outside of the parties and the young men. And even if you go back into it when you go home, as you probably will, Katharine, it won't do any harm for you to have had a year to stop and think, and talk matters over, before plunging into the 'scrabble,' as you call it."

"It seemed so queer, when I first came East," said Katharine, as she took up her work again, "to see you and Molly sit down and talk for an hour at a time. Mamma hasn't ever done it with us, only to joke with us, or ask about our lessons once in a while. But everything that comes up, Molly and Polly Adams say, 'Mamma says so,' or 'Mamma thinks so.'"

She sewed steadily for a few moments, then she broke off, to ask, with an air of mock tragedy,—

"Mamma says she wants me to marry at eighteen; but what in the world should I do, auntie, if nobody should ask me?"

"Not get married, I suppose," returned her aunt composedly.

Katharine's face fell.

"What! be an old maid, like Polly's Aunt Jane!" she exclaimed.

"It isn't necessary that you should be like her, even if you shouldn't marry." And Mrs. Hapgood laughed at the horror in Katharine's tone. Then she went on, seriously, "Katharine, may I talk very plainly with you, just as if you were really my daughter?"

"Please do, auntie." And Katharine drew her chair a little closer to her aunt's.

"You were just saying that your mother and I look at things differently, Katharine, and it is true that we do. I wouldn't find fault with her for anything, for she has been a dear, good sister to me; but it seems to me that she has made a little bit of a mistake in letting your head get filled with all these thoughts of being married. You are only a child yet, my dear, and it is years before such ideas ought to come to you. But now they are here, I am going to tell you just what I think about it all. Not all women are fitted to marry; some would be happier and better without it. The day is long past when a woman must either marry or be laughed at as an old maid. What I want my girls to do is to grow into strong, noble women who are fitted to fill any position that opens before them, and to fill it well, with no thought of self, but only for the good of others. Then, if the time ever comes that you are asked to be the wife of a man, for the sake of whose love and companionship you are ready to give up all else, then you will do right to marry him, but not until then."

There was another pause. Mrs. Hapgood went on,—

"And since we are on the subject, Katharine, there is one more word to say. If the time ever comes for you, remember, in making your great decision, that married life is not all sunshine, but that there are the same little every-day worries after marriage as there were before. If a woman is strong enough to be a true, devoted wife, she can have no happier, better life than in her own home. But she has no right to promise without thinking it all over, whether she can sacrifice and work, can suffer hardship and even wrong for her husband's sake. Those are solemn words, dear, and should never be spoken thoughtlessly: 'For better for worse, for richer for poorer, in sickness and in health—'"

"You make it all mean so much more than mamma did," said Katharine thoughtfully. "She never talked to me like this. You make me half afraid of it, auntie."

"So much the better," her aunt replied. "It isn't anything that you can do one day, and undo the next; but it is a matter of life—and death," she added, as if to herself. Then she went on, with an entire change of tone, "Now, Kit, we have been talking about a very serious matter, and I am nearly through. But we may never speak of it again, so before we leave it, I want to just say that I wish you could put this whole subject out of your head for years, until the great question comes to you,—better still, if it had never been put into your head in the first place. However, that mischief is done. Still, try as hard as you can, for this year at least, to forget all about it. Then, if you must remember it at all, remember it as we have spoken of it, a serious question which must be settled between you and your conscience. In the meantime, do the very best you can to develop yourself into a helpful woman, ready for any call that may come. Your call will come, in one way or another, and all you have to do is to be prepared to answer 'ready.' And the grand secret of this preparation lies in perfect unconsciousness of self. It is all hidden in you, Kit, if you only try to make the most of it. And now I shouldn't at all wonder if we were better friends than ever for this frank talk, should you?"

The girl did not speak, but, bending over, she kissed her aunt impulsively and left the room.

"The child is finding her soul at last," said Mrs. Hapgood to herself. "Kate had smothered it and buried it under her false ideas of womanhood; but it is there, and Katharine might so easily make a woman to be proud of, with her warm, loving nature, if only she could be kept out of the 'scrabble' for a few years longer. Well, my son, what is it?" she added aloud, as Alan came in, yawning and stretching, and dropped into the chair just vacated by Katharine.

"Nothing, only I'm sick of reading, and came in for my share in the talk. Has Kit gone?"

"She just went up-stairs," answered his mother, surveying her boy with fond pride, for, in all truth, Alan was good to look at as he sat there, a real bonnie boy who might gladden any mother's heart. Mother-like, she passed a caressing hand over his yellow hair, and straightened out his coat-collar, but she only said, "Alan, you are positively growing tall, every single day."

"Am I?" asked the boy absently. Then he went on. "Speaking of Kit, mother, has it struck you that she is leaving off a little of her airs and graces? She isn't near as silly as she was when she first came."

"I don't think Katharine is silly," his mother replied; "it is only a little way she has. You are too critical of her, Alan."

"Well, she makes me tired," responded the boy, rolling up his eyes at his mother, whose deep-seated objection to that phrase he well knew. "She wants to be the very middle of things when we're together, and must have just so much fuss made over her. She'd be well enough, if it wasn't for that."

"Katharine has a great deal of character, after all," said his mother. "You aren't quite fair to her, Alan. If Polly or Florence did the same things she does, you would think it was all right."

"Polly and Kit aren't to be spoken of in the same breath," answered Alan energetically. "Florence doesn't count, one way or the other; but Polly is a splendid girl, and about the best friend I have. She always fights for me, and it would be mean if I didn't return the compliment once in a while. Here comes Mrs. Adams now," he added, as he glanced out of the window.

It was only an errand, not a call, she hurriedly explained.

Friday night was going to be Hallowe'en, and wouldn't Alan and the girls come over to celebrate, as a surprise to Polly? Jean and Florence would be there, too. Then she went away again, leaving Alan to discuss the matter with his mother.

Friday evening came, and the surprise was kept a profound secret. Mrs. Adams had called Polly up-stairs to try on a new gown which she had just finished, and Polly was still revolving in front of the mirror, making vain attempts to view her back, when the bell rang.

"You go down, Polly," said her mother. "I am all covered with basting-threads."

So Polly, in all the glory of her new gown, went running down the stairs to the door, and started back in astonishment as her six guests came solemnly marching into the house, dressed in their best, to do honor to the occasion.

"Why, what are you doing here?" she was beginning rather inhospitably, when her mother unexpectedly came to her relief and invited the girls to take off their things.

"We're a party, Polly," exclaimed Jessie. "How stupid you are not to see it!"

"It's Hallowe'en," added Florence; "and we've been asked to come to celebrate it."

"Oh-h-h!" And a new light dawned on Polly. "It's a surprise party, is it? Who started it? You, Jerusalem?"

"Why don't you take your little friends into the parlor and converse with them, Polly?" asked Aunt Jane's prim voice. "Don't you know that it isn't polite to leave them standing here?"

A sharp reply was trembling on the tip of Polly's tongue; but she caught her mother's warning glance, so she resolutely turned her back on the blue satin bow which Aunt Jane had donned for the party, and led the way into the parlor.

Then the fun began, for Mrs. Adams had studied to find all the amusing tricks, whether they belonged to Hallowe'en or not. She was the gayest of the gay, entering into all the frolic, and doing her best to make Aunt Jane unbend and have a share in the games. But there must be a skeleton at every feast, and Miss Roberts played the part to perfection, sitting back against the wall, and only smiling indulgently, now and then, as the room rang with the shouts of the young people. It all started with a tub and a plate of apples which mysteriously appeared in the dining-room, and soon they were all in a kneeling circle around the tub, bobbing for the apples, that took a malicious delight in ducking under the water and rolling away, just as the white teeth were ready to seize the stem. The captured apples were only just pared and the seeds counted, when Mrs. Adams called them away to try their fate on one single apple which hung by a string from the top of the room.

"It is an unfailing test," she said. "If you can take a bite out of this apple without touching it, except with your teeth, you will live to get married. Otherwise, you will die an old maid."

Now, it sounds like a very easy matter to bite an apple; but when it is free to swing this way and that as you touch it, the success is not so sure. Alan first chased the apple up and down, gnashed his teeth and retired. Next Florence took her turn, with no better success. Jessie, too, failed to get a taste, even of the skin. Then Jean advanced to the charge.

"Now watch," she said, laughing. "I'm going at this on

scientific principles. See here!"

She hit the apple with such force as to throw it far up and out, waited with wide-open mouth until, pendulum-like, it swung back and, at the instant of its reaching her, before it had turned, she struck her strong, young teeth into the side and brought away a generous mouthful.

"There!" said she triumphantly, as she marched back to her place. "I defy anybody to do better than that."

They melted lead and poured it into water, to learn from the shape as it cooled the secret of their future work; they floated needles on water, watching them sink, or swim and gather in groups; they roasted nuts in the ashes, and tried the old, old test of the three dishes of water. But the prettiest trick of all was one that brought them back to the great tub once more, to float the walnut-shell boats, with their burning candles fixed in each. As the girls took their pairs of shells, one with a pink, the other with a blue candle placed in the middle like a mast, it was curious to see the difference in their ways of launching them on this mimic ocean of life. Jean and Jessie dropped theirs in thoughtlessly, only intent on the fun of the moment. Florence put hers in daintily and with care not to wet her fingers, and Molly and Katharine launched theirs out boldly, following them up with a little ripple which sent them rocking away into the midst of the tiny fleet. But Polly, Polly who did not believe in signs, had an anxious pucker about her eyebrows as she started out her wee vessels, and hurried them all their way with a mighty splash which threatened to capsize them, there and then.

Mrs. Adams stood back, watching the group of bright-colored gowns and eager faces, as the young people gathered more closely about the tub to see the fate of their lights, now exclaiming in chorus at some crisis, now in anxious silence while they waited for new developments.

"My light has failed, first of all," said Katharine regretfully.

"Which is it?" asked Mrs. Adams.

"The pink one."

"That is the man," she answered, bending over to look at the poor little end of candle, with only a smouldering wick to show that any life was left.

"It may come up again, Kit," said Florence consolingly. "While there's life, there's hope."

"They are alive as long as they float," Mrs. Adams interpreted. "When they sink, they are dead; but this one is only ill, or else his plans have failed."

"That's almost as bad," said Jean. "But isn't this just like Florence? Her two have cuddled up side by side, and are blazing away in a corner, all by themselves." "Look at Polly's and mine," said Molly. "We have joined hands. We must be going to live together, all four of us."

"In a New York tenement house," suggested Alan unkindly.

"No such thing," returned Polly. "Molly shall keep house, and I'll board with her. I hope my man will be proprietor of a restaurant, though," she added, in an aside to Alan.

Suddenly there came a wail from Jessie.

"Girls, girls! Just look at mine!"

"Where are they?" asked Molly.

"Here." And Jessie pointed tragically to one side of the tub, where the blue candle lay at the bottom of the sea, and the pink one, though still floating above it, had burned out and tilted to one side in an attitude of profound dejection.

"Where was Moses when the light went out?
Where was Moses, what was he about?"

sang Alan teasingly.

But even while he was singing, an energetic wave from Jean's side overturned his own small ships and left them floating bottom upwards.

"Just my luck!" he remarked, as he rose. "I knew I should come to some untimely end. As Poll says, I don't believe in signs, anyway."

The chocolate and wafers had been passed, and the fateful loaf of cake had been cut, bringing the ring to Florence, and the thimble, fitting symbol of single blessedness, to Jean; and still there was time for a little more of the fun. Some one suggested a game of forfeits, and a pile of them was soon collected, to be held over the head of Jessie who was chosen judge, as being the youngest girl present. Her ingenuity was endless, and she kept them laughing over her ridiculous fines, until nearly all had been redeemed.

"Only two or three more," said Jean encouragingly. "Here's one of them, now."

"Fine or superfine?"

"Fine."

"Fine? Let's see, I know whose 'tis," meditated Jessie. "Oh, I haven't any ideas left! Let him.

"Bow to the wittiest,
Kneel to the prettiest,
And kiss the one he loves best."

Like most sensible mothers, Mrs. Adams had a horror of anything like kissing games; and now she frowned a little, in spite of herself. No one of the V, she felt sure, would have pronounced this fine. She turned to glance at Alan who stood for a moment, blushing as his eye moved over the group. Then he walked up to Polly and bowed low, passed on to Katharine's chair where he dropped on one knee, and then, walking straight to Mrs. Adams, he bent down and kissed her cheek with a heartiness which was not all play. She put out her hand and drew him down on the sofa, at her side.

"Thank you, dear," she whispered. "It was a pretty compliment, and we old people enjoy such things, you may be sure."

"It was true," said Alan simply, as he settled himself beside her with a confiding, little-boyish motion.

The last forfeit had not been redeemed, when the heavy portieres swung open, and a figure swathed in dark draperies and with a veil over her face came slowly into the room. The girls gazed doubtfully at this ghostly apparition, till a brown hand—was extended and a deep voice spoke from under the veil,—

"I am here to reveal the future. To-night is the time to know the secret of your coming lives. Let the oldest advance first."

Katharine, still a little in awe of the mysterious stranger, stepped forward and laid her hand on the dark one before her. The being scanned it closely.

"A long life," she said, "and a happy one, for you will slowly learn the joy of doing good to those around you and forgetting yourself for others. Then, wherever you go, you will be surrounded with friends and your name will long be remembered."

Katharine smiled, as she stepped back and Jean took her place.

"You will have the best possession the earth can give, a contented mind. I see in the future a little house presided over by a strong, quiet woman whose life is in her home."

Then Molly's turn came. Her fate was quickly spoken.

"Yours is a husband six feet tall, and your children will number nineteen, as they sit about your meagre table."

Molly groaned, as she yielded her place to Florence.

"I see a lordly house, richly furnished and filled with servants. Within is a devoted husband who watches over a wife with golden hair."

"How elegant!" said Polly. "Now it's my turn." And she held out her hand with a smile.

"You will suffer much and have much happiness," the voice went on. "You will love deeply and be loved in return, and the end will more than repay the beginning."

"Isn't that queer!" And Polly withdrew, to ponder on her mystical fortune.

"Now Jessie," said Mrs. Adams; "see what fate has in store for you."

"I'm half afraid," she said, laughing.

"Love, happiness, and sunshine," was what she heard. "A tiny cottage simply furnished with a teapot and eleven cats."

There was a shout.

"Now, Alan."

The brown hand trembled a little, and the eyes under the veil looked right into Alan's, as she spoke. "Some pain, much joy; a slow, even growth into a glorious manhood that knows no wrong, but lives for truth. Whatever else maybe is hidden from my sight."

"What a splendid one, Alan!" exclaimed Polly, her face flushing, as she took in all the meaning of the words.

And Katharine added quietly,—

"You have read us very well, Aunt Ruth."

"Mamma?" exclaimed Molly and Alan, in a breath.

"Yes, mamma," answered Mrs. Hapgood's voice, as she quickly shed her wrappings. "I thought I would have a finger in this pie, too. But how did you know me so soon, Katharine?"

"I knew nobody else would say what you did, for it was just a part of our talk the other day," she replied, as she unpinned the thick veil from Mrs. Hapgood's hair.

"Good-night, Mrs. Adams," said Jean, as they stood grouped about her in the hall. "This has been a lovely Hallowe'en, and I shall always remember it, I know."

"I hope you will, too, till next year," added Alan suggestively, as he went out into the bright starlight.

Anna Chapin Ray

CHAPTER IX

THE NEW READING CLUB

"The beautiful summer of All Saints" was at its height, and the soft haze lay upon the blue hills and rested lightly over the meadows along the river. Such days were tempting enough to entice a hermit from his cell, and Mrs. Adams and the young people had agreed to devote Saturday afternoon to a long drive. Soon after their early lunch they had started off, Job leading the way, with Mrs. Adams, Jessie, Molly, and Jean, followed by Cob, the wiry little mustang that Mr. Shepard had sent East for his daughters' use, drawing Katharine, Florence, Polly, and Alan. Their destination was the nearer of the two mountains, a drive to the foot and then a scramble to the tip-top house, for the sake of one last look down upon the beautiful valley, before winter should shut it in. Unfortunately, Job was in one of his languid moods that day, and in spite of warning checks and flapping of lines, and even a mild application of the whip, he refused to break into a trot; but, with bowed head and discouraged mien, he plodded onward with as much apparent effort as if each motion of his aged frame were to be his last. In vain Katharine again and again reined in Cob, to wait for his companion; the old horse lagged farther and farther in the rear. At length Mrs. Adams called,—

"This is unbearable, Katharine! I am afraid we shall have to give up and go home. Job acts as if he couldn't crawl another step. I'm sorry," she added to her passengers, "to spoil our plan, but I dare not drive this old fellow any further, for fear he might never get home."

But even the turning back again failed to inspire Job as it usually did. In her secret heart, Mrs. Adams regarded this as an ominous symptom, and felt an ever-increasing anxiety lest he should never reach home alive. They were less than two miles from the town, but it was a long hour before Job dragged his weary way up the street, in at the gate, and tottered feebly up to the open door of the barn. By making little side excursions up and down the country, the other carriage had managed to keep respectfully in the rear; and Katharine now tied Cob outside the gate, while the others crowded around Job to watch with pitying eyes, as Mrs. Adams unharnessed this feeble veteran who had probably gone on his final march. The last strap was unbuckled and allowed to fall to the ground, while Mrs. Adams invitingly held up the worn old halter, to slip it on Job's nose. Perhaps she was slower than usual, perhaps some sudden thought of a neglected opportunity shot through Job's brain. However that might be, there was a quick scattering of the group, as two iron-shod heels flew up into the air, the brown head was playfully tossed from side to side, and Job, the feeble, the lifeless, went frisking away across the lawn, now galloping furiously up and down, with a lofty disregard of the holes he was tearing in the soft, dry turf, now stopping to roll on his back and kick his aged legs ecstatically in the air, with all the joyous abandonment of a young colt, then scrambling up again, to go pounding away, straight across a brilliant bed of chrysanthemums and only pausing, for a moment, to gaze pensively out over the front gate.

"Whoa, Job! Whoa, boy!" Mrs. Adams was calling in vain,

Anna Chapin Ray

while Jean exclaimed spitefully,—

"Mean old thing! I'll never be sorry for him again! I didn't lean back all the time we were gone, but just sat on the very front edge of the seat and tried to make myself as light as I could."

Then followed an exciting chase, for Job appeared to have regained all the agility of his far-off ancestors that roamed the plains at their own sweet will. Such sudden wheelings! Such wild leaps! Such frantic kicks! He refused to be coaxed; he cocked up his ears in derisive scorn when they scolded him and requested him to whoa. He had no intention of whoaing. He recognized from afar that a snare lay hidden somewhere in the measure of oats which Mrs. Adams held out before him, and he drew back his lips in a contemptuous smile, as he capered away to the remotest corner of the grounds. The pursuit lasted for an hour, and at the end of that time, Job appeared to be far fresher than his pursuers, fresher even than he had been at the start.

It was plain that nothing was to be gained in this way, so Mrs. Adams and the girls retired to the house to take counsel, leaving Alan to drive Job to the stable, and come back to dinner with the others.

"I am tired, if he isn't," sighed Mrs. Adams, dropping into a chair by the window overlooking the lawn.

"Has he ever done it before?" asked Florence sympathetically.

"Never with me; but he used to get away from John, when he was younger. Now he has started, I am afraid he will repeat the experiment, he has had such a good time to-day. It just makes me want to whip him!" And Mrs. Adams glared out at the unconscious Job who was quietly cropping a tuft of green grass.

It may be that the stolen fruit was not so sweet to his tongue as Job had expected, or his conscience may at length have begun to act once more. He slowly raised his head and gazed longingly up and down the street, as if yearning to try a wider field for his gymnastics. Then apparently his sense of duty carried the day for, turning reluctantly, he plodded away to the open stable door, and quietly marched into his accustomed place.

"Run, Polly, quick! Run and fasten the door!" her mother exclaimed, as she hurried away to tie up the prodigal, to prevent any fresh wanderings.

When the doctor came home to dinner and heard the story, he was merciless in his teasing.

"One woman, six girls, and one boy, all to be outwitted by one poor old horse twenty-nine years old! "he exclaimed.

"Now, that's not so!" interposed his wife.

"Job isn't but twenty-three, so don't put any more years on his devoted head."

Dr. Adams laughed. He took a sinful pleasure in reminding his wife of Job's advanced age.

"Twenty-nine last June," he said, as he gave Polly her second piece of meat. "If you are careful of him and keep him for a few years longer, you can sell him out at a high price, to be exhibited as a curiosity."

"Sell Job! Never!" protested Mrs. Adams. "I would almost as

soon sell Polly. No money could ever make up for that old fellow's intelligence, and for the real love he gives me."

"Yes," added Alan sympathetically; "and no money could buy his obedience to you, this afternoon, when he was loose."

While the table was being cleared for the dessert, the doctor suddenly turned to his daughter.

"Well, Polly," he asked; "how comes on the reading club?"

"Finely, papa. Why?"

"I didn't know but you were tired of it, by this time, and wanted something else."

"Oh, no; we have such good times," said Jean enthusiastically. "And if we gave it up, you never would get your stockings darned, either."

"Oh!" And the doctor lapsed into silence.

"What made you ask, papa?" inquired Polly.

"Mere curiosity."

"I know better than that," she said, seizing his hand as it lay on the table. "Now, popsy Adams, you just tell us what you are driving at."

"What is the use?" asked the doctor provokingly. "I did have another plan; but if you are all satisfied, I'll offer it to some of the other girls, or perhaps Aunt Jane will take it in charge."

This was too much for Polly.

"Do tell us," she begged. "We'll do it too, whatever it is; won't we girls?"

"But what if it is something that isn't funny at all, something for which you have to give up your own good times?"

Polly's face fell, but she answered steadily,—

"We'll do it, just the same."

"I am glad to hear you say so," remarked Aunt Jane approvingly. "I have felt that it was high time you girls were made to take an interest in something really useful."

"What is it, Dr. Adams?" implored Jessie, whose curiosity was by this time fired.

"Well, it's just this: down in the hospital there's a girl about Katharine's age shut up in a room by herself, where she must stay a year. She isn't pretty; she isn't especially bright; she is an Irish girl from one of the hill towns in the northern part of the state. But she has something the matter with her back, so all she can do is to lie there on a sort of frame, and look at the wall of her room."

The doctor paused. While he had been talking, he had watched the faces of the girls, curious to see the effect which his short story would have on them. Polly's cheeks were flushed, Jean's eyes were shining with her interest, but Katharine's lashes drooped on her cheek, and were a little moist. He nodded approvingly to himself, as he looked at her.

"Go on, papa," urged Polly.

"There isn't much more to say," returned her father, resting his arm on the back of her chair. "It occurred to me to-day to wonder if you girls couldn't each of you take a day a week,— there are just the six of you, you know,—and run in to see her for a few minutes after school. She is perfectly well, except for her back, and you can imagine how dull it must be for her there. Now, suppose you could drop in for half an hour and get acquainted with her, or read something simple to her? She's not up to 'Pilgrim's Progress' yet." And he pinched Polly's cheek playfully.

He stopped again. This time there was a murmur of assent from his hearers. Then he resumed,—

"Now, talk this over among yourselves and see what you think of it. I don't say you ought to do it, remember; you all have a good deal to do, I know. I only suggest the chance to you. I would think of it well, for unless you could be regular, it might be worse than nothing, for she would come to depend on it, and be disappointed. I warn you, she isn't very attractive, she is only ill and lonely."

"What's her name?" asked Florence, as the doctor started to leave the table.

"Bridget O'Keefe."

"What!" And in spite of herself, Jessie wrinkled her nose in disgust.

"Yes, I told you she was Irish, you know," answered the doctor briskly. "Now I must be off. Think it over till Monday and then let me know."

And a moment later, the front door shut behind him.

Aunt Jane went out after dinner, and Mrs. Adams made an excuse to leave the girls to themselves. Gathered around the parlor fire, they had an animated discussion, and, with many a practical suggestion from Alan, their plan of work was agreed upon. Each was to take her own day, and give up half an hour after school to a call on this other girl, who was condemned to lie still and know that the world was going on around her just as usual. There was no difficulty in planning for the first five days of the week; but the girls, though fired with a desire to do good, yet drew back from pledging themselves to break into their Saturday afternoons, the one holiday of the week.

"What's the use of going Saturday?" said Florence. "If we go to see her every other day but that, it ought to be enough."

"I don't want any half-way work," said Jean decidedly, "and yet, it does seem too bad to upset our fun when we've always been together. What if we draw lots for it?"

But Alan objected.

"That's kind of a shirky way to do. If I'm ever ill, I don't want you drawing lots which shall go to my funeral. I'll go Saturday, myself."

"You can't, Alan; you aren't a girl," said Molly. "No," added Katharine, as she leaned over to lay her small, slim hand on his; "the boy can't go, but he can teach the girls a lesson in generosity. I'll take Saturday myself, girls."

Alan turned to her impulsively.

"Good for you, Kit!" he said warmly. "I'm proud to have you for a cousin."

Katharine laughed lightly.

"It's nothing, after all. I have more time than most of you, and it's only a little while, anyway."

It was only a little thing, as Katharine had said, but by it she gained far more than the one short half-hour a week would ever cost her; and, too, from that time onward, Alan looked on his cousin with a new admiration which her beauty and her attempts to win his liking could never have brought.

The girls entered into their work heartily, charmed by the novelty of their experiment. It was an unknown sensation to them to feel sure that some one was eagerly listening for their step in the outer room, to see the dull, plain face before them brighten with a new life, as they came through the door. For the first few weeks, they begged to be allowed to prolong the half-hour; but the doctor, mindful of the fate of "Pilgrim's Progress," and knowing that a reaction would probably come, checked their zeal, and only encouraged their shorter visits. How much good they did to their young patient, they never knew. The healthy, out-of-door atmosphere which they brought in, their scraps of news, and their gay chatter did as much to brighten the rest of the long, lonely days, as the one or two pictures they brought did towards beautifying the plain, white walls of the little room where Bridget was learning her lesson of patience. Still less did they realize how much they themselves were gaining from the quiet half-hour in the corner of the great hospital. The little self-sacrifice, the interest in this girl so far removed from their usual world, their girlish desire to gain her liking, and the womanly tact which was needed to win her from her rough shyness, all these had their influence on their young maidenhood, an influence which lasted far on through their lives.

And by degrees their interest widened. At first they had shrunk from the suffering around them, dreading and almost fearing to look on its outward signs. But as they became more accustomed to the place and its associations, they no longer hurried along the corridors, with their eyes fixed on the ground; but glanced in, now and again, through some open door, to see the long lines of little beds and the white-capped nurses moving quietly about the room, or sewing cosily by the sunny window. Winter was not half over before the girls used to turn aside, now to spend a few moments among the forlorn midgets in the children's ward, then to pass slowly along through the accident ward, giving a pleasant word or two in exchange for the smiles that never failed to greet their coming. Each one of them had her own particular circle of friends whom she gravely discussed with the doctor, learning much of the history and needs of these fellow-beings, for whom, until lately, they had thought and cared so little. Molly and Jessie devoted themselves to the little girls, Polly lavished all her attentions on three or four small boys, while the others preferred the older patients. But all this was only incidental, and the girls considered Bridget as their especial property, the younger ones regarding her as a superior sort of toy, to take the place of the dolls which they had cast aside.

However, Katharine, who was older and more mature than the others, had come to understand Bridget and to be friends with her, before any of the others. At first she could feel nothing but repugnance for this uncultivated, unwholesome-looking girl, a repugnance which she struggled hard to conceal; but, little by little, as she talked to her, she was won by her quiet endurance and courage. At length, one day, Katharine coaxed the girl's story from her, how she was left an orphan with younger children to care for; how she had fallen and hurt her back; how she had strained it with overwork, when it was still weak; how she had struggled to keep on, until the doctor had brought her where she was; and how she must hurry to get well, in order to earn money to pay the neighbors for caring for the little children. It was a homely tale and simply told; but when it was ended, Katharine was surprised to find her eyes full of tears, as she bent over and touched her lips to the girl's forehead. "I am glad you told me this, Bridget," she said. "Now we can talk about it together, and it will make us better friends."

And Bridget answered gratefully, as she looked up into the clear eyes above her own,—"Thank you, miss. It's nice to have a body know all about it. Somehow it helps along."

Three weeks later, as Katharine went into the room and dropped two or three scarlet carnations on the girl's idle hand, she was saluted with exciting news.

"A letter from home, to-day, Miss, and somebody has sent money enough to pay the children's board for ever and ever so long; and they don't know at all who it is. Isn't it wonderful!"

Not so wonderful, perhaps, as it appeared to the simple girl. No one but Katharine and her parents ever saw the letter that went hurrying westward to remind her father that Christmas was coming, and to tell him in what way she would prefer to take her present. The secret was kept, and no thanks were ever spoken; but Katharine cared for none. It was enough to watch the girl's happy content, now that her one anxiety was removed. Mrs. Hapgood, alone, had a suspicion, when Molly told her of the affair; but she wisely asked no questions, and in silence rejoiced over the broader sympathy her niece was daily gaining.

"How queer it is, the way things are divided up!" Katharine said to Molly, one day when they were out driving.

It was a clear, cold December day, and Cob trotted briskly over the frozen ground, as if he too, as well as the girls themselves, were enjoying the air and motion.

"What is divided up?" asked Molly vaguely, rousing herself from a half-formed plan for Alan's Christmas present.

"Oh, everything,—at least, everything isn't divided," returned Katharine a little incoherently. "Some of us have so much more fun out of things than other people do. There's us; and then there's Bridget and that little pet of Polly's, Dicky what's-his-name. You know the one I mean. And then, just in our set, there's ever so much difference. Jessie and I have everything we want, and Jean has to pinch and scrimp; Jean is as strong as a bear, and Alan can't do anything at all, without being laid up to pay for it; Polly wails for a family of young brothers, and Jean has more of them to take care of than the old woman that lived in a shoe. Now what's the reason things are so mixed up, I'd like to know."

"I can't see why myself," said Molly, tucking in the robe about herself and her cousin. "Maybe, if we knew all about it, they aren't as mixed up as they seem."

"Yes, they are," Katharine insisted. "If they weren't, some people wouldn't have everything, and some go without, as they do. I don't suppose there is much of anything in the world I couldn't do, if I wanted to, and tried hard enough for it; but everybody isn't so."

"I have sort of an idea," answered Molly profoundly, "that most everybody can get what she wants, if she is willing to work and wait long enough. It's only a question of what you want."

CHAPTER X

POLLY'S POEM

"Molly, don't you want to come and take a walk with me?" asked Polly, appearing in the door one Saturday morning.

Molly sprang up and tossed her book down on the table.

"Yes, indeed I do. It's too pleasant to stay in the house such a day as this. I'll go and call the others."

"But I don't want the others, at least, not this morning," said Polly mysteriously. "I want you all to myself, for I've something to tell you, to show you.". Polly blushed and stammered a little.

"What is it, Poll?" asked Molly curiously.

"Oh, nothing much; at least, I'll tell you by and by. Go and get your hat, and come on."

"The Bridget Society" as Alan disrespectfully called it, had been in operation for about two weeks now; but though it had proved an absorbing subject to the girls, yet it took very little of their time, and left them nearly as free as ever for their usual occupations. Their common interest in the one work, however, had bound the six girls even more closely together than before, until they depended on one another's help and sympathy, in any and every question that arose.

It was a clear, bracing day, so cold that the white frost was still glittering on the grass-blades in the more sheltered corners, so clear that the bare, rough ledges of the western mountain looked so near that one could toss a stone up to the pile of broken rocks which marked the line of their bases; while far across the river valley, the sun lay warm upon the roofs and towers of the town nestling on the hillside, and touched with a golden light the tall, slender spire of the little church. The girls walked briskly away through the town and out towards the river, a mile away. Polly appeared to be unusually excited, whether by the crisp air or by her new winter coat, Molly was at a loss to decide. It was a fine day, surely; but the more Molly studied the long dark-blue coat trimmed with chinchilla, and the saucy little blue cap edged with the same soft fur, and cocked on the back of Polly's curls, she came to the conclusion that Polly's spirits were affected by her becoming suit. That being the case, it was plainly her duty to remove Polly's worldly pride.

"Do try to walk like a civilized being, Polly!" she exclaimed, as her friend suddenly pounced into the midst of a flock of hens that were pluming themselves in a sunny fence-corner. "People will think you're crazy, if you act so."

"Well, what if they do?" said Polly, laughing. "I don't care what they think, I wanted to astonish those hens. Shoo!" And she charged upon them again, brandishing a dry stick which she had picked up by the roadside.

In spite of herself Molly laughed as she clutched her friend firmly by the elbow and dragged her onward, out of temptation's way.

"You'll have the jailer and the fire department out after you," she said, as she guided Polly's erring footsteps back into the concrete path of virtue. "Do come along! Besides, you had something to tell me."

Polly's face grew suddenly grave, and the hot blood rushed to her cheeks. When she spoke, her voice was trembling with suppressed excitement.

"Wait till we get out on the bridge, Molly," she begged. "We'll be all alone there."

So it wasn't the new coat, after all. Molly's brow cleared.

"How queer you are, Polly!" she said. "I can't stand it to wait, I am so wild to know. Come on, let's have a race to the bridge, then."

"But you just said I mustn't run," protested Polly, hanging back.

"Not after hens, when the owner is looking on," answered Molly; "but it's our own affair, if we want to run a race. Come on."

She threw the last word back over her shoulder as she went darting away, followed by Polly who soon passed her, laughing and breathless. In the middle of the long, white bridge she stopped and looked about her, struck by the beauty of the familiar scene around, the soft hills at the north, the shining, river as it wound along through the russet meadow grass, and cut its way between the southern mountains, over which slowly flitted the clouds above. A few belated crows rose and sank down again over the deserted corn-fields, while, from the red house on the river bank, the great black dog barked an answer to their hoarse cries. No other living thing was in sight as Molly joined her friend, and they stood leaning against the iron rail, with their backs turned to the cutting wind that came down upon them from the northern hills.

"Now, Polly." And Molly paused expectantly.

From rosy red, Polly's face grew very white, and her breath came short and hurried. She hesitated for an instant, then plunged her mittened hand into her coat pocket, and pulled out a dingy sheet of paper whose folds, worn till they were transparent, showed the marks of long service. With trembling hands, she smoothed it out, tearing it a little, in her excitement. Then she turned to Molly.

"Now, Molly Hapgood," she said solemnly; "will you promise never to tell, if I tell you something that there doesn't anybody else know, that I've never even shown to mamma?"

"Go on, Polly!" urged her friend impatiently, trying to steal a glance at the worn-out sheet, which was covered with Polly's irregular, childish writing. But Polly edged cautiously away.

"Now remember," she said again; "you're the only single soul in the world that knows this, Molly; and I am telling you my secret because I know you love me. I've—" there was a catch in her breath—"I've written a poem!"

"Really!" And Molly's eyes grew round with astonishment and respectful awe.

"Yes," Polly went on more calmly, now the great secret was out; "I knew I could, and it was just as easy as could be."

"How did you ever know how?" inquired Molly, with a

vague idea that she had never before appreciated this gifted friend.

"I didn't know how, at first," answered Polly, kindly exposing her methods of work to her friend's gaze. "I just knew that there ought to be some rhymes, and then I must say something or other to fill up the lines. One Sunday in church I read lots of hymns,—Aunt Jane wasn't there, you know,—and then I went to work."

"Are you going to have it printed?" asked Molly.

"Not yet," said Polly. "I thought at first I would send it to the *News*, but I've a better plan. I'm going to copy it all out, and write my name on it and my age and how I came to write it, and put it away. After I'm dead and famous, somebody will find it, and it will be printed. Then people will make a fuss over it and call me a child prodigy and all sorts of nice things."

"But what's the use?" queried Molly. "When you're all nicely dead and buried, it can't do you any good."

"But just think how proud my children and grandchildren will be!" exclaimed Polly enthusiastically.

"Maybe you won't have any," suggested Molly sceptically. "People that write are generally old maids, unless they are men."

Polly's face fell. Here was a flaw in her plans.

"Well, go on," said Molly. "Aren't you going to read it?"

Polly looked at the paper in her hand, cleared her throat nervously, drew a long breath, and cleared her throat again.

"What's the matter?" asked Molly unsympathetically. She had never written a poem, and had no idea of the mingled fear and pride that were waging war in Polly's mind. She spoke as the calm critic who waits to sit in judgment.

"I'm just going to begin now," said Polly faintly. Then, nerving herself to the task, she read aloud,—

> "The children went chestnutting once,
> Out in the woods to stay all day,
> There's Maude and Sue and James and Kate,
> All there, for there's no school to-day."

Polly stopped to catch breath.

"Where'd you get your names?" inquired Molly critically.

Polly looked up with a startled air.

"Why, out of my head, of course."

"Oh, did you?" Molly's tone was not reassuring. "Go on," she added.

"Maybe you'll like the next verse better," faltered Polly.

> "The good, kind mothers pack the lunch
> Of bread and butter, meat and cake,
> So off they start at ten o'clock,
> For it is hot when it is late."

This time, Polly found her friend looking at her, with a scornful curl to her lips.

"I thought you said it was a poem," she said, with cutting emphasis; "but it sounds just exactly like a bill of fare."

Anna Chapin Ray

This was too much for Polly. Her temper flashed up like a fire among dead twigs.

"Molly Hapgood, you're as mean as mean can be, to make fun of me! I've a good mind never to speak to you again as long as I live."

As usual, the more Polly became excited, the more Molly grew cool and collected.

"Don't be a goose, Polly," she said provokingly. "You're no more able to write a poem than Job is."

"What do you mean?" demanded Polly, facing her friend with gleaming eyes and frowning brow.

"What do I mean!" echoed Molly mercilessly, "I mean just this: your old poem isn't any poem at all. It doesn't rhyme more than half way, and there's no more poetry about it than there is about one of your freckles. Poetry is all about spring and clouds and butterflies, or else death or—" Molly paused for an idea. Not finding it, she hastily concluded, "Besides, I've heard something just like that before."

Polly choked down her rising sobs.

"Very well," she said, through her clenched teeth. "This is all I want of you, Molly Hapgood."

Deliberately she pulled off her mittens and put them into her pocket; then, with shaking hands and with her face drawn as if in pain, but with her eyes steadily fixed on Molly's face, she slowly tore the paper into long, narrow strips, gathered the strips together and tore them into tiny squares, and defiantly threw them away over the side of the bridge into the swift blue stream below. But even before the first floating square had touched the surface of the water, the reaction had set in, and Polly could have cried for the loss of her first and only poem. For a moment, she gazed after the white bits drifting away from her; then, biting her lip to steady it and struggling to keep back the tears, she turned on her heel, without a word, and walked away towards home, leaving Molly to follow or not, as she chose.

The tears came fast now, as she hurried on, avoiding the main streets as best she could. No one was in sight when she reached the house, so she could run up the stairs unnoticed, and throw herself down across the foot of the bed for a long, hearty cry. She had hoped so much from Molly's sympathy! But, after all, now the opportunity had come, the tears were not so ready as they had been, and she did not feel quite so much as if the world had abused her, as she did when she was standing on the bridge, watching the white dots on the river below. At least, no great harm was done, for she remembered the whole poem and could easily write it out again. As this thought came to her, she sprang up once more, seized a pencil and a bit of paper and rewrote the words which had caused her so much joy and so much pain. She was still sitting with her forehead resting on her clasped hands, reading the verses over and over and dreaming of the future day when fame should come to her, when she heard her mother's voice outside.

"Polly! Polly! are you there?"

"Yes, I'm here," answered Polly, moving across the room to open the door, with a secret hope that her mother would see that she had been crying, and ask the reason of her tears.

But Mrs. Adams was too intent on the matter in hand to give more than a passing glance at her daughter.

"Polly, Aunt Jane wants you to run down to Mrs. Hapgood's and ask her if she can't take in some ministers next week, over the convention. She would like her to take four, if she can."

"Oh dear!" grumbled Polly. "I do wish Aunt Jane would go on her own old errands, and not keep me running all over town for her."

"Polly dear," Mrs. Adams's tone was very gentle; "Polly, aren't you forgetting yourself a little?"

"No, I'm not," returned Polly rebelliously. "I hate Aunt Jane."

"Polly!"

This time there was no mistaking her mother's meaning. After an instant, she added,—

"I wish you to go at once, my daughter, and to go pleasantly. Aunt Jane is a good, kind aunt to you." Polly raised her eyebrows, but dared not speak; "and I am sorry you are so ungrateful as not to be willing to do this little errand for her."

Polly turned away and obediently started on her errand, but as she went down the stairs, her mother heard her murmuring to herself words that were not altogether complimentary to Aunt Jane and the coming ministers.

It was one of the days when everything went wrong, Polly said to herself as she went out of the gate and down the silent street. Molly had laughed at her, Aunt Jane had abused her, and, worst of all, her mother had spoken to her more seriously than she had done for a long time. That was the way it generally was with geniuses, she thought, and reflected with a vindictive joy that some day or other they would all be sorry for it. At this point she was interrupted by hearing her name called in boyish tones,—

"Polly! Polly! I say, wait for a fellow; can't you?"

Turning, she saw Alan running after her, with his overcoat waving in the breeze and his soft felt hat pulled low on his forehead.

"Where going?" he inquired briefly, as he overtook her and fell into step by her side.

"To your house," she answered as briefly, not yet able to return to her usual sunny manner.

"That's good," returned Alan cheerfully; then, as he surveyed her, he added, "What's up, Polly? You don't seem to be particularly festive this morning. Have you and Molly been having another pow-wow?"

"A little one," confessed Polly.

"That's too bad," said Alan, with a paternal air of consolation. "If Molly's been teasing you, I'll give her fits when she comes back from Florence's. She's there now."

"Oh, I suppose it was both of us," responded Polly, cheered by his understanding of the situation.

"I presume 'twas," said Alan candidly. "Molly is an awful tease; she gets after me once in a while, so I know. You're snappish, Poll; but you don't keep fussing at a fellow and hitting him when he's down."

They walked on in silence for a few steps. Then Alan

remarked, as he looked at her critically,—

"That's a gay little cap, Polly, and suits you first rate. New, isn't it?"

Polly nodded smilingly. Alan's sympathy had smoothed out all the wrinkles in her temper, and she was once more her own merry self, so by the time she went in at the Hapgood house, she was laughing and talking as brightly as if she and Molly had never taken their walk to the bridge.

"Oh, dear!" sighed Jessie, as she glanced down from the window of their room. "Here come Alan and Polly Adams. What a nuisance!"

The two sisters, left to themselves for the morning, had been having a private feast of lemonade and crackers in their own room, where they had been alternately reading and nibbling, for the past hour.

"Why is it a nuisance?" inquired Katharine, getting up to look out of the window, over her sister who was curled up in one of the deep window-seats, regardless of the delicate frost ferns that were thinly scattered over the panes.

"Just see here," replied Jessie, as she stretched out her arm for the pitcher and tilted it expressively, exposing to view a few bare, dry slices of lemon in the bottom. "They'll be sure to come up here, and it's rather shabby not to give them any."

"I'd make some more," said Katharine, pensively surveying the ruins of the feast; "but I put our very last lemon into this, and I can't. Maybe they won't care for any, it's so cold," she added, with an air of relief.

"I'll tell you, put in some more water, and mix it up pretty well," said Jessie hastily, as she heard Alan calling from below. "It was almost too strong before, so it won't be so bad, and we really ought to treat, I think."

Katharine laughed silently, as she obeyed her sister's instructions, while Jessie surveyed the operation with dancing eyes.

"Let's see," she said gravely, as she poured out a few drops into a glass.

With frowning solemnity she tasted it, then set down the glass with an air of decision.

"It's real good truly, Kit. I'll get out some more crackers, and then you call them up. Boys are never very fussy, when it's something to eat; and Polly will like the fun." And as she opened the box and took out a fresh plateful of their dainty crackers, Katharine invited up her guests who came willingly enough, never dreaming of the straits to which their friends' hospitality had put them.

"Whose autograph album is this?" exclaimed Polly, pouncing on a flaming red and gold volume that lay on the table.

"It belongs to one of the girls up at school," answered Jessie. "Just see here, and here, and here," she continued, turning over the leaves and pointing to several well-known names. "You see, she lives in Boston and her father knows all these people, so she could get them."

"How splendid!" And Polly bent over to gaze more closely on the signature of a writer clear to all childish hearts. "I'd give almost anything for that," she sighed.

"Which is that?" asked Katharine, leaning over to glance at the page. "Yes, I wouldn't much mind having that one. But, after all, autograph albums are a bore. I used to care for them, years ago, but they are all just alike. I had one friend who wrote the same verse in every album she took, only she changed the name in it. Have some more lemonade, Polly." And she waved the pitcher which was nearly empty for the second time.

"No, thank you," answered Polly gratefully; "but it's been ever so good. I haven't had any since last summer, so this tasted better than usual, and I always like it."

"I am so glad," responded Katharine heartily, though with a sly glance at her sister.

"But I don't think autographs are stupid," said Jessie, returning to the subject of the book in her hand. "I wish I had all these. Why, sometimes they are sold and bring perfectly enormous prices."

"I know that," said Katharine; "but they make ever so much fun of the people that ask for them."

"I don't care if they do," said Jessie; "I'm going to have one, pretty soon, that will make you all envy me."

"Whose?" asked Alan.

"That's telling," responded Jessie mysteriously.

"How are you going to get it?" inquired Polly.

"I've asked for it," replied Jessie, with a knowing smile.

"Is it somebody I know?" asked her sister.

"No, not exactly; but it's somebody that everyone in this

whole world knows about."

"Jessie Shepard, what crazy thing have you been doing?" demanded Katharine.

"I shan't tell." And Jessie shut her lips defiantly.

"Oh, come on, Jessie, tell us," urged Alan, while Katharine added,—

"If you don't tell me, Jessie, I shall speak to auntie. I know you have done something you are ashamed of."

Jessie laughed good-naturedly.

"Don't be silly and make such a fuss over nothing, Kit. I only wanted to tease you a little; I'd just as soon tell as not. I'll give you each a guess, and then, if you don't get it, I'll tell you. That's fair, isn't it? Who'll you guess, Kit?"

"Oliver Wendell Holmes," said Katharine promptly.

Jessie smiled disdainfully.

"Wrong. What should I want of him?"

"I should think anybody would want him," returned Katharine. "He's the greatest person I could think of; and besides, you've just been studying about him."

"Well, he isn't the one," said Jessie. "Go on, Alan."

"The President of these United States," suggested Alan pompously.

"Never!" responded Jessie fervently. "I'm a Democrat, you

know, so I don't want him. But you're in the right track. Polly, who is it?"

"General Grant," said Polly.

"He died ever so long ago, Polly," corrected Alan.

"Oh, yes, so he did. Well, let's see. The Mayor of Omaha?"

"No! No! No!" said Jessie. "I didn't say it was a man, any way. It's a woman; she's an English-man and she's a queen."

"Jessie!" And Katharine dropped into a chair, too much horrified to say more.

"You don't mean to say," queried Polly, "that you've been and gone and asked Queen Victoria to send you her autograph?"

Jessie nodded triumphantly.

"Well, she won't," returned Polly, with deliberate emphasis, while Alan laughed, and laughed again at the absurd idea.

Then Jessie showed her trump card.

"Yes, she will," she said, with a firmness born of conviction; "she will too, for I put in a two-cent stamp for her to answer with. There!"

CHAPTER XI

JEAN'S CHRISTMAS EVE

Christmas mystery was in the air. For weeks the girls had been busy over all sorts of gay trifles which were whisked out of sight, now and then, to avoid some particular pair of curious eyes that were not intended to see them until the proper moment came.

"What's the use of making such a time about it?" inquired Alan, in some disgust one day.

He had rushed breathlessly into the room to announce the first skating of the season, and was greeted with four protesting voices, as the girls tried to cover up the stripes of the afghan they were making for his own especial use.

"Making such a time about it, you heathen!" retorted Polly, diving after a ball of golden-yellow wool; "you know perfectly well that all the fun of Christmas is in surprising people. I'd rather have a paper of pins, and have the fun of being astonished over it, than get the most elegant present in creation and know all about it beforehand."

"That's all very fine, Poll; but I haven't been able to come near you girls for a month, without your all howling at me," objected Alan. "Now, of course I know you aren't doing all this for me, but you won't let me see anything. I'll start up some secrets, too; see if I don't!"

"Poor boy, does he want to see?" said Katharine protectingly. "Well, I'll show you one thing, Alan, if you'll promise not to tease any more."

"Depends on what 'tis," returned Alan grudgingly. "One is better than nothing, so go ahead."

Katharine gathered up her work under the light shawl which lay across her shoulders, and went away out of the room. Presently she came back again, with a pile of something soft and red in her arms.

"There now!" she said, shaking out the folds with conscious pride. "This is our grandest secret of all. It's a dressing-gown for Bridget, and we girls have cut and made it ourselves, every stitch. It's well made, too; you can look, if you know enough to judge."

"We!" echoed Polly. "Katharine has done 'most all of the work."

Alan eyed it critically.

"I say, that's something worth having," he remarked. "I wish I was Miss O'Finnigan; I know that color would be becoming to me, and it's so soft and warm." And before the girls could guess his intention, he had slipped on the long, loose garment, and was parading up and down the room in it, with all the airs of a young peacock.

"Tell me some more," he implored them; "tell me what you were doing when I came in."

"Never!" said Jessie sternly. "You know more now than you deserve. You'll have to wait for the rest."

"A whole week?" groaned Alan. "I never can stand it. Never you mind, though; I know one thing you don't, and I was going to tell you, and now I shan't. It's something awfully nice, too, and it's about Christmas."

"Tell me, Alan," said Katharine. "You know I showed you this, so it's only fair you should let me be the one to hear your secret."

"All right, Kit; I'll tell you for the sake of making the rest jealous." And Alan glared defiantly at the other girls, as he bent over and whispered a few words in Katharine's ear.

"Really, Alan? What fun!"

"Isn't it?" And they exchanged significant smiles.

"Where's Jean, these days?" inquired Alan, a few minutes later, as he settled himself on the sofa, with his shoes on the pillow. "I haven't seen her for a coon's age."

"Poor Jean!" said Polly. "She's having a hard time. Ever since her father had that fall, two weeks ago, Mrs. Dwight has been busy with taking care of him, and Jean has had to do all the work, and see to those four boys, besides."

"That's hard luck," said Alan sympathetically.

"I did feel so sorry for her, the other day," said Jessie, moving into the sofa corner to let Alan rest his yellow head in her lap. "I asked her what she was going to do Christmas, and she said, 'Nothing at all.' She laughed; she always does that, but she looked as sober as could be, and it did sound so forlorn."

There was a silence throughout the group for a moment.

"I say!" exclaimed Alan so suddenly that Jessie, who was bending over to part his hair into little squares, started violently.

"Well?" inquired Molly, who was tranquilly rocking back and forth by the window.

"I say, girls, let's give her a Christmas surprise." "Good, Alan!" And Jessie sprang up in an excited fashion that nearly dislocated the boy's neck. "This is the best plan yet. It's ever so much more fun than Bridget; and Jean is working so hard now, that she needs a little good time to make up for it. What shall we do?"

"Oh, have some kind of a lark Christmas eve," answered Alan. "We can't do it Christmas day because—Well, I may as well tell the rest of you—mamma has just asked Polly and all the other Adamses to come here for dinner and the evening, so we can have our fun, all of us together."

"Oh-h-h!" remarked Polly rapturously.

"So you see," the boy went on; "whatever we do must come in on the night before; but I think we could manage it. Let's call mamma in, to take counsel."

"Would Florence help us along, I wonder," said Jessie thoughtfully.

"Yes, I know she will," Katharine responded quickly; "I'll answer for her. We'll have to work, girls, to get this done, with all our other plans; but I am sure we can do it."

"Oh, dear! I've got to finish up my scrapbook for my hospital boys," sighed Polly; "and the corners peel up faster than I can stick them down."

"I'll do it for you, Polly," Alan offered. "I can't sew, but I can stick beautifully."

"That's so," said Molly, in an undertone to Polly. "He upset the mucilage bottle into the dictionary, the other day, and now we have to take a knife and pry, if we want to look up anything from I to Q."

"Oh, Polly, I almost forgot to tell you," said Alan suddenly. "I was coming up past your house, just now, and saw Mr. Baxter going in at the gate. You'd better hurry home, and tell him something more about Job."

Polly laughed at the memory.

"He has called once since then," she said. "I don't see what has started his doing that, and he comes to see Aunt Jane, of all people. This time I was telling about, he went on in the queerest way about his children, as if he didn't care anything for them. I wish you could have heard him. He said that they had very peculiar dispositions, and his wife never did know how to bring them up. But go call your mother, there's a dear boy. I do want to plan about Jean."

For the next hour there was held a council into which Mrs. Hapgood entered with spirit, restraining the girls' ardor, offering all manner of assistance, and making many a useful suggestion for the success of their frolic, which was to be extended to include something for the little brothers, as well as for Jean. There was no time to be lost, for there was only a week before Christmas, and there was much to be done. At dinner time the girls separated, with many vows of secrecy.

Christmas fell on Thursday that year. It had been cloudy all the early part of the week, and on Wednesday morning Jean had opened her eyes in the cold, gray dawn, to see the air filled with whirling snowflakes that went dancing and skurrying this way and that before the noisy wind. Such a tempting morning to pull the blankets over one's shoulders and nestle down for another nap! But there was no such luxury for Jean; she scarcely had time to realize that this was the dawn of the Christmas eve. A careless step on a slippery roof, a cutting wind which had numbed him too much to let him save himself, these had given her father a bad fall so that work was out of the question for a long time to come. Her mother was busy caring for her husband and doing a little sewing at odd moments, so the main charge of the house and of the children had fallen on Jean's strong young shoulders, which were bearing the load with a merry willingness that is so much more helpful than mere patient endurance. And really, if it had not been for Christmas, Jean would not have minded it so much. But it was hard to think of the fun the other girls were having over their mysterious plans; and though she had no time to join them, in fancy she pictured their merry afternoons together, while Alan dodged about them, pretending to pry and peep into the carefully covered work-baskets. Harder still it was to imagine the disappointment of her own young brothers, when Christmas morning should reveal the empty little stockings that Santa Claus had forgotten to fill.

"No, Jean," Mrs. Dwight had said sadly; "we can't have any Christmas this year. I'm sorry to disappoint you and the children; but with the uncertainty about father's going to work again, I feel that it would be really wrong for us to use our money for presents, when before winter is over, we may have to borrow some for food or clothes."

And Jean saw the right of it. Still, she cried herself to sleep that night, not so much for herself, as for the boys who had talked of the children's fur-clad saint for a month past. But by the next morning, Jean's inspiration had come. As soon as her work was done, she shut herself into her room and ransacked her few small stores. At least the boys should not be disappointed she thought, as she selected this treasure and that from the meagre number which she had hoarded with such care. A little planning and contriving changed them to fit the present need, and Jean had put them away until Christmas eve with the happy certainty that, at any rate, the toes of the stockings would bulge a little, even if the legs hung empty and lean.

But now it was the morning of Christmas eve, and breakfast was waiting until Jean should get it ready, so she sprang up and hastily dressed herself. Then, with her cheeks glowing from the shock of the icy water, and her fingers aching with cold, she ran across the hall to rouse the boys. But they were sitting up in bed, calling back and forth to each other through the open door between their rooms, in all the joyous excitement of the approaching Christmas tide; so Jean only stopped to caution them not to disturb their father, and hurried away down-stairs, to start the fire for their morning meal. The house was so cold, in the dim light, for the fire had burned low and the wind seemed to blow in through all the cracks and corners. But Jean never minded that; she was thinking with a quiet satisfaction of the little box up-stairs, and as she knelt on the bare floor to shake down the ashes in the kitchen stove, she was humming contentedly to herself,—

"And pray a gladsome Christmas
On all good Christian men;
Carol, brothers, carol,
Christmas day again!"

Anna Chapin Ray

Her mother's step interrupted her.

"Good morning, mammy!" she exclaimed, jumping up. "Why in the world didn't you stay in bed till the house was a little warmer?"

"It's no colder for me than it is for you," her mother answered. "Your nose is blue and your ears are red. Are the boys getting up?"

"Oh, yes; they must be nearly dressed," answered Jean. "They started as soon as I did."

Breakfast was all ready to put on the table, and still the boys had not come down. Jean had heard them running about their rooms; but now, for some time, all had been silent. Suddenly there was a shout.

"Jean! Jean! *Jean!*"

"Well," answered Jean, going to the foot of the back stairs, with the toasting-fork in one hand and a slice of bread in the other.

"I can't find but one stocking. You come and look for it for me."

"I'm busy, Erne," she called. "Ask Willie to help you."

"He won't. He's gone back to bed, 'cause it's cold," responded the childish voice.

Jean glanced at her mother in despair. Then she put down her toast and went up to the boy's room. Mrs. Dwight could hear her coaxing, laughing, and merrily scolding the boys, as she found the missing garments, routed Willie out from his warm nest in the middle of the bed, and triumphantly marshalled the four children downstairs to their seats at the breakfast table.

It was the beginning of a long, hard day, and Jean was forced, again and again, to hold herself in check while she bethought herself of the true Christmas spirit: good will to men. The boys had not the least intention of being naughty; but the storm kept them shut up in the house, and they were overflowing with fun and mischief, which was somewhat increased by the vague holiday feeling that is in the very air around us at Christmas time. Jean did her part well, restraining their boisterous shouts, making peace in their small quarrels, proposing new entertainments when the old ones had been worn threadbare, and, in the afternoon, calling them all into a corner of the dining-room and telling them marvellous old-time stories, to keep them quiet while their father took his nap in the next room. Not much of a Christmas eve, perhaps, compared with the stir and bustle of preparation at the Hapgoods', or with the elaborate gifts which Mr. and Mrs. Lang had bought for their only child; but after all, blessed be drudgery! and the hard work and stern self-denial were doing much to round Jean's character into the perfect womanhood, for which all our girls were striving.

Slowly the day wore away; an endless one it appeared to Jean who, with tired hands and weary head, longed for the hour when the little ones should be tucked away for the night, and she could give her nerves and her patience a little rest. It came soon after supper, for the boys were more than ready to go to bed, hoping in this way to encourage an early visit from Santa Claus and so have the first choice of gifts from his overflowing pack. There was a little sadness in Jean's smile, as she watched them eagerly fastening their long stockings around the kitchen chimney, with many a sleepy dispute about the best place and to whom it should be given. Then they clattered up the stairs and pulled off their clothes, tossing them in a promiscuous pile on the floor, to be sorted out again by Jean while they lay huddled under the blankets. The last good night was said, the last "Merry Christmas" exchanged in anticipation of the morrow, and Jean went away and left them.

She crossed into her own room, took up the little box, and went down-stairs again and out into the kitchen. How poor and mean her gifts looked, after all, and how lonely in the toes of the long, thin stockings! She could have cried, as she stood there looking at them; but what was the use of crying? Tears wouldn't bring Willie the air-rifle for which he sighed, nor Ernest the fine new sled and knife that he had so innocently mentioned in his prayers. No, crying wouldn't help the matter any; so she smiled instead, as she went back to the sitting-room; but it was a wan, lifeless smile, after all.

For a few moments she stood at the window, looking out into the night and listening to the sleepy murmurs from the room above. It would be good sleighing for Santa Claus, she thought, and then smiled at the childishness of the idea. The storm had died away at sunset, and the soft, light snow lay white on the ground, and piled high on the evergreen hedge at the side of the house. In the cold, still air, the stars glittered like little, pricking points of steel, throwing a faint light over the town below; while, far down in the quiet western sky, lay the tiny silver thread of the baby moon, as if anxious to linger above the horizon for a peep into the happy Christmas world, when the midnight bells should ring in the glad news, centuries old, yet ever coming to us with all the fresh joy of that first eastern Christmas dawn.

Jean's eyes wandered from the snow below to the sky above, then dropped again to the distant lights that were shining out from the upper rooms of the Hapgood house. Even the attic was ablaze, for Mrs. Hapgood still kept to the old-fashioned custom of illuminating the house on Christmas eve. How Jean wished she could peep in to see what they were all doing! She had missed her friends and their frolics during these past weeks, missed them more than any one knew but her pillow, to which alone she confided her troubles.

Then she turned away from the window and threw herself down on the scratchy old haircloth sofa, with her arms folded under her head, to stare at the ceiling and think it all over. She had kept her temper that day, at least; for so much she could be thankful. But now she would have given worlds to run away out of the house and down the street, to spend the evening with Polly or Molly, or even Florence. Mrs. Dwight was busy with her husband, so Jean was quite alone and could be as forlorn as she pleased.

Suddenly she sprang up and listened intently. There was the rhythmic beat of footsteps on the sidewalk which Willie had cleared, and a chorus of blithe young voices rang out on the quiet air.

> "Hark! Hark! Upon the frosty air of night
> A joyful anthem swells!
> A song of gladness and delight,
> The bells ring out with all their might,
> And echo o'er the fields, with snow all bright,
> The merry Christmas bells!"

"It's a carol!" And Jean strained her ears to listen, while the steps and the voices came nearer, and still nearer.

> "Hark! Hark! About the gray old belfry tower
> Their gladsome notes resound,
> And carol through the moonlight hour,

O'er snowy sward and glist'ning bower,
The glory of the Lord, whose saving power
On earth to-night was found."

They were very near now, nearer than Jean realized, for, as the last line died away, the front door swung open and the singers appeared on the threshold, with rosy cheeks and shining eyes, exclaiming in a jovial chorus,—

"Merry Christmas, Jean!"

And Jean stood in amazement, while Alan and Polly set down the great basket that they carried, and the six friends pulled off their coats and hats and prepared to spend a long evening.

What need to linger over the unpacking of the great basket, to listen to the fun as the simple presents and absurd jokes came to light, one after another, while Jean now wiped away a tear or two over Katharine's dainty gift, now laughed convulsively over some ridiculous prank of Alan's plotting? And all the time, the chorus went on, now explaining, now joking, but always bringing to Jean the welcome assurance that her friends did not forget her even in her absence.

It was a successful evening, they all said again and again, as they gathered at the door in the starlight; and Jean stood looking after them with happy eyes as they marched off through the snow, gaily singing the dear old carol,—

"God rest ye, merry gentlemen,
Let nothing you dismay,
For Jesus Christ, the Saviour,
Was born upon this day."

That night when the Christ child came silently over the

mountains and down into the sleeping town, he lingered beside their pillows, to whisper to Jean words of encouragement for the coming days of toil, to paint bright visions of the well-filled stockings which the boys were to find in the morning, and to bring to five girls and one young lad his thanks for their helping to do his work here upon the earth. And if the morning brought the merry Christmas to them all, to none it came more truly than to Jean as she watched the children's rapture over their lumpy, shapeless stockings, while she turned, again and again, to look over and caress her own generous share of gifts which the Christmas eve had brought her.

Anna Chapin Ray

CHAPTER XII

HALF A DOZEN COOKS

Christmas had come and gone, and the new year was well started in its course. The time was passing rapidly for the seven young people, who were making the very most of the cold, bracing winter weather. There were coasting frolics and skating parties, long walks and longer sleigh-rides, and even one grand snowball fight which was brought to an untimely end by a carelessly aimed ball that flew straight from Jessie's hand to the back of Aunt Jane's stately neck, just as that good woman was starting for the jail with a large package of tracts clasped in her black-gloved hands. The calls on Bridget still continued and the long-talked-of play was slowly approaching completion. Jean had worked on it at intervals during her father's illness, and it was now so nearly done that the girls had thought it was advisable to begin rehearsing on the first part of it at once.

And best of all the good times were the long, cosey evenings, when they gathered around the open fire, either at the Hapgood house, or else in Mrs. Adams's parlor, to talk over the events of the day or tell stories, while they roasted apples and popped corn over the coals, regardless of the fact that much better results and much fewer burns would have come from the same labors performed over the kitchen stove.

They were all settled at Polly's one snowy evening, Mrs. Adams sewing by the lamp, Polly, Jessie, and Alan curled up on the rug, and the others in low chairs, when Aunt Jane came into the room, looking like a funereal sort of spook in her long, shiny black waterproof.

"What now, Jane?" inquired her sister, glancing up from her work.

"Mothers' Meeting," responded Aunt Jane, disdainfully eying the home-like group before her.

"Oh, Jane, I wouldn't take that long walk on such a stormy night," urged Mrs. Adams.

"If these children can come here for mere pleasure, it certainly is not too stormy for me to go out on an errand of duty," answered Aunt Jane, with dignity. "And, Isabel, I really think it is your duty, too, as a mother, to go to these meetings. They are very helpful and improving, and would be a great source of comfort to you in training Polly."

"Perhaps they might be, if I went," replied her sister gently; "but you can never make me believe, Jane, that I ought to go away and leave Polly alone, one night in every week."

"Don't go, Mrs. Adams," implored Alan, in an undertone.

"I haven't the least idea of it, Alan," she answered, as the door closed behind Aunt Jane. "People don't all think alike about these things, and your mother and I both believe that we can do more good by staying at home, and trying to know and understand our own boys and girls, than by leaving them while we tell somebody else how to bring up her children that we have never seen." And Mrs. Adams gave a little nod of conviction, as Katharine moved her chair back to the table, saying heartily,—

"I quite agree with you, auntie."

"Perhaps if you'd always been to the meetings, Jerusalem, I'd have been more of a success," remarked Polly pensively, as she settled herself more comfortably with her head in Jean's lap.

"No use wasting one's time on poor material," said Alan philosophically, while he shielded his face from the blaze with the shovel.

"Molly, do you remember what a time we had one night, trying to make this fire burn?" inquired Polly, thoughtlessly betraying the secret of their experiences.

"Don't I, though!" answered Molly fervently.

"When was that?" asked Florence.

"Last fall, when mamma went to New York," answered Polly. "We wouldn't tell you then, but I don't care now, do you, Molly?"

"You'd better let me tell it," put in Alan. "You girls won't half do it justice. Now listen." And he told the tale of their housekeeping experiences, suppressing nothing, but, on the contrary, making such additions as his fertile brain and an utter disregard of the facts could suggest.

By the time his story was done, Polly and Molly were blushing and protesting, while the other girls were lying back in their seats, exhausted with laughing.

"Is that all?" asked Katharine, as her cousin ceased speaking.

"All! I should think it was, and more too," said Molly. "He made up half of that, and the other half he exaggerated so that it couldn't recognize itself, if it tried."

"How many of you girls would do any better?" added Polly.

"I can't cook the first solitary thing," admitted Florence; "but I had a cousin that used to make bread when she was ten years old."

"Much good that does you," remarked Alan disrespectfully. "My grandmother was a splendid cook, but I never found that it helped Molly any."

"I can cook," said Jean, with manifest pride; "I know how to do meat and lots of things; but I don't suppose I should, if I hadn't had to."

"I always wanted to get into the kitchen, when I was a little girl," said Florence. "We had one girl that used to let me roll out pie-crust and stir up muffins; but mamma caught me one day, with a new gown all covered with flour and bits of dough, and after that there was no kitchen for me."

"Ask Alan how he boiled some meat once," said Molly.

Alan hung his head in confusion.

"I'll tell you, if he won't," went on his sister mercilessly. "Two years ago we had some company just before Thanksgiving, and mamma wanted to boil some meat for mince pies. We hadn't any girl, so when we went to ride, she told Alan, to watch it and put in more water when it needed it, so it shouldn't burn. He went off to play ball and forgot it, and—"Molly made an impressive pause.

"Go on, Molly," urged Polly, delighted that the tables were turned, and Alan's failings to be brought to light.

"Well," resumed Molly, ignoring her brother's threatening glances; "as soon as we turned the corner, coming home, we noticed a most awful smell. It grew worse, the nearer we came to the house; and then we saw the kitchen door wide open, and the smoke just pouring out in streams." Molly's metaphors were becoming mixed, but the girls never minded that, as she continued, "Mamma was dreadfully frightened, for she thought the house was on fire. We rushed in, and there was the meat frizzling away on the stove, and Alan so excited that he was just hopping up and down and crying, and letting it burn away, because he didn't dare take it off. It was more than a week before the smoke was out of the house."

A gentle snore from Alan greeted the end of the story. He had rolled over on his face, and was apparently sound asleep.

"There!" said Polly, with an accent of relief. "I'm glad we aren't the only know-nothings in the world, Molly."

"The question is, how are we going to know something," said Katharine thoughtfully.

"Let's turn our reading club into a cooking club," suggested Jessie; "that is, if Mrs. Adams is willing."

"Yes, and poison ourselves, or else die of indigestion," interrupted Alan, waking abruptly to make this remark.

"Oh, you go to sleep again!" said Polly, rolling a hassock at him.

But Alan appropriated the weapon, and at once put it to use

as a pillow, while his sister said reflectively,—

"I wish we could do something of the kind. I don't know as we can; but I should so like to know how to do enough cooking so that Polly and I won't starve to death, next time we keep house."

While they were talking, Mrs. Adams had been hastily thinking over the possibility of giving the girls a few lessons in plain cooking. Such a plan would take some of her time, and involve much trouble and waste, besides, as Alan had suggested, imperilling the digestions of the family. But, on the other hand, Mrs. Adams had always felt that any woman, no matter how many servants she might keep, should have enough experience as a cook to direct the servants intelligently, and to be able to provide food for her family, if the hour of need should ever come. It was high time that Polly should be gaining a little of this experience, so why not extend her lessons to include all the girls? It would probably be the only chance that Florence and the Shepards would ever have. She resolved to try the experiment, for a time at least.

"What's the use of it, anyway?" Florence was saying. "A servant always does the cooking."

"Yes," Mrs. Adams answered, suddenly breaking in on the conversation once more; "but perhaps you won't always be able to keep a servant, perhaps you'll have a poor one. I knew of one unfortunate young wife who knew so little about cooking that, before she could teach her servant, she used to have to study her cook-book and recite the rules to her husband, to be sure she had learned them. Now I don't want any of my girls to be in such an absurd position, so I'm going to give you a few lessons, just to try and see if they are a success. Come next Saturday morning, and bring your gingham aprons."

"Yes," added a voice from the next room, where the doctor had just settled down to his evening paper; "and I'll promise to give two prizes, one to the first girl that will bring me a perfect loaf of bread of her own making, the other to the first one who invites me to a dinner which she herself has cooked."

"That's not fair, papa," remonstrated Polly.

"Jean knows all about it now, and can take both prizes."

"She doesn't know the first thing about bread," returned Jean, "and she never knew till to-night that elastic starch was good for puddings."

The following Saturday morning proved to be the first of a long series of similar meetings. The girls entered into the subject enthusiastically, delighted with the new interest which bade fair to rival Bridget in their estimation; and week after week they gathered in Mrs. Adams's great kitchen to mix and to stir, to bake and to brew. Mistakes were numerous and failures frequent; but Mrs. Adams was an admirable teacher, praising the girls when she could, encouraging them when her conscience forbade her to praise, and they toiled on, regardless of burns, and not even deterred by the prospect of the dish-washing, which always ended their morning's work. Alan was not permitted to cook, but he acted alternately in the capacities of errand-boy and taster-in-chief, and his hearty boy appetite carried him through the operation, unharmed. Polly's experiments were, perhaps, the most original and striking of any that were made. On one occasion, she neglected to sweeten her muffins till they were in the oven and began to bake. The rule called for sugar, and most cooks would have regarded the attempt as a failure; not so with Polly. Slyly opening the oven door, she added a generous teaspoonful of sugar to every separate muffin, greatly to the surprise of the others, when they broke them open, to find a solid lump mysteriously arranged in the top of every one. The teasing she had to endure when the truth was known, was only equalled by that which fell to her lot a week later when, as if to make amends for past extravagance, she forgot to put any sugar at all in her sponge cake. Even Alan's appetite failed to compass the result of this venture.

Slowly the plan extended until, as spring came on, Mrs. Adams used to take her flock on marketing expeditions, letting each in turn select the dinner at her will. These Saturday mornings were regarded by the girls as the crowning frolic of the week, for the simple domestic lessons which they were learning were made so gay and attractive that it was not until long years had passed and they were in charge of homes of their own, that most of them realized all that Mrs. Adams had done for them.

At length, during the latter part of April and the first week in May, the spirit of hospitality appeared to have run riot among the young cooks, for Dr. Adams was invited to a series of six grand dinner parties, each one more elaborate than the last. Jean, as the veteran cook of the club, opened the course, and it was good to see her air of importance as she presided over the long table, in the chair of state from which her mother was for the once deposed. It was all delicious, the doctor declared, and he filled Jean with satisfaction by asking to be helped a third time to her macaroni and cheese, and praised the roast until the other girls exchanged envious glances.

Florence's dinner followed, and was a surprise to them all, for this dainty, helpless girl, who had been brought up to know nothing of the practical side of life, had developed a real genius for cookery; and during the past two months she had spent many a happy hour in the kitchen, helping the cook to concoct her elaborate dishes with a skill which won the praise of even that accomplished tyrant, and Florence was making rapid progress towards being able to take charge of the house and servants which had been promised to her on Hallowe'en.

Polly's turn came last of all, and she had determined to retire from the contest covered with glory in all their eyes. She had chosen the first Saturday in May for her party, and she had gained her mother's somewhat reluctant consent to extend her invitations to include Mrs. Dwight, Mrs. Lang, and Mrs. Hapgood, as well as the other girls and Alan, who had been the usual guests.

It proved to be one of the warm, heavy days which come in the early part of May, a day that is delightful to those who can be absolutely idle, but which is singularly oppressive to the unfortunate majority who have duties to which they must attend. Though the dinner hour was not until six o'clock, Polly was up betimes, and went rushing about the house and slamming doors, with a profound disregard of Aunt Jane's morning nap.

By eleven o'clock the house was in festal array, and the most delicate of lemon puddings was cooling on the ice. Nothing more could be done for hours; but Polly resisted all her mother's efforts to induce her to rest, and roamed excitedly up and down the rooms, now and again pausing to flick a few grains of dust from the mantel, or to rearrange one of the graceful bunches of flowers that decorated the house.

"Now, Polly," said Aunt Jane, at length, with an encouraging trust in human nature; "you'll be utterly tired out to-morrow, and you know that always makes you cross. I really think you'd better go and lie down, or else sit down quietly and read."

But Polly scorned the suggestion. She was longing for the hour to come when she could retire to the kitchen. At length it came and, leaving her new spring gown spread on the bed, to be hastily put on at the last minute, she went running down the stairs. In the hall she paused, horror-stricken, as she heard a familiar voice from the next room, saying to her mother,—

"I always have heard say that his brother hadn't enough principle to save even the little tail of his soul, but nobody ever thought the worse of Solomon Baxter for all that. Folks can't help their relations; it's their friends that tells the story."

Miss Deborah Bean had come to dinner.

With a sinking heart, Polly went on to the kitchen and sat down on one edge of the table, to collect her ideas. If anything did go wrong, she knew, from past experiences, that Miss Bean would not hesitate to mention the fact. But nothing should go wrong; and as Polly gave the roast of beef a vigorous push ovenward, she resolved to do or die. When she went to bed that night, she felt that she had very nearly done both, the doing and the dying.

In the first place, the fire obstinately refused to burn, and in working over that, Polly entirely forgot her vegetables until some time after they should have been put on to cook; so the dinner was delayed for a long half-hour, while Polly was haunted by spectral visions of her guests falling from their chairs, in the faintness of slow starvation. At length all was ready, and leaving the girl to take up the tomato soup which Polly regarded as her one infallible dish, she ran up-stairs to dress herself and appear before her expectant guests, with a flushed face and ruffled curls.

If she had any misgivings as she marshalled her friends to the table and pointed Miss Bean to an extra seat beside Florence, she certainly concealed them with a tact worthy of an older housekeeper. The truth was, Polly felt no uncertainty as to the beginning and the end of her feast. The soup had never failed her, the pudding she knew to be good; so she could bear with the tough and stringy roast and the hard, lumpy potatoes with a fair grace. There was a hush of interested expectancy, as Polly dipped the ladle into the creamy, foamy soup. Then, when she poured it out into the plate, the conversation hastily started up again, but not so soon as to cover a sudden giggle from Alan, which he would have given worlds to recall when he saw Polly's tragic expression, as she surveyed the thin, watery compound and the white lumps floating in it.

The mothers present accepted their shares in silence and were heroically preparing to eat them, when Miss Bean was heard to speak.

"No, thank you," she said, as she waved her plate away; "I don't care for any; it don't look very good. I reckon it wheyed a little mite, didn't it?" she asked, turning to Mrs. Adams inquiringly.

But the doctor mercifully led her off into a tide of reminiscence, and his daughter was spared for the time being. The dinner went on from bad to worse, but the guests were most polite, and tried their best to keep up a brisk conversation, while they nibbled at the underdone potatoes and picked at the overdone asparagus. Miss Bean alone was unconscious of the true state of affairs, for Mrs. Adams had thought it unnecessary to inform her of the cause for the party, and she commented with a perfect unconcern, ending with the final verdict,—

"Well, Mis' Adams, though I do say it that shouldn't, I do think your cook has fallen off considerable since I was here before. No wonder Polly looks kind o' peaked."

The sudden buzz of conversation rose again, as if to cover Polly's confusion, while Alan gave her hand a sympathetic pinch under the tablecloth. However, Polly was supported through these trials by the thought of her final triumph when the pudding should appear. At last the meat was removed, and the clearing of the table was only interrupted by a quick cry of "Scat!" from Mary, as she was taking the last plates from the room.

"Now," thought Polly, straightening up and raising her eyes defiantly, "now I'll show them that there's one thing I can do well, anyway."

Alas for Polly! Some one else had thought her pudding a success. It came in, borne by Mary, who set it down, disclosing a round hole in it, near one end of the dish, and bent to whisper in Polly's ear.

"What?" gasped Polly, as the bright color rushed into her cheeks, and then faded again.

Mary repeated her whisper, more loudly this time, and the company plainly heard the one word *cat*.

It was too true. The Adams cat was an animal of refined tastes and, preferring pudding to her ordinary diet of bread and milk, she had watched her chance when Mary's back was turned, and mounting to the table, she had helped herself to the dainty dish, which was for the moment unguarded.

Tears stood in Polly's eyes, and another minute would have brought them down in a shower, had not the doctor burst out laughing, as he exclaimed,—

"It's too bad, and I am sorry for you, Polly; but I don't believe we any of us ever enjoyed a dinner more than we have this one."

And Mrs. Hapgood added hastily,—

"Yes, and we mothers have all been through it ourselves so many times, too."

All this was like Hebrew to Miss Bean, who was at a loss to see why they should all be administering comfort to Polly. But there could be no doubt that something was wrong, so she inquired, with an air of stony censure,—

"What is the matter, for the land sakes? If Polly can't eat what's set before her, she can go without."

That settled the question of Polly's tears, and she began to laugh hysterically, while the others joined in until the dining-room rang with their mirth.

"Well," said the doctor, as he pushed back his chair, half an hour later; "if Florence takes the prize for the best cooking, Polly ought to have the one for the best entertainment."

The guests went away early, and Polly ran upstairs to take off her best gown and slip on a comfortable dark blue wrapper. When she returned to the parlor, her mother was sitting in front of the fire, in a wide sleepy-hollow chair. She turned her head, as Polly entered the room.

"Come, dear," she said; "there's room for two here."

And Polly came.

The motherly arm around her shoulders felt very comforting to her just then; and, like a little, tired child, she cried it all out, all the weariness and mortification and sense of failure. But while the tears were still falling, she began to laugh once more.

"Oh, Jerusalem Adams!" she said; "did you ever see anything so funny as Miss Bean was about my soup?"

Her mother smiled, but before she had time to reply, Polly went on tragically,—

"But wasn't it all dreadful, mamma? Seems to me I never can look any of them in the face again, Mrs. Lang and all. And just when I thought I was going to be so smart and show off all I knew!"

If Aunt Jane had been there, she would doubtless have reminded Polly that pride must have a fall, and that this was a just reward for trying to outdo her friends. Mrs. Adams did no such thing, however. She only drew the curly head over against her shoulder and stroked it gently, as she said, with a half-laughing tenderness,—

"My poor little Polly! You tried to do more than you had strength for. But, after all, it's as true a side of life as Florence's successful dinner was; and every housekeeper must go through just such experiences, again and again. You are no more likely to fail the next time, because your dinner to-day wasn't a good one. It is only one of the unlucky days that we all must have."

"You, mamma?" And Polly raised her head in wonder.

"Yes, I've had my fair share of just such times." And Mrs. Adams laughed quietly, as she thought of similar chapters in her own housekeeping. Then she added, "But I was proud to see my little girl bear it so well, without breaking down or getting vexed at Miss Bean. That's worth a dozen elegant dinners, Polly. But now it's high time my cook was in bed and asleep, without a dream of soups or puddings or disagreeable guests who come uninvited. Some day you and I will have another dinner, and astonish the natives."

A few moments later, she followed Polly upstairs to tuck the blankets around her and cuddle her, and kiss away the few tears that lay on her cheeks. Then she went back to the parlor, where she and her husband laughed heartily and long over Polly's grand dinner party.

CHAPTER XIII

ALAN AND POLLY HAVE A DRESS REHEARSAL

It was still in the early days of the cooking club, and February's snows lay soft over the mountain sides, the smooth, open places throwing into bold relief the long rows of trees, which looked blue and hazy against their dazzling background. The town was snow-covered, too, and the frozen river, and wherever one went, the air was full of the gay jingle-jangle of countless sleighbells, while the streets were thronged with a motley collection of equipages, from the luxuriously upholstered double sleigh with its swaying robes and floating plumes, down to the shapeless home-made "pung" with its ragged, unlined buffalo skin snugly tucked in about the shawled and veiled grandma, who smilingly awaited her good man while he purchased the week's supply of groceries.

Such cold, clear days, such glorious sleighing were not to be resisted; and on this particular Saturday afternoon, Katharine had driven around with Cob, to take Mrs. Adams out for an hour or two, before time for her usual call on Bridget. The day had long passed when Job could be driven on the snow. Mrs. Adams had made one or two attempts in previous winters, but the poor old animal had toddled along so gingerly, slipping and sliding in every direction, that she had

180   Anna Chapin Ray

resigned herself to the inevitable, and put the old horse into winter quarters, much as she did her fan, or her lace bonnet. Such a course had its disadvantages, too, for the long time of standing in his stall stiffened up Job's venerable joints to such an extent that it took him a large share of the summer to regain the free use of his members. However, Katharine had been very generous with Cob, and Mrs. Adams had had a fair share of the sleighing. That day, though she was in the midst of writing a letter when Katharine came, the gay little sleigh and the lively mustang proved too attractive, and she had thrown aside her pen and put on her fur coat without a moment's hesitation.

Polly had gone down to the hospital that afternoon. Her cooking in the morning had been so successful that she had begged to be allowed to take a taste of it to Bridget; so, with a little basket in one hand and a carefully arranged posy in the other, she had gone away down the street, soon after lunch. Once there, she had lingered, chatting with Bridget, who was in an unusually dismal frame of mind, owing to a letter which, had come that morning, telling her that the youngest child she had left had suddenly developed a fractious turn of mind, and that her temporary guardian was "kilt entirely wid the care of her." Naturally enough, this news was preying upon Bridget, and when Polly went in, she found her resolving to leave the hospital and all the good it was doing her, and go home to see to the unmanageable infant. For this reason, Polly had stayed for some time, soothing Bridget's anxiety and trying to distract her mind from her worries by telling her all the funny stories she could remember or invent. By degrees Bridget's face brightened, and, charmed with her success, Polly talked on and on till the clock in the church tower near by chimed three. Then she rose in haste, surprised to find it so late.

"I don't care if 'tis three," she said to herself, as she went along the corridor; "I'll just look in on the babies now I'm here. I haven't been near them, for an age."

As she turned in at the door of the children's ward, what was her astonishment to find Alan sitting there, quite at his ease, surrounded by half a dozen small boys who were in a high state of glee over this new playfellow.

"What! You here?" And Polly's face grew expressionless with her amazement.

"I seem to be, don't I?" responded Alan, a little shamefaced at being caught, while he carefully set down the four-year-old urchin on his knee and rose to join her, regardless of the protestations of his small hosts.

"You see," he went on, as they walked away down the corridor together; "I thought it would be a good scheme to have a full dress rehearsal of our scenes in the play, so I went to your house, bag and baggage. They told me that you weren't at home, that you'd gone on an errand to Bridget, so I followed on after you. I waited round outside for a good while; but it was so cold that I nearly froze, so I rang the bell and asked if you were here. You were such a forever-lasting time that I'd begun to think you had gone out by some other door."

"No danger of that," returned Policy, as he paused. "I'm a snob and only take the front door. But go on; what did you do then?" "I asked if you were here," the boy resumed; "and the woman said you were, and took me up into that room, for she said I could see you go past the door when you came out. I don't see what possessed her to put me in there, and I hadn't any idea of taking any notice of those babies, but somehow or other they got round me."

Anna Chapin Ray

There was an apologetic tone to Alan's voice as he spoke the last words, which made Polly say heartily,—

"I am so glad they did, Alan. They don't often get hold of a boy in there, and they'll remember it ever and ever so long. It won't hurt you any, just for once, and it delighted them."

"I hope it did," said Alan, frankly adding, "I did feel no end silly, though, when you came out and caught me at it, playing child's nurse."

"I wonder why it is," returned Polly reflectively, as they went down the steps, "that a man always acts ashamed of doing what a woman is expected to do, day in and day out. I don't see why we shouldn't take turns and mix things up."

They walked along in silence for a little way. Alan's chin and ears were buried in his wide coatcollar, but the part of his face that showed was very sober.

"I say, Polly," lie said suddenly; "you don't know how kind of squirmy it made me feel, in there to-day, with all those little fellows, the one with the brace on his ankle, and the one with his eye tied up where they'd taken out a piece, and all the rest of them. I couldn't stand it to just sit there and stare at them, as if they were a show; that was too mean, when I couldn't do anything to help them out. What's the use of it all, any way?"

"I'm sure I don't know," answered Polly, as she tucked her mittened hand confidingly down into his, as it lay in the side pocket of his over-coat. "I felt just the same way when I began to go, last fall; but now I'm used to it, and don't mind so much."

"But what's the use, I'd like to know?" persisted Alan.

"What's the use of your having so much rheumatism in your bones?" responded Polly, answering question with question.

"How should I know?" returned Alan. "To make me cross as a bear, and give mother something to worry about, as much as anything, I suppose."

"I don't believe that's all the reason," said Polly seriously; "but as long as these things are round, and have to be, just think how splendid it must be to be a doctor!"

In spite of himself, Alan shivered at the thought. The scenes of the past hour had made a strong impression on his quick, sensitive nature.

"No," he said, "I don't want to spend my whole time among such things. It would be dreadful, Poll."

"I don't think so," said Polly energetically, as she snatched at the blue cap which a sudden gust of wind was lifting from her curls. "I don't want to be one myself, but I'm glad papa is a doctor, and I've always wished I had a brother to be one, too. I know the side of it you mean, Alan, and it is dreadful at first; but after a little, you'd get used to that, and I think there could be nothing grander than to spend all your life in mending broken bones, and cutting people to pieces to take out bad places, and helping them to grow all strong and well. I'd rather be a real good doctor than the President in the White House, and I don't believe but what I'd do more good."

While she was speaking, Alan watched her with admiration, for her eyes had grown dark and deep, and her whole face was alive with the earnestness of her words.

"You ought to have been a nurse, Poll," he said, when she had finished her outburst. "That's what makes you so nice and comfortable when I'm sick. I'd rather have you than Molly any day. But don't let's talk about it any longer; I can't keep those poor babies out of my head. They just seem to stick there."

"Go to see them again, and perhaps they won't," suggested Polly quickly.

"I'll see about it," said Alan; "but it strikes me I had enough of it this morning to last me for one while." And he lapsed into silence once more, while Polly eyed him stealthily, trying to read his thought.

When he spoke again, it was on an entirely different subject, and with an evident effort to dismiss the matter from his mind. Polly did her best to fall in with his mood, with an instinctive feeling that, boy-fashion, Alan did not care to put into words all that he thought; so by the time they reached the house, they were lightly discussing all sorts of unimportant matters; the weather, the sleighing, their play, and even Job, and Alan had thrown off his momentary seriousness and become as gay as ever.

"Where did you put your war-paint and feathers?" asked Polly, as they ran. up the steps, rosy and breathless from facing the strong wind.

"My war-paint, ma'am! It's yours. I'm a civilized white man, named Smith," returned Alan, as he pulled off his coat in the hall. "I left them in a corner of the dining-room."

"I'll get them." And Polly vanished.

"You see," Alan went on, as she reappeared. "We know our parts well enough, I suppose; but I wanted to get used to seeing you in full rig, before the time came. I was afraid, if you suddenly appeared to me, I should laugh and spoil our best scene."

"Don't you dare do that!" returned Polly sternly. "If you laugh, I'll let Jean cut off your head, and not try to save you. But it's a good idea to have a chance to go through it, while we are all alone by ourselves. Our parts are best of all, and I want to do them as well as we can for Jean's sake, she has taken so much pains to write it up."

"Yes," added the captain ungratefully, "and I'd like to have you try over that rushing out and tumbling down on top of me. The last time you did it, you. nearly knocked the breath out of my body. You'd better go a little slower, Poll, or you'll kill me as surely as Jean would,—and I don't know but what her way would be about as comfortable as yours."

"We've plenty of time and the house to ourselves," said Polly meekly; "so we can try it over and over, till I get it right."

"What a prospect!" groaned Alan. "When we get through, you'll have to take me to the hospital and put me in with those youngsters, where I was to-day."

"All right," returned Polly, laughing; "but if I ever do kill you, don't expect me to tell of it. Now let's come up into mamma's room and dress in front of her long mirror."

The dressing was a prolonged and hilarious operation, for each in turn helped the other to don his costume, stopping now and then to burst out laughing at the results of their labors. Alan, it is true, made a very attractive young captain, though, with a fine disregard for dates, he was attired in the moth-eaten, faded uniform with tarnished brass buttons and epaulettes which one of his ancestors had worn during the Revolutionary War. But the ancestor had been several sizes larger than his nineteenth century descendant, and the uniform lay in generous folds over the back and shoulders, and was turned up at wrist and ankle, while the great cocked hat, pushed back to show the yellow hair in front, rested on the boy's shoulders behind. However, a truer, tenderer, more valiant heart never beat in old-time captain, than was throbbing in Alan's breast that day, when he held forlorn little Dicky Morris on his knee.

But Polly! In arranging her costume, the girls had let their individual tastes have full sway, and beyond the general notion that Indians like bright color, they had paid no attention to the traditional ideas of dress among the noble red men. Pocahontas, as she is usually pictured in her quill-embroidered tunic and dull, heavy mantle, would have laughed outright at the appearance of this vision of silk and satin, of purple and scarlet and vivid green, which was solemnly parading up and down the room, in all the enjoyment of her finery.

"'Tis splendid, isn't it, Alan?" she asked, turning, with a purely feminine delight, to survey her long red satin train as it swept about her feet.

Alan looked at her doubtfully.

"Why, yes; it's very splendid, Poll, but somehow it doesn't look much like an Indian. I didn't know they wore satin trails a mile long."

Polly's brow clouded.

"But princesses do, Alan, and I'm a princess, just as much as I'm an Indian. It's such fun to wear this. Don't you suppose it will do?"

"Yes, perhaps," said Alan, with an heroic disregard of the truth. "It isn't just like the pictures; but you look first-rate in it, honestly, Poll. Now let me fix your head."

Polly beamed under his praise, and dropped into a chair where she sat passive until he had fastened on the lofty coronet of feathers which would have formed an honorable decoration for the brow of a Sioux brave. A little red chalk supplied the complexion, and a few dashes of blue on the cheeks and forehead added what Alan was pleased to term "a little style" to the whole. Then Polly sprang up, caught her skirt in both hands, and dropped a sweeping courtesy to her friend, saying merrily,—

"Prythee, how now, Captain Smith; is it well with thee?"

And the bold captain returned, in some embarrassment, as he removed his wide-spreading hat,—

"Yes'm. Same to you, ma'am."

There was something at once so quaint and so ridiculous in the pair, that they gazed at each other for a moment, and then, sinking clown on the floor regardless of their finery, they burst out laughing.

"Oh, Alan, you're so absurd!" gasped Polly.

"You're another," responded Alan; "only you're worse." And they went off into a fresh paroxysm of giggles.

At last Polly sprang up with decision.

"How silly you are, Alan!" she said, as she marched up to the glass once more.

Anna Chapin Ray

"Am I?" inquired Alan meekly. "How do you like the looks, Polly?"

Polly stared at herself closely and long, and a scornful expression gathered about her lips.

"It doesn't match," she said concisely, as she turned away.

It certainly did not. The face and head-dress, suggestive of the free, roving life of the plains, rose above a gown which was only suited to comic opera. Clearly, Pocahontas had made a mistake when she arranged her costume.

"What shall we do about it?" she asked disconsolately, as she faced Alan once more.

"Do? If I were in your place I'd get myself up as a real genuine Pocahontas, and not go trailing around in any such trumpery as that," returned Alan, scornfully kicking at the end of the train, as it lay across his toes.

"I suppose it would be better," said Polly faintly. "This doesn't seem to suit the part very well, but I did want to wear it." And she gazed regretfully down at her despised finery.

"I'll tell you what," suggested Alan, "why not wear this when you are at court? You'll have your face washed and your feathers off there, and this will be just the thing. When you first come on, you can have a real Indian dress. How would that go?"

"Good, Alan!" And Polly swept up and down the room once more, watching her train, over her shoulder, and listening with a rapturous countenance to the silken swish of her skirts.

"Now," said Alan, who was beginning to be tired of the question of dress, "let's begin and go over our scenes."

"We ought to have Jean here," said Polly, as she regretfully turned away from the mirror.

"No matter, we can do a good deal as 'tis. Let's take this end of the room for a stage." And Alan stretched himself out on the floor, prepared to die heroically, and began a sentimental speech of farewell to his distant home and friends.

"Now, Poll, we'll leave out what comes next. Your word is 'And so farewell! Let the fatal drop fall!'"

The most critical audience could have found no fault with the way Polly rushed in and cast herself upon the neck of the valiant captain, while she alternately defied her father, the irate Powhatan, and in elaborate broken English, cooed loving words into the ear of her "own dear John," who lay coughing and strangling in her clutches. As soon as he could regain his breath, he responded as a gallant Englishman should, and the scene went on smoothly, with many a coquettish bit of by-play on Polly's part, and a stern resolve, on the captain's side, to reduce it all to the footing of high tragedy.

"That went well!" said Polly, when they had reached their closing tableau, with John Smith on his knees, kissing the French kid shoe of Pocahontas. "I do hope it will go all right next week, for mamma says we may each invite four people, and I don't want to fail."

"We're going to have it here, after all, are we?" asked Alan.

"Yes. Florence wanted it, but her mother wasn't willing, so we're going to use the library for a stage, and put the people

Anna Chapin Ray

in the parlor. It will hold ever so many, that way. Tuesday night we're going to rehearse it there."

"I wish we could try our parts there, now," said Alan.

"Why not do it?" asked Polly. "We can, just as well as not, for there isn't a soul in the house but ourselves. Come on." And she led the way to the head of the stairs.

"Sure there isn't anybody there?" asked. Alan.

"Nobody, I am certain."

"All right, here goes, then." And followed by Polly, Alan raced down the stairs, singing at the top of his lungs,—

"Oh, my wife and my dear children!
Oh, the deaths they both did die!
One got lost, and one got drownded,
And one got choked on pumpkin pie!"

Hi-yi-whoop-*ee*!" he added, with a threatening war-whoop, as he opened the parlor door and dashed in.

There, side by side on the sofa, sat Aunt Jane and Mr. Solomon Baxter, looking up in surprise at the vision which had suddenly burst in upon their quiet conversation.

The children stopped abruptly, just across the threshold, and gazed in speechless horror, first at Aunt Jane and her caller, then at each other. For a moment, no one made any attempt to speak. Alan was the first to recover his senses.

"Good afternoon, Miss Roberts," he said, advancing, hat in hand, with one of his peculiarly bright, attractive smiles. "I hope we haven't disturbed you, but Polly said there wasn't anybody here."

Aunt Jane relaxed nothing of her rigidity, and Mr. Baxter answered for her, in an excited, nervous tone, while he waved his cane on which he had hung his stiff black hat, as if in grotesque imitation of his own long, lean body,—

"What in the world are you children doing, anyway, making such a noise? Polly—that's your name, isn't it?—you look as if you'd just come out of the mad-house."

In her astonishment at finding the parlor occupied, Polly had forgotten all about her remarkable gown, her ruddy countenance, and her towering headgear. Now, at the sudden recollection of it, she blushed until it was visible even under the chalk, and gave a vigorous pull, in the hope of removing her coronet, while she said penitently,—"I truly didn't know you were here, Aunt Jane. We were going to rehearse part of the play, and—"

"That will do, Polly," interrupted Aunt Jane stonily; "you needn't say any more about it. Go and get me a glass of water. Solo—Mr. Baxter, wouldn't you like some, too?"

"Calls him Solo—Mr. Baxter, does she!" remarked Alan, as the door closed behind the culprits. "Depend on it, Poll, there's something up in that quarter."

"I wonder if there is," said Polly. "I'm sorry for him, if it's true. But, Alan, think of our rushing in on them, looking like a pair of heathen, and that song and all! How could we!"

Anna Chapin Ray

CHAPTER XIV

POLLY'S DARK DAY

The next Monday noon, Polly stood on the top of a tall step-ladder, with the hose in her hand, washing off the parlor blinds. It was a warm, clear day, so warm that there was no possible discomfort in her work, and yet Polly was in a state of great disgust over her present employment. If it had been the back blinds, even! But to Polly, it seemed that her position on the ladder, within full view of the street, was extremely undignified, and she had protested vigorously when her mother sent her out.

"It won't take but a few minutes, Polly," Mrs. Adams had said; "and they need it badly. There's no knowing when we shall have another day that is warm enough, so run right out and do it now."

Polly went, for she dared not disobey; but she went with a frowning face, and after she had slammed the door behind her, she further freed her mind by remarking, with incautious emphasis,—"I don't care, I think it's too mean!"

Of course Aunt Jane chanced to be passing along through the hall, just then. She stopped directly in Polly's pathway and said, with deliberate, cutting severity,—

"Think your mamma is mean! Why, Polly Adams, I am surprised at you! I shall feel it my duty to speak to your mother about this."

Then Polly lost all self-control.

"I think you're meaner than she is!" And the outside door banged even more loudly than the other had done.

By the time she was on the steps, Polly longed to sit down and cry. Her temples were throbbing violently, and her throat felt swollen and aching. There were days when everything seemed to go wrong, she thought desperately; she had gone to school feeling so happy, that morning, but she had torn her gown at recess, and had failed in her history lesson, and now she must go out and wash those hateful old blinds. Well, some day when she was all nicely dead of overwork and too many scoldings, she knew they'd be sorry. Who the *they* in question were, she did not stop to analyze, but, forcing back the angry tears, she went away in search of the step-ladder. Soon she returned, dragging it after her and bumping it with unnecessary force against all the trees and corners of the house in her way, and, planting it in position, she slowly mounted to the top, hose in hand. She was just balanced up there, when she saw Alan come in through the gate.

"Hullo! What you up to, Poll?" he called.

"I should think you might be able to see for yourself," replied Polly, with dignity.

Alan surveyed her in astonishment, then asked,—

"Can't I help you?"

"No!" snapped Polly shortly.

The boy gave a long, low whistle, the meaning of which was so obvious as to be anything but soothing to Polly's ruffled feelings.

"Got a pain in your temper? Didn't you sleep well last night?" he inquired, with mock sympathy.

Polly vouchsafed no reply.

"Perhaps you lay awake to write another poem," he went on. "How was it, it went: 'The children went chestnutting—'?"

What unlucky chance had implanted in Alan's mind the spirit of teasing, and in Polly's, at the same moment, the spirit of perversity? What ever was the cause, the result was the same; and Polly, in her present mood, could not endure this slighting reference to her poem which she had fondly imagined was a secret between Molly and herself. Her face grew white to the very lips, as she faced the lad below.

"Alan Hapgood!" she exclaimed; "what right have you to say so? If you don't keep still, I'll turn the water on you."

"All right," said the boy composedly, never dreaming how excited she really was; "fire ahead, if 'twill give you any satisfaction. I suppose poets are always rather peppery."

The next instant, the strong, full jet of icy cold water struck him directly in the chest. Polly's aim was accurate, the force of the water great, so a few seconds had drenched the boy from his neck to his shoes. How long it might have lasted was uncertain, but a hasty misstep sent Polly head foremost to the ground, where she lay for an instant, stunned by her fall. Unmindful of his wetting, Alan ran to her side.

"Polly, are you hurt? Where is it?" he exclaimed.

But Polly sprang up fiercely.

"Go away, Alan! You needn't come here again till I send for you." And she ran into the house, and up to the safe refuge of her own room.

Once there, in quiet and alone, she quickly came to her senses and realized, with a horrible fear, all that she had done, all that it might yet do. It was her first serious quarrel with Alan, and for such a little cause she had turned upon her favorite companion. And then, with his rheumatism, what effect would the wetting have on him? Filled with this unbearable anxiety, she submitted to her mother's reproof for her words to Aunt Jane, without making any attempt to excuse herself, and silently left the house, without telling the secret of her last, worst outbreak. Lessons had begun, when she entered the schoolroom, and as she seated herself, she stole a quick glance at Alan's place. It was vacant.

She had no opportunity to see Molly alone, that afternoon, and no mention of Alan was made. After school, she walked quickly home without waiting for the girls, and taking up a book, she sat for an hour, not speaking, not reading a word, but with her eyes fixed on the roof of the Hapgood house, going over and over the scenes of the noon, longing to run to Alan and beg his forgiveness, yet too proud to do so, so soon. How she wanted to tell her mother the whole story, and ask her how to undo the harm she had done! But she dreaded to see her mother's shocked, pained face, so she held her peace. The long hours till bedtime slowly dragged away, and for once Polly went up-stairs without her usual goodnight talk. But, for some reason, sleep would not come to her, even then. Instead of that, she lay with wide-open eyes, staring into the darkness and picturing Alan as she saw him turn away, with the cold water dripping from his clothing. Suddenly she heard the bell ring sharply, violently.

Anna Chapin Ray

Springing out of bed, she stole noiselessly to the head of the stairs to listen, sure that it was a message of bad news. She was not mistaken, for she heard Molly's voice saying hurriedly,—

"Can Dr. Adams come right away? Alan is terribly ill."

Yes, he was ill, and perhaps he was going to die, and she had done it! Polly fled desperately back to bed and, pulling the blankets tightly over her head to smother the sound, she burst out crying as she had never before cried, in her life, crying with shame for herself and sorrow for her boy friend.

As soon as her first outburst was over, she raised herself on her elbow and strained her ears to listen for the sound of her father's return, convinced that he must and would bring good news. It was nothing serious, she reasoned, they were unnecessarily alarmed, for it would be too unjust for Alan to be ill, when she alone had been the one to blame.

It was long that her father was gone. A dozen times Polly had been sure that she heard his steps, but the moments dragged on and on, without bringing him. At length the door opened and he entered. Polly was out of bed in an instant and crouching at the head of the stairs, shivering with cold and fear, while she waited to hear his first words to her mother. She thought he would never get his coat off and go into the parlor. When he did, she heard something that seemed to stop her breath.

"I've only just pulled Alan through, to-night," the doctor was saying to his wife. "When I went in, I thought there wasn't much chance for him; but the worst is over, for the present."

"What was it?" asked his wife anxiously.

"Acute pneumonia, as much as anything," answered the doctor; "but it's mixed up with his rheumatism till he's a poor, forlorn little bundle of aches and pains. They sent for me just in time, too. If they'd waited till morning, we should have lost our Alan."

"What brought it on?" asked Mrs. Adams, and her voice was a little unsteady as she spoke.

"That is the strangest part of it," replied her husband. "He came in this noon, dripping wet, and Mrs. Hapgood hasn't been able to make him tell what had happened."

"Oh, mamma!"

The doctor and his wife both started up, at the sound of the strange, stifled voice. In the door directly behind them stood Polly, barefooted and with her teeth chattering violently, while her face was so swollen with tears as to be almost unrecogizable.

"Polly!"

Mrs. Adams sprang towards her, but Polly waved her off.

"Don't touch me, mamma! Don't kiss me, till you know all about it, what I've done! I'm to blame about Alan."

Without speaking Mrs. Adams caught up the afghan from the sofa and wrapped it closely about her daughter. Then, leading her to the bright wood fire, she sat down before it and took Polly into her lap, as if she had been a little child. The gentleness of her manner, the unspoken sympathy for some trouble which she did not yet know, had started Polly's tears to flowing again, and for a long time she could only cling to her mother and sob, with her head against the soft, warm cheek and a loving arm about her shoulders.

For some moments, the quiet of the room was only broken by the measured ticking of the clock on the mantel and the snapping of the fire on the andirons. At length Mrs. Adams said gently,—

"Now, Polly, tell me all about it."

And Polly told, sparing herself in no way, but giving all the details with a merciless truthfulness, and ending, with a sob,—

"And after all that, mamma, he tried to help me up when I fell, and I drove him off, and now—Oh, what shall I do! Scold me, if you want to; you ought to! I tried to tell you before, but I couldn't."

Mrs. Adams's arms grew tighter about her daughter, while she said gravely, very gravely,—

"Polly, dear, I am much too sorry for you, to scold you."

As she spoke, the doctor rose quietly and left the room, for he felt that what would follow was for mother and daughter alone, and even he had no right to sit by and listen to their words.

"I am sorry for you, dear," her mother went on, after a moment; "not so much for what you are suffering now, as I am because, little by little, you have let your temper get the better of you until to-day, for just this trifle, you have forgotten yourself entirely. The pain you have borne tonight on Alan's account is only a blessing to you, the natural punishment for what you have done, and it will help you to remember this another time, when you are angry. Each one of these fits of temper leaves a scar, Polly, that nothing can ever entirely heal; and I want no such scars on my Polly's womanhood, which must be above reproach. You are very dear to me, my daughter, and my whole life is bound up in my hopes for your future."

"Oh, how can I remember!" sobbed Polly. "It is all over, so in a minute, and then I just hate myself, but it doesn't do the least bit of good."

"It can't be done in a day, Polly; it will take years and years; perhaps it may be the work of a whole lifetime. But if, by watching yourself and struggling to keep back the quick words that come to you, after long years you could cure this temper, wouldn't the 'well done' be yours just as truly as if, for instance, you went on some mission abroad? It is often far more to rule yourself, than it is to spend your life working among the poor and wicked, and takes more courage and selfdenial. That may be the work which is laid out for my little daughter, and I pray that she may do it bravely and well, so that in time I may be as proud and happy in my Polly as I now am fond of her."

As her mother spoke, she rested her face against Polly's curls, and one bright tear sparkled among the soft little rings. Then she resumed,—

"And now, about Alan. I shall not scold you, Polly, for your punishment has come, as it always does, and is hard enough to bear, without my adding a word. But the danger was great, and you have only just escaped the most terrible sorrow that can ever come to any human being. Still, Alan is very ill, and may be for a long, long time to come. Anything that you can do, to make up to him for this, must be at once your duty and your pleasure, and I know that you will feel it to be so."

The talk lasted for a long time, until the fire burned out into cold, white ashes, and Polly shivered in her mother's arms. When she went up-stairs again, Mrs. Adams went with her, and always after the last quiet words in the dark, silent room, Polly felt a new reverence for her mother which never left her in the future years.

Polly went down-stairs to breakfast, the next morning, filled with gloomy forebodings, for she feared Aunt Jane's sharp glances and sharper words. But the doctor had had a plain, decided talk with Miss Roberts, the evening before, and had forbidden her to allude to Polly's trouble, so for once Aunt Jane held her peace. Soon after they left the table, Polly appeared before her mother, with her coat and cap on.

"I'm going, mamma!"

"Where?" inquired Mrs. Adams, in some surprise.

"To Mrs. Hapgood's," answered Polly, nerving herself to speak steadily. "I think I ought to tell her what I did to Alan, for he's keeping it a secret to save me, and she ought to know. Besides, I must hear how he is."

Mrs. Adams made no attempt to dissuade her, and Polly went down the street, walking more and more slowly as she neared the house, for she felt her courage fast leaving her. At the gate she paused to glance up at the window of Alan's room. The shades were drawn down, and no familiar boy face appeared there, to give her a welcome. How she dreaded to go in! The cold, raw wind swept past her, as she stood there, and it seemed to Polly that the day was strangely in harmony with her life, just then, for the warm, bright air of the morning before had given place to dull, heavy clouds which lay in long, low banners along the mountain side. As she looked up at the window above, she felt a strong, unreasoning desire to turn again and run away towards home; but just then the side door below opened softly, and Mrs. Hapgood stepped out on the piazza.

"Come in, my dear," she said. "I have good news for you; Alan had a fairly comfortable night, and now he is asleep."

"Oh, Mrs. Hapgood!" And Polly told her the story in an excited, breathless fashion, with the same unhesitating truth she had shown in talking to her mother.

If Mrs. Adams had been kind, so was Mrs. Hapgood, as well. She spoke no word of blame, but gathered the forlorn little figure into her arms, and soothed and comforted the child with assurances of her forgiveness and Alan's, too.

"Now, Polly," she said, as she rose, "I must go back up-stairs to my boy again. And if I were in your place, I would let this matter rest a secret between ourselves, your parents and Alan. I promise you that Molly and the other girls shall never know. But I am glad that you felt you could come and tell me about it. We will hope we can have Alan down-stairs before many days, and then you must run in to see him."

Two days later, a note came for Polly, just as she was starting for school.

"Alan wants to see you," it said; "come in for a few minutes."

Polly needed no second bidding, but hurried away, glad at the thought of seeing her friend once more. Mrs. Hapgood saw her coming and met her at the door, to lead her up-stairs to Alan's room. The boy was propped up with pillows, and his face looked rather white and worn, but it lighted as Polly entered, and he stretched out his hand to her eagerly.

"Hullo, Poll!" he exclaimed. "I'm no end glad to see you."

Mrs. Hapgood had left them alone together, but Polly did not stop to notice that, as she darted impulsively to the bed, saying,—

"Oh, Alan!"

Alan understood, but, being a boy, he only squeezed her hand between his, as he said lightly,—

"Bother all that stuff, Polly! Molly was mean to tell, and I was meaner to laugh at you, so I deserved to have my face washed. I sent for you because I knew you'd hear I was sick and worry about it. I didn't mean anybody to know, though."

When Mrs. Hapgood came back again, after a few moments, she found Polly sitting beside the bed, with a happier face than she had worn since the memorable Monday noon, while Alan looked as blissful as she; and when Polly took her departure, a little later, the boy called after her,—

"Come again as soon as you can, Poll. You're a jolly little nurse, and I like to have you round."

CHAPTER XV

THE PLAY

It was the last week in March, and the time had finally come for giving the long-discussed play, which had been delayed for some weeks on account of Alan's illness. After the first acute attack had passed, there followed, as a result of his drenching, a slow, tedious form of rheumatism which kept him shut up in the house, where he was forced to amuse himself as best he might. His sister and cousins did what they could to make the time pass quickly and pleasantly; but between school and their cooking club and their frequent calls on Bridget, they had little time for the boy except during the evenings, and he was mainly left to the society of his mother. This had been the state of affairs for more than a week, and Alan was becoming somewhat restless. He was not a saint, but only one of the next best things, a bright, lovable boy; and having rather exhausted his resources of reading, playing solitaire, and talking to his mother, the evening usually found him decidedly cross after his dull day, and he only half responded to the girls' attempts to be entertaining.

"I don't see what's come over Alan," said Molly, one afternoon, as the girls were walking home from school together. "Pie's always been so jolly, and now he's cross as

Anna Chapin Ray

can be. He doesn't act as if he wanted to have anything to say to us, and goes off to bed as soon as he can, after supper. I told him last night I thought he'd better be ashamed of himself."

As Molly spoke, they were just passing the Hapgood house. Polly glanced up at Alan's window, in the wing, to see the back of a yellow head, inside the glass. Molly followed the direction of her eyes, and said, by way of explanation,—

"Alan's not down-stairs to-day. He said he didn't feel like it."

"He isn't?"

Polly paused irresolutely at the gate, then turned in.

"What are you going to do, Polly?" asked Florence.

"I'm going up to see Alan," responded Polly.

"But I thought we were all going down to see Bridget."

"Bother Bridget!" returned Polly, with some energy. "The rest of you can go all the time, if you want to; but it's my impression that charity begins at home. Here we've all of us had that everlasting old Bridget on the brain, and let Alan get along as best he can."

"But Alan has mamma, and Bridget hasn't anybody but us," said Molly, in a virtuous tone of self-denial.

"I don't care if she hasn't," retorted Polly vehemently; "she has five of you to coddle her, and you just go there because you like the fun and think it sounds goody. There are enough of you without me, and one of you can take my afternoon, till Alan gets better."

"That's just like Polly," said Molly teasingly. "She always has liked boys better than girls."

Polly's face flushed.

"You know that's not so, Molly! I've done my fair share with Bridget, but now I think it isn't just right to go chasing off after her when we're leaving Alan all alone. If you knew—" Polly checked herself abruptly, then added more quietly, "I'll tell you what, girls, it isn't like Alan to be cross, and if he is, there's some good reason for it, so I think it's our place to find out what's the matter." And turning away, she went into the house, leaving her companions to go on to the hospital discussing, as they walked along, "Polly's last freak."

She stopped a moment to speak to Mrs, Hapgood, then ran directly up-stairs and looked in at the partly open door. Alan was half sitting, half lying on the sofa, with his book dropped, face downward, on his knee, and his hands clasped at the back of his head. Too much absorbed in his thoughts to notice her light step, his face was turned away from the door, and he was scowling moodily at a distant corner of the ceiling.

"May I come in, or are you making up a poem and don't want to be disturbed?" inquired Polly gaily, pushing the door wide open.

The boy started up with quick enthusiasm.

"Poll! How jolly of you to come in to see a fellow!"

"Then I'm not in the way?" she asked, as she pulled off her coat.

"What an idea! I was desperately lonesome, and somehow

Anna Chapin Ray

you always seem to fit in better than the others. Molly teases, and Jessie tires me. Katharine is better, only she's a little given to gushing, and boys don't like that sort of thing, you know," returned Alan frankly.

"I'm very glad if I suit you," said Polly, devoutly hoping she could succeed in avoiding the sin of teasing on the one hand, and of sentimentality on the other.

"Well, you do," replied Alan, with a heartiness which he did not often show, for he was not much given to direct praise. "You're first-rate company, Poll, and I'd been hoping you'd get time to run in, for it's stupid in the house. I knew you would, when you got round to it."

"Oh, Alan, you just make me ashamed!" said Polly contritely. "I ought to have been here before, and 'specially when I was the one to blame for all this, too."

"No use crying over spilt milk," answered Alan candidly. "I did think you'd come before this; but you're here now, and so it's all right. I've grown meek and am glad of small favors," he added, with a merry, sidelong glance from his gray eyes.

After that, not a day passed without a call from Polly. Now that her conscience was awakened, she realized that she had rather neglected her friend, and did all that lay in her power to make amends for her past forgetfulness. Her mother encouraged her visits, for she had learned from Mrs. Hapgood that they were a benefit to Alan and a help to herself, so Polly dropped in at her will, morning, noon, or night, and never failed to find a hearty welcome. The other girls laughed a little at her devotion, but it had no effect, so they went on their way, giving the boy the odds and ends of their time, while Polly and Alan spent long, cosy hours together, reading or playing games, with a perfect enjoyment of each other's society which left them no opportunity to miss their absent friends. Damon and Pythias, the girls called them, and never were two friends more closely united, with a simple, true affection, which, however, had no trace of the consciousness that one was a boy, the other a girl. Two boys could not have been more free from sentimentality, two girls were never farther from any suggestion of budding flirtation. They were just well-tried friends of long standing; and when, after four weeks, Alan went back into school again, his loyalty to Polly was, if possible, increased by the knowledge of the good times she had given up for his sake.

Aside from Alan's illness, the past weeks had brought to light another cause for excitement. Aunt Jane was about to become the second Mrs. Solomon Baxter. How, when, or where the fateful words were spoken was never known. What powerful arguments Mr. Baxter had brought to bear upon her, to overcome her aversion, to domestic life, was never revealed. However, a week after Miss Roberts had, in the presence of the children, addressed her guest as "Solo— Mr. Baxter," she had taken her sister into her confidence, and long before Alan was in school again, the matter was publicly announced by Mr. Baxter's escorting her to church, one Sunday morning, and marching up the aisle by her side, in full view of the assembled congregation.

This was the reason that, on the night of the play, Miss Roberts and Mr. Baxter occupied two armchairs placed side by side in the very front row of spectators, and that the captain's opening speech was interrupted by a little giggle, as his eyes fell on the faces before him.

The curtain, rose on a "glade in the forest primaeval," as was announced by the dozen playbills which did duty for the audience. Evergreen boughs, a few potted plants, and a dingy, greenish carpet were supposed to transform the stage

Anna Chapin Ray

into the glade in question; but the audience had little time to study the scenery, for the prompt entrance of the captain and a chosen companion called up a hearty burst of applause. The over-critical might have objected that English sailors do not, as a rule, have braids of brown hair escaping from their hats, and that the brave captain and explorer walked with some difficulty; but the speech and action of the sailor were spirited, and the captain's halting step was doubtless owing to temporary fatigue. Moreover, one glance at the boyish face under the great cocked hat was enough to make the most carping critic forget all other defects while, in strangely modern idioms and with a lofty disregard for dates, the old-time hero reminded his comrade of their long and perilous voyage over the sea, of the great wilderness which lay before them, and of the glory of reclaiming that wilderness to the civilization of the Virgin Queen. The sailor resisted his eloquence and refused to proceed, uttering mutinous threats. against his leader's life. But even in this crisis, the captain's presence of mind did not fail him, and, seeing that his persuasions and commands were of no avail, he promptly bound the sailor, hand and foot, and was preparing to carry him forward on his shoulders, when a fierce war-whopp was heard, and three ferocious savages rushed in upon them, just as the curtain fell.

The second scene, was regarded by the actors as being their most elaborate attempt. The room was darkened, and at the back of the stage, three or four dusky braves were crouched about their camp fire which, for the moment, had taken the form of an oil stove; while in the foreground lay Alan and Jessie, bound and motionless, awaiting the death which seemed inevitable. Jean had expended all her energies on this scene, and the warriors smoked the peace-pipe, inspected their medicines, and danced a war-dance with befitting solemnity, while the captain writhed uneasily, not so much with mental anguish as on account of the rheumatic twinges which his cramped position had set to running up and down his legs and back. Then, with a close fidelity to the old histories, an imposing throne was brought in, and Jean, as Powhatan, mounted the insecure structure; two stones were rolled into place at her feet, the captives' heads were arranged on these comfortless pillows, and a brave, ball-club in hand, took his place beside each. The sailor proved himself a coward, but the captain was bold to the last, and alternately defied the king and encouraged his weaker companion, who was whimpering by his side. Then, in one long speech which, absurdly out of keeping with the surroundings as it was, yet had the ring of true pathos, the captain bade farewell to home, wife, and children, and welcomed death in the name and for the honor of queen and country. Even Aunt Jane's face grew a little gentler as the boy voice went on to the close, and there was a momentary hush, followed by a hearty burst of applause, while Mrs. Adams, at the side, held Polly back, that her too hasty entrance should not mar the scene. Then Pocahontas dashed wildly in and, regardless of consequences, cast herself down on the captain's prostrate body with a force that elicited a sudden "Ow!" from the hero who had just dared to defy a savage king. But his anguish was quickly repressed, and the scene went finely to its close, when the fair Pocahontas herself loosed his fetters, raised him to his feet, and once more threw herself into his arms, while Powhatan embraced them both, with many paternal remarks uttered in the choicest Indian gutterals. While the stage was being arranged for the next scene, John and his Pocahontas were called before the curtain to receive the applause they had fully earned.

In the next two scenes, Jean had departed widely from the traditional story. In the former one, the captain took the stage alone and told over the story of his past life, dwelling with especial emphasis on his charming wife and thirteen

Anna Chapin Ray

beautiful children at home in mother England. His soliloquy was interrupted by the entrance of a messenger from a ship just landed, and, after a little political discussion, the messenger incidentally told him of a cyclone which had blown down his house and destroyed his entire family. The agony of the captain was tragic to behold, and moved Mr. Baxter to wipe his eyes sympathetically, and then cast a furtive glance at Aunt Jane who was apparently unmoved by this strange similarity of fate. Perhaps she was reserving her sympathy for Pocahontas. However, the captain's grief spent itself, and he finally recovered himself with the novel consolation that "thirteen always was an unlucky number." Then, dismissing the messenger, he proceeded to walk up and down his cabin and take counsel with his heart, how best to comfort himself in the future. After suggesting many a plan and rejecting it as soon as suggested, he resolved to set off immediately to Powhatan and ask for the fair hand of Pocahontas. As the curtain fell on this third scene, no one applauded more enthusiastically than Mr. Baxter.

The next scene opened with the preparations for the marriage of Pocahontas to the young planter, John Rolfe, which were interrupted by the sudden appearance of the captain, who bent on one knee before Powhatan, to ask his daughter's hand. Powhatan consented joyfully, and when Rolfe quite naturally objected, the captain proposed a duel, and killed his rival, under the very eyes of Pocahontas, who smiled rapturously as she watched the expiring agonies of her former lover. Then, turning to the captain, she said confidingly,—

"And now, dear John, everything is all prepared, so what if we get married at once?"

Accordingly, the marriage was at once solemnized, with the warriors as witnesses, while Powhatan descended from the throne to give the bride away, and Rolfe opportunely came back to life in time to serve as the clergyman who performed the ceremony.

There was a long delay between the marriage and the closing scene of the play; and while the audience discussed the past scenes, there went on a great commotion behind the curtain, sounds of murmuring and of moving furniture, mingled with excited whispers,—

"Where is my crown?"

"Do somebody see if my train is all right!"

"Where is my sword?"

"Hush! Hush!"

All this was enough to rouse the expectations of the audience, but even they were not prepared for the blaze of glory which met their eyes as the curtain rose on the court of England. Katharine and Florence sat on the throne, as pretty and dainty a royal couple as could be imagined. The play-bills had announced it as the court of Queen Elizabeth, and Florence looked the queen to perfection, in her trailing white silk gown, and with her mother's diamonds blazing in her golden hair; but opinions varied as to the identity of the haughty king by her side, for no one present was aware that Elizabeth's kingdom had any such lordly appendage. Still, it was all very picturesque and, as Polly had said, a great deal could be attributed to poetical license, so nobody complained, if the throne was a little overcrowded. Back of the queen were grouped three maids of honor, elaborately and richly dressed in gowns that rivalled the rainbow in variety and brilliancy of color; while at the king's left, as a fitting symbol of the British Lion, crouched old Leo, the Langs's great Saint Bernard. After a long pause to allow the

Anna Chapin Ray

audience to study this gorgeous scene, Pocahontas and her captain swept in and knelt at the foot of the throne. The queen bowed gracefully, in recognition of their homage, and bade them rise. Then, addressing the Lion and the maids, she called them "the free men of England" and, bidding them recall the captain's services to her realm, she announced her determination to knight him on the spot. The captain and his bride knelt again, while the queen not only gave him the royal accolade and dubbed him Sir John, but went on to extend the ceremony to his devoted wife, and saluted her as "My Lady Pocahontas, the fairest savage in all London town." Then the royal pair stepped down from the throne and, joining hands with My Lord, My Lady, and the maids, and escorted by the British Lion who amiably wagged his tail in token of approval, they advanced and bowed low to the audience as the curtain fell on the play. The applause was enthusiastic and prolonged, and the actors were rejoicing in their success when, as the clapping of hands died away, Aunt Jane's voice was heard, solemnly remarking,—

"Well, I do hope those children realize that all this story about Pocahontas has been proved to be entirely without foundation. It seems to me a great waste of time to get up a play that hasn't a word of truth in it."

"Isn't that just like Aunt Jane!" whispered Pocahontas in disgust. "I wonder if she'd have liked it any better, if we'd acted out all about her and her Mr. Baxter."

A few moments later, the actors appeared, all in costume, to bring small trays laden with good things for the refreshment of their guests, and to receive congratulations on their play. Then they gathered in the dining-room to have their share of the goodies and discuss the evening, feeling that the best part of the whole was the merry time of talking it over afterwards.

"Oh," groaned Alan, taking off his hat as he helped himself to a macaroon; "I didn't much think I should ever breathe again, to say nothing of eating, after Pocahontas came down on me. Polly, I do wish you'd go and get weighed, in the morning." "There's one favor I'd like to ask," said Jessie. "If we ever play it over again, I wish that when you get ready to kill us, you'd put us inside the curtain. You were so eager about untying Alan that you forgot all about me, and when the curtain came down, I was half inside it and half outside, so that Mrs. Adams had to come and pull me back, before I could get up."

"If we ever play it again!" echoed Jean. "But you never will, with my consent. I thought 'twas splendid, while I was writing it; when we were rehearsing it, I thought 'twas pretty good; but while we were playing it to-night before all those people, I thought it was simply dreadful, and I was ashamed of myself for ever trying to write such trash."

"If you don't like it, you can write us another," said Jessie; "but, for my part, this is good enough for me."

"Are you through eating, children?" asked Mrs. Adams, putting her head in at the door. "Mrs. Hapgood wants you all to sing something, just to finish up the evening."

It was an unexpected request, and for a moment, the actors demurred, then held a hasty consultation. A few minutes later, they appeared in Indian file, John Smith and his sailor leading the way, and the rest following in their Indian costumes. Katharine sat down at the piano and played a few solemn, slow chords, then the others took up the chorus, the words of which they had adapted for the occasion:

"John Smith had a little Injun,
One little Injun girl."

CHAPTER XVI

JOB GOES TO A FUNERAL

"Do you know what a first-rate substitute for roast oysters these are?" asked Alan, twirling the great metal spider with purplish back and spiral wire legs that hung from the gas fixture.

"No, nor you either, Alan," said Jessie. "They do, now honestly. If you heat them up real hot, they smell just like roast oysters. I knew a family once, that always kept one on hand, and when provisions ran low, they'd set it to frying, and all sit round and smell of it. It was 'most as good as eating them," persisted the boy soberly.

"Alan Hapgood," said his sister, "if you tell any more such taradiddles, I'll send you home."

"But what if I don't choose to go?" returned Alan. "Mrs. Adams asked me here to spend the afternoon, and you wouldn't any of you have known what was going on, if it hadn't been for me."

"You shall stay and tell all the stories you like, Alan," said Polly, coming to his defence as usual. "And if Molly doesn't like it, she shall go home, her own self."

"Come, Alan," urged Florence; "tell us another story, a real long one, to help pass the time."

"Hm! Let's see," mused Alan. "I don't know as I know any. I'll tell you, I read one a while ago that I liked pretty well, and if I get hard up, I can put in some of that. How'll that do?"

"Beautifully," said Polly, with enthusiasm. "You do tell such splendid stories, Alan."

The group in Mrs. Adams's parlor had gathered there for a strange purpose, that day. An old negro, well-known throughout the town, had died, two days before, and Alan had discovered, only that noon, that the man was to be buried with military honors. The line of march to the cemetery lay past the Adams house, so Mrs. Adams had asked them all to come there, to watch the solemn pageant. It was a cold, gray April day, threatening rain at any moment. As the girls and Alan reached the gate, they had paused, for a minute, to watch the fast-gathering crowd as it hurried away up the street to the old brown house, just visible in the distance, whose end, jutting out on the street, was surrounded with the members of the company, who had assembled to pay the last honors to their sleeping comrade. Under the dull, leaden sky, and in the shade of the arching elms, the old house and the road and the gray-coated men looked to the children as if the heavy shadow which rested over the silent room within had extended over them all, and was enveloping them in its sombre gloom. Though only a moment before, they had been laughing and talking in mere curious interest, they grew suddenly quiet, as they realized that the swift, mysterious summons had come to old Pete, whom they had known so well.

"And they say," said Alan, as Polly joined them at the gate,

Anna Chapin Ray

and they lingered there, "that Pete's little dog won't leave the room one minute, but just lies there and watches him. They tried to get him away, for the funeral, but he snarled at them so they had to let him be."

Katharine's face softened.

"That's a friend worth having," said she thoughtfully. "Some people say 'only a dog,' but if he is faithful to his master, even after death has come, what more can he do?"

"Oh, dear me; there's Job!" exclaimed Polly suddenly, as the old creature stalked into sight. "How did he get out?"

"I wonder if we could get him in," said Alan.

"It's no use; he'd only kick you," returned Polly. "We may as well come into the house, and let him alone; then perhaps he'll go in. He's awfully obstinate, you know."

"I think I've noticed something of the kind," said Jessie, as they ran up the steps, and left Job to the quiet workings of his conscience.

By the time they were gathered in the parlor windows, their momentary quiet was over, and they were talking as gaily as ever while they gazed up the street, watching for the first signs of the procession. But the funeral services were long, and the girls' patience was rapidly becoming exhausted when Florence had suggested Alan's telling them a story, to while away the time of waiting. The girls arranged themselves before the two long front windows, to look and listen at the same time, Katharine, Florence, and Jean at one, Molly and Jessie at the other, with Alan and Polly on the floor at their feet, and the lad began his tale.

"Once upon a time, about sixty-seven years and nine months ago, there was a young man in England that was rich and handsome and brave and good, and his name was—Oh, give us a name for him, Poll."

"Mortimer Vincent Augustin Thome," responded Polly promptly. "I think that's a lovely name."

"Too long," objected Alan. "Something shorter, not but one."

"Malcolm, then; will that suit?" asked Florence, from the other side of the room.

"Yes, that's good. Well, his name was Malcolm, and he fell in love with a girl named—"

"Gertrude," suggested Jean, without waiting to be asked.

"No, Margaret," said Polly. "That's ever so much better."

"All right, call her Margaret," said Alan; "but if you girls don't keep still, I never can tell you any story. Malcolm loved Margaret and wanted her to be his bride, but she was kept a captive in a tower, by a wicked uncle who had gone on a crusade to the Holy Land."

"But they didn't go on crusades sixty-seven years ago," said Jean, whose strong point was history.

"Will you keep still, Jean?" said Polly. "This isn't a true story, and he has as good a right to poetical license as you had in the play."

"The Holy Land," resumed Alan, not noticing the interruption; "and he had taken the keys to the tower in his pocket, so Malcolm didn't really know just what to do. At

Anna Chapin Ray

last, after he had tried all sorts of things, he took his banjo and went under the tower window and sang a little song that Margaret had made up, when they were children together." Here Alan paused to smile meaningly at Polly, before he went on. "It was a very sweet song, and his voice was loud enough so Margaret heard him and opened a window to peek out. She knew him as soon as she saw him, and she wrote a letter and tied it to a string and let it down to him. He read it and wrote an answer, and was just getting ready to send it up, the same way, when a great, fierce ruffian with a bloodhound pounced on him, and threw him into the very darkest dungeon in the cellar of the tower. He was pretty much scared, for he was all in the dark, and he was without any food or anything to drink, and he only had his banjo to comfort him. But he was so glad it wasn't Margaret that was there, that he didn't much mind anything else. But that wasn't the worst of it. His prison walls kept growing smaller and smaller, till by and by it began to get so tight that it hurt him. It didn't stop, even then, but it grew so small that his bones began to break, till finally he found that he only had one whole one left. That stirred him up, and he said to himself, 'If I don't find a way out, I shall be a dead man!' So he pounded on the walls, to see what they were made of, and found they were iron; but he knew the floor was earth, so he began to dig as fast as he could, and he used his banjo for a scoop, to carry off the earth in."

"Where'd he carry it to?" inquired Jessie. "I thought he didn't have any room to move round."

"He didn't, very much," said Alan; "but he made the most of every little corner, and before long he had dug down far enough to come to just the jolliest little secret passage you ever saw. He slipped down into it, and followed it along and along ever so far, till at last he came up to the light again, outside the walls of the tower. He swung his hat in the air and shouted, 'Three cheers for Queen Victoria!' and then he ran round under Margaret's window and took his banjo and sang the song once more, to let her know he was alive. Then, without wasting any more time, he ran off through the forest. But when he came to the top of the very first hill, he looked back and saw Margaret leaning out of the window, waving a pale blue flag with the word courage on it, in gilt letters."

"Where did she get such a thing?" asked Jean.

"Oh, she'd been making it, while he was in the dungeon," answered Alan. "So he went away to the Holy Land, to look for the wicked uncle. He walked every step of the way, and swam rivers and climbed up mountains and slid down on avalanches on the other side, and at last he came to Jerusalem. He found the uncle just leading four regiments against the city gates, mounted on a splendid white horse. And he looked down and smiled scornfully and said, 'What ho, Malcolm! You here?' That made Malcolm very mad, so he pulled the uncle off his horse and hit him, thump! with his banjo, and killed him. Then he looked in his pockets and found ever so much money; but, hard up as he was, for he'd had his pockets picked on the way, he didn't take the money, for he wanted something else. It was found at last, a little gold key hung round his neck on a silver chain; so Malcolm took the key and went home, riding the uncle's horse, and let out Margaret, and they lived happy and died happy, and she was heir to all the tower and the servants. But the first thing she did was to block the walls of the dungeon, so they couldn't move any more."

"Oh, Alan, Alan! Where did you get such a story?" said Katharine, laughing until the tears came.

"Get it? Made it up, of course," returned the boy, with evident pride in his tale.

"It must be splendid to be able to make up such stories!" sighed Polly enviously. "I'd give almost anything if I could do it."

"I should hope if you tried, yours would hang together a little better," said Molly who, in virtue of her relationship, felt privileged to be as critical as she chose. "It's a mystery to me how he could move round to dig up the floor when all his bones were broken, and I never heard that you could use a banjo for a shovel and then play on it, or hit a man hard enough to kill him, and not break it."

"I don't care for all that," said Polly enthusiastically. "Anybody could tell a story and get rid of those things. What I like is the things he did, he was so brave and so true, and then his not touching any of the uncle's money was the best part of it all, when he needed it so much."

"But he stole the uncle's horse," objected Jean.

"He didn't steal it, he only took it home. And speaking of horses, I wonder what's become of Job." And Polly leaned forward to peer out of the window.

"There he is, over in the next lot," said Jessie.

Dr. Adams's house stood far back from the street, and next to it was a deep, vacant lot at the very rear of which Job was aimlessly wandering about, pausing now and then to nip at the tender green blades that were pushing their way up through the brown, dead turf.

"What ever sent him in there!" said Polly. "I don't see how we can get him home."

"Let him alone long enough, and he'll come," predicted

Molly. "It's no use to chase him round and round, and if you drive him out into the street, he'll run away."

"I wish he would," said Polly explosively, "and never come back again! He's more trouble than he's worth, and he knows more than all the rest of us put together."

"Give him to Aunt Jane for a wedding present," Alan proposed.

"She'd think 'twas signing her death warrant," answered Polly, laughing. "You know he did duty at the funeral of Mrs. Baxter the first."

"Oh dear, it seems as if they never would come!" sighed Jessie impatiently. "What does keep them so long?"

"Do somebody tell another story," said Florence. "Can't you, Katharine?"

"I should never dare, after Alan's wonderful success," replied Katharine lightly, as she took out the daffodil she had been wearing in her buttonhole and tossed it over to her cousin. Then she added soberly, "It isn't any story at all, but I believe, while we wait, I'll tell you about the saddest funeral I ever saw in my life."

"Go on, Kit; you have the floor," said Alan encouragingly.

"It isn't much to tell, but you've no idea how pitiful it was to see," the girl went on thoughtfully. "Just a year ago this spring, papa had to go West on business, and he took me with him. We had to stay two or three days in a little bit of a town up in the Rocky Mountains, and while we were there, a young woman died. She had only been married a month, and had just come out from New England, to live in the cunning little new house that her husband had built. It was a winter of very deep snow, even for that region, and when it melted, it grew soft all the way down through, before it seemed to go away, any at all. The cemetery was away from the town, up on the side of the mountain, just the loneliest, most desolate place you can imagine; and it seemed so sad to take her away and leave her there all alone. It was a long, long procession, and papa and I stood at the window to watch it, as it went through the town, and on out into the open country, where no road had been broken. Then, for a mile or two, the long black line crawled along over the snow, while the horses floundered about, half buried in the drifts, and the hearse tipped this way and that, as first one wheel would sink down out of sight, and then another. At last it wound around the foot of the hill, and we couldn't see it any more; but I kept feeling so sorry for the poor little wife and for the lonely husband in his new house."

Katharine paused, but there was no word spoken, so she went on,—

"A month later we spent Sunday there, on our way home. The snow had all melted and, in the afternoon, I teased papa to walk up to the cemetery with me. We remembered the name, so we could find the grave easily enough. It was perfectly bare, without any grass on it, but at the head was a rough little cross made of two boards nailed together, with her name painted on it, in black letters that were a little unsteady, as if somebody's hand shook when he was making them; and at the foot of the cross lay one tiny bunch of white immortelles, to show that she wasn't quite forgotten. But when we turned to look at the view, it didn't seem sad, any more. The little, low, dingy town lay below us, as if she had risen above it, and all around us, the great, soft, kind mountains stood up in the sun to guard her and watch over her, in her sleep. The shabby cross and the little posy and the magnificent brown mountains were all so much more kind and loving than our piles of marble and fussy flowers arranged for show, that when I came down the hill, I didn't feel sorry for her, any longer."

The hush that followed Katharine's simple story was unbroken for some moments. Then Polly sprang up excitedly,—

"The drums! Don't you hear them?" And she rushed away to call her mother.

The procession was moving, at last, and the distant roll of muffled drums could be plainly heard by the girls, as they pressed closely to the window. Touched, as they had been, by the account of that far-away funeral among the mountains, they were in just the mood to be impressed by the scene which was passing before them. And, in truth, any one who stood looking on, that day, must have felt the impressiveness of the long line as it slowly filed down the broad street under the graceful arches of the tall old elms, in the cold light of the cloudy afternoon. First came the drum corps, with wailing fife and muffled drum; next appeared the gray uniforms of the company who marched two by two, with bowed heads and reversed arms, to escort the hearse in their midst. Directly behind the hearse trotted a small, yellow figure, at sight of whom Alan stealthily drew his hand across his eyes. It was Pete's faithful friend, the little Scotch terrier, who was following his master to his last resting-place, with a sturdy determination not to leave his good old master with whom he had spent such a happy little life. Then followed the line of carriages and the straggling groups on foot; but the girls paid little heed to them, for Polly said, in a sudden whisper,—"Just look at Job!"

For a long time the old horse had been quietly grazing,

Anna Chapin Ray

without so much as raising his head to take breath and look about him, so greedy was he for the first tender grass-blades of the spring. Suddenly he heard the roll of the drums and threw up his head to listen, with eager ears and dilating eyes, as if the sound recalled to him some vague memory of his far-off youth. So proud and spirited he looked as he stood there, that it was evident that, in fancy, he was living over his former days, perhaps listening to the triumphant strains of music which heralded the close of the rebellion. As the sound came nearer, and yet nearer, he appeared to be under its spell and slowly moved down towards the street, arching his glossy neck and stepping high, in perfect time to the music. Fifty feet from the fence, he stopped and gazed at the scene before him, still spellbound by the martial sounds and the memories they called up in his mind, while the group in the Adams's windows watched him intently, amazed at the life and fire in the old creature's pose and manner. Still Job stood watching the soldiers, listening to the band until it had moved onward, past the spot where he was. Then his eyes fell on the hearse, and he took one eager step forward. Surely that was a familiar sight! The carriages came next, and by that time there was no hesitancy in his mind; for at length he recognized all the solemn import of the procession. It was a funeral, and in funerals Job had often borne a conspicuous part. The band was doubtless his call to duty; and should any one say that he had failed, even in his old age, to respond to this call? He took another step forward, paused again, for only one instant; then, just as the last carriage passed the gate, he swung his aged tail round and round, in two rapturous, joyful whisks, and with tossing head and flying mane, he trotted rapidly out into the street, overtook the procession and, dropping into a decorous walk just as his nose touched the back of the rear carriage, he marched solemnly off down the street, with patient resignation and unending sadness depicted in every line of his old brown body.

Inside the parlor the girls, without a thought of their past interest in Pete's funeral, turned and gazed at each other in silence for a moment, then sank to the floor, in uncontrollable, though noiseless laughter.

CHAPTER XVII

MISS BEAN'S VISIT IS RETURNED

Still another month had passed and it was late in May when, one bright Saturday morning, Jessie, Polly, and Alan drove away through the town and out over the western hills. Cob was as full of life and spirits as they were, and they went gaily onward with no particular destination in view, but only intent on enjoying the soft, warm air and the abundance of spring life all about them. Birds in every tree, green leaves and bright blossoms on every hand, and over them all the clear, yellow sunlight, these were enough for the happy young people in the carriage.

"Dear me!" sighed Polly. "When we begin to have days like this, it does seem as if vacation never, never would come. I can't bear to stay in school and work over books in such weather. I'd much rather stay outside and watch things grow."

"Let's cut school for the rest of the term, Polly," suggested Alan, "and take Job and drive off out of the world some-where, and not come back till winter."

"Thank you, no. I'll take Cob, if Jessie is willing, for we couldn't get outside of the town with *Job*, if we had *any* idea of getting *back* by Christmas," rejoined Polly, laughing.

"Take Cob and welcome, if I can go with you," said Jessie. "Seems to me I never felt so before, but I don't want to stay in school any more than Polly does. Perhaps it's because your springs are pleasanter than ours."

"I shouldn't wonder if they were," said Polly reflectively, as regardless of freckles, she took off her hat and let the sun strike full upon her ruddy curls. "Isn't this perfect?" she added, with a sigh of content. "I do believe everything is nicer in Massachusetts than it is anywhere else. I'm glad I happened to be born in the Bay State."

Jessie laughed outright at the fervor of her tone. Then she said, as she drew Cob down to a slow walk, to enjoy a bit of road that lay under a group of tall pines,—

"After all, I shall be sorry to have vacation come, for as soon as this term is over, we shall have to go home, and I don't want to, one bit."

"Sorry to leave me, aren't you, Cousin Jessie?" asked Alan, with, mock sentiment.

"Don't flatter yourself, young man," said Polly, in parenthesis, as Jessie went on. seriously,—

"Why, yes, I suppose I shall miss you, Alan; but it's the girls that I care most for. We've had such good times doing things together, and next year I shall be forlorn enough, for Kit will come out, and I shall be left all to myself."

"Come back here," suggested Alan quite hospitably, considering the frank way in which Jessie had spoken of her slight regret at leaving him.

Anna Chapin Ray

"Without Kit? Never!" replied Jessie earnestly. "I'd rather be with her and have only a dozen words a day from her, than have to be separated from her. I've always been fond of her, but it seems to me she was never half so lovely as she's been this last year."

Polly stepped on Alan's toe, under cover of the robe, and was met by an answering flash from the gray eyes, but neither spoke, as Jessie continued,—"You do so many more things here, and have so much better times, you girls, that Kit and I both wish papa and mamma would come back here to live. Omaha is pleasant enough, and the river is lovely,—when it isn't muddy; but I shall miss these hills and the elms and the lazy look of the old town. I like old things best. And what do you suppose I shall miss, most of all?"

"Job" and "Aunt Jane," suggested Alan and Polly, in a breath.

"You're too bad to laugh at me." And Jessie tried to pout, but it was too hard work, so she gave up the attempt and laughed instead. "No, it's the garret at your house, Alan, with all the old spinning wheels and warming pans. Some day, when I get my cats, I'll come back here to live, see if I don't." And Jessie nodded with decision as she started up Cob once more.

"Oh, dear! Next year doesn't mean much fun for me," groaned Polly. "I shall have to begin Latin and Greek and all sorts of dreadful things, so as to get ready for college."

"Then you are really going," said Jessie. "What makes you do it, if you don't want to?"

"It's been the family plan ever since I was a baby," said Polly; "and there's no use in trying to change it. Besides, I don't think I mind it much, or shan't when I once get there. I want to know a few things when. I'm grown up, even if I'm not a lawyer or a doctor,—but I'm going to leave that for Alan,"

"Don't worry about that, Polly," said Alan. "At present rate of progress, if I lose a month or two of school every winter, I shouldn't get through college till long after you were dead and out of the way. And then, I don't think I want to be a doctor, anyway."

"Now, Alan," retorted Polly; "that's not quite fair of you, when you know how my heart is set on having you. a splendid doctor, and in time taking papa's place. I've told you, time and time again, that if I had a brother, he would have to be one; and, as long as I haven't, you're the next best thing. You'd make such a splendid one, too. I know, for I asked papa if you wouldn't, and he said yes. He said—" Polly came to a sudden pause.

"Said what, Poll? Out with it."

"I wasn't going to tell, for fear 'twould make you conceited," returned Polly; "but if I thought it would make any difference with your plans, I'd run the risk, only you must be really in earnest about it, Alan, and think it all over. He said you had just the character that goes to make a good doctor, brave and true and unselfish, and always gentle and calm and jolly. Now doesn't that make you want to be something grand?" And Polly turned to look at the boy, with all her earnestness, all her love for him lighting her face and beautifying it, in spite of the brown freckles on her cheeks.

Alan's face flushed and his eyes were shining, as he asked eagerly,—

"Did Dr. Adams really say all that about me?"

Anna Chapin Ray

"Yes, he said so only the other day, and I suppose I oughtn't to have told you; but, ever since our talk one day last winter when you'd been to the hospital, I've been hoping and hoping that some day you'd be just the right kind of a doctor, one that cures his patients, whether they can pay or not, and makes them love him, in spite of the horrid things he has to do to them. If you'd only do that, Alan, I should be so proud of you."

"Should you, Poll? Well, I'll think about it, but it's too soon to make up my mind yet. Mother wants me to be a minister."

"You a minister! Why, Alan, you'd laugh, even in the middle of a sermon; and I know you'd never go to a funeral without thinking how Job went, the other day. And anyway, I'd a great deal rather be a doctor, for they do more good. Ministers *talk;* doctors *do*."

"Some ministers *do*," said Jessie.

"Yes, some of them; but it's their business to preach, and that's all most of them try to do. You won't hear of many ministers that get up, cold winter nights, every night for a week, to go to see one poor little croupy baby, just for love of it, and not expecting to get a cent. I don't believe that, taken year in and year out, there are many missionaries that work harder or do more good than papa does."

"Not many doctors, either," suggested Alan.

"That may be; but just his doing it proves that it can be done, if anybody is willing to try. Don't shirk that way, Alan; it isn't like you. You can do it just as well as he can, and I mean you shall, some day, if teasing can do any good."

"Do you know, Polly," said Jessie; "you've talked about it till you make me want to be a doctor, myself. I don't suppose mamma would ever let me, but I'd like to try, and I think I could do it."

"Why don't you, then?" asked Polly heartily. "I don't want to myself, and I shouldn't succeed. I should be like the old doctor papa tells about, that used to swear at his patients when they didn't mind him. I never could keep cool when things went wrong. Besides, I think it's a man's work, more than a woman's."

"I'd like to be one, and prove that you are wrong," returned Jessie, with some spirit.

"If I really made up my mind to be a doctor, I'd be a good one, if I had to give up everything else for the sake of it; but it isn't in my line," said Polly a little regretfully. "But when you and Alan are famous all over the world, I'll go around telling everybody how I was the first one to start you in that line; and they'll all be grateful to me, even if I haven't any career, see if they aren't."

"In the meantime," said Alan, suddenly breaking off the conversation, "has anybody the slightest idea where we are?"

"I haven't," said Jessie, pulling up Cob abruptly. "I've been so busy talking and thinking that I haven't paid any attention to where we were going."

"I never saw this road before," said Polly. "It's too far out of town for Job's wanderings. But go on; we shall come to a house or a guideboard before long."

"To judge by the sun and by my appetite," remarked Alan pensively, "it must be almost noon."

"Oh, that makes me think!" exclaimed Polly. "Get up, Alan; you're right on them!"

"On what?" inquired the boy lazily, without stirring.

"On the gingersnaps. Mamma gave me some to put in my pocket, in case we should get hungry, and here you've been sitting on top of them, all the way!" There was an accent of despair in Polly's tone.

Alan rose, and she plunged her hand into her pocket.

"Just look here!" she said accusingly, as she drew out a crumpled paper bag.

Alan caught it from her hand and peered down into it.

"Pulverized gingersnaps!" he exclaimed. "Want some, Jessie?"

"I'm so hungry, I'm thankful for anything," she replied. "Let's eat up the largest pieces ourselves, Polly, and make Alan take the dust for his share, for he was the one to blame."

"I know it, and now he'll never know how good they were," returned Polly relentlessly, as the girls devoured the contents of the bag, even to the last crumb. "He deserves to go hungry."

"But what's that building over there?" asked Jessie, a little later, pointing to a great red house on the side of a distant hill.

"That? That's the poorhouse," replied Polly, after studying it for a minute or two. "I came here once with papa, ever so long ago. I'd like to know how we ever managed to get here;

it's seven or eight miles from town."

"Seven or eight miles from town! And we are dying of starvation," said Alan.

"Speak for yourself, please; Jessie and I have had lunch," said Polly. "But," she went on, struck with a sudden thought, "let's go and see Miss Bean, and maybe she'll invite us to dinner. She ought to, for she's been fed at our house often enough."

Jessie fell in with the idea.

"Let's try it, anyway," she said. "I've always wanted to see what they do in such a place, and I don't believe there would be any harm in it."

"What harm could there be?" said Polly. "We needn't tell her we've come to dinner; only, if she should happen to ask us, we could stay, after she's teased a little."

Turning from the main road, they drove under the great gateway and followed a winding drive up to the very door of the house. A few old crones sat in a row by the door, chattering like so many venerable crows; but when they caught sight of the children, their voices sank to whispers, as they watched Alan spring to the ground, hold up his arms to help Polly and Jessie, and then deliberately tie Cob to the nearest post.

At sight of the women in their plain white caps and dark calico gowns, Jessie was seized with a nervous desire to laugh, and hid behind Polly, whispering,—

"You do the talking, Polly; I can't."

"But what shall I say?" returned Polly, in the same tone.

"Isn't there a matron or something?" said Jessie doubtfully. "Ask for her."

By this time, Alan had joined them and they held a hasty consultation, as a result of which Alan walked straight up to the old women. Hat in hand, and a smile on his bright, boyish face, he bowed low before them and asked if he could be directed to the matron's room. Alan's smile never failed to move a woman's heart, no matter whether she was old or young. In the present instance, one of the aged dames tottered to her feet, saying,—

"Bless your heart, sonny! I'll show you, myself, to pay for your sweet manners." And she toddled away, followed by the girls and by Alan whose sweet manners had collapsed into a stifled giggle at the unlooked-for compliment.

They were taken into a long, wide hall through the middle of which ran a strip of rag carpet, edged with plain wooden settees. Everything was scrupulously neat and clean, but the only ornament in sight was a stuffed poodle under a glass case, above which hung the somewhat inappropriate motto: *God loveth a cheerful giver*. Here they were told to sit down, while the old woman went in search of the matron. The next few moments were rather uncomfortable for all three of the children. Now that they were really inside the institution, they were a little frightened at what they had done; and yet the ridiculous side of their being there struck them so keenly that they dared not speak, for fear of being found laughing, when the all-powerful matron should make her appearance. At length she came, a trim little woman, with an earnest face and a business-like manner. At Polly's request to be allowed to see Miss Bean, she shook her head doubtfully.

"It isn't one of our regular visiting days," she began." Was your errand an important one?"

"Not very," returned Polly, with a lingering accent on the second word, as she caught the sound of a distant clatter of dishes and breathed in a vague odor of boiled beef.

"I am sorry to disappoint you," the matron went on; "and if you have come all the way from town, it is too bad to send you back without seeing her, for a minute. Call Miss Bean," she said to a servant. "What name shall I tell her?" she asked Polly.

"Polly Adams, ma'am," answered Polly.

The matron became suddenly cordial, like a snowbank under the rays of the spring sun.

"Isn't this Dr. Adams's daughter?" she asked. "I thought I saw a familiar look about the lower part of the face."

"Yes, Dr. Adams is my father," said Polly, whose hopes of staying sprang into life once more.

"Indeed! I am very glad to see you for his sake," returned the matron. "Perhaps he sent you?"

"No—o, he didn't send us; we came," faltered Polly.

"Never mind; I am glad to see you, anyway. And these are your young friends, I suppose. Wouldn't you all like to stay and have dinner here? It is almost ready," she added, in a generous burst of hospitality.

"Thank you, we should be delighted," said Alan hastily, fearing Polly might lose the opportunity by politely hesitating.

Anna Chapin Ray

"Well, Polly Adams, where in the name of time did you come from?" asked Miss Bean's voice behind her.

Polly turned around. Could this be Miss Bean, this little, withered figure in the calico gown and white cap? Where was the green and black gown? Where were the lace mitts and the shaker bonnet? However, there could be no doubt of Miss Bean's identity when she said, in her usual abrupt manner,—

"How's your ma? And who are these children?"

"This is Alan Hapgood," replied Polly, introducing her friends; "and this is Jessie Shepard."

"You don't say so! Henry and Kate Shepard's daughter, from out in Omaha?"

"Yes."

Miss Bean completed Jessie's embarrassment by critically scrutinizing her from head to foot, then asking suddenly,—

"Do they dress much out in. Omaha?"

This unexpected question sent Alan, off to examine the stuffed poodle, while Miss Bean turned to Polly again.

"Did your ma send you?"

"No, ma'am," said Polly.

"Then what did you come for?" was the hospitable query.

"We were driving this way, and so we stopped to see you," answered Polly, with a feeling of shame at her own insincerity.

"Much obliged," returned Miss Bean, with grim sarcasm; then she added, "How's your Uncle Solomon? I always thought he and Miss Roberts would come round, if I only just put 'em in a way to think of it."

Miss Bean's questions bade fair to last indefinitely, but fortunately the dinner bell sounded, and the matron came back to lead her young guests into the great dining-room, at one end of which she had arranged a small table with seats for them, and for Miss Bean who was regarded with no small degree of envy, as she took her place in this honored circle. The matron seated herself with Alan, and Jessie at her left, Polly and Miss Bean at her right, and the simple dinner of boiled beef and vegetables was brought in. Except for an occasional request for food, the meal was eaten in silence, while the old people curiously watched the matron's group, and listened eagerly to the conversation they kept up. Polly, too, was silent, gazing with a curious fascination at the long line of aged faces, some peaceful, others querulous, but all so alike that the row of them seemed to become an endless perspective of white caps and wagging jaws. Her reverie was interrupted by Miss Bean, who leaned across the table to say reprovingly to Jessie, as she refused the boiled cabbage,—

"Folks that go a-visiting hadn't ought to be difficult with their victuals."

"Can you imagine anything more dreadful than to live in such a place?" exclaimed Polly, as they drove away, after being conducted over the establishment. "I'd work and scrimp, year after year, rather than, just sit down and be supported by the town."

"Yes," answered Jessie; "but I suppose they do have real good times, in their way."

"So does a cat that eats her milk, and then goes to sleep in the sun," returned Polly. "That may be their way, but I'm thankful it isn't mine."

"I presume all they care for is to have enough to eat, and to keep warm in winter and cool in summer," said Alan. "Some of them looked as old as the Rocky Mountains, and I don't see why they shouldn't live forever, doing nothing but sun themselves."

"I'd rather live a little shorter time, and live a little harder, while I'm about it," said Polly. "I think I prefer wearing out to rusting out."

It was late in the afternoon when they reached the town once more, and drove up the street to Polly's house. Mrs. Adams was at the gate, watching for them.

"At last!" she exclaimed. "I was really getting quite anxious about you, for fear Cob had run away, or you were lost. Aren't you hungry? Where have you been?"

"Oh, no, we aren't hungry," said Alan, as he jumped out to help Polly to the ground. "We've been to dinner at the poorhouse, and Jessie has disgraced us all, by refusing to eat cabbage."

CHAPTER XVIII

MR. BAXTER TAKES A NAP

They had all been at the Langs's that afternoon. The third of June was Florence's fourteenth birthday, and Mrs. Lang had celebrated the day by giving a little afternoon tea on the broad piazza, overlooking the grounds. It had been a pretty sight, with the dainty gowns of the girls, and the active figures of the few boys who had been favored with invitations to share in the games on the lawn. The ever-present amateur photographer had thought so too, apparently, and from his position in the street, he had already aimed his detective camera at them, when Alan discovered him and gave the alarm, only just in time to prevent his stolen success.

Polly and Jean walked home with the Hapgoods in the early twilight, and, refusing Mrs. Hapgood's invitation to go into the house, the girls settled themselves on the two high-backed seats at either side of the broad front porch, and gave themselves up to the luxury of talking over the event of the day.

"It must be fun to be able to have company, and do it up in such splendid style as Mrs. Lang does," said Jean a little enviously, as she pulled out the bunch of pink clover she had

Anna Chapin Ray

worn at her belt.

"It was lovely, wasn't it?" assented Molly. "Mrs. Lang doesn't do it often, but when she does have a party, it is always perfect."

"After all," said Katharine, "it's all from the outside, somehow. I don't know whether you understand what I mean, but I know, myself."

"I'm glad you do, Kit," said her sister disrespectfully; "for it's certain that nobody else does. Remember that we are young, and explain yourself a little."

"I did really mean something, Jessie," said Katharine. "With Mrs. Lang, it seems as if she set the day and gave her orders to the servants, and that's all there was about it. Of course she entertains charmingly, and all that; but it makes me feel, all the time, as if she did it to pay her debts, and not because she likes to have us there. When we go to—well, to Polly's, for instance, I. never think of that, for Mrs. Adams always acts as if she enjoyed us as much as we enjoy being there."

"She does," answered Polly, with conviction. "She says she never half grew up, for she likes young people now better than she does those of her own age."

"It must be horrid to have to give parties, whether you want to or not, just because somebody else has invited you," remarked Molly.

"That's the way they all do in society, though," said Jessie, with a knowing air.

"Well, if that's society, then. I don't want any of it," said Polly ungratefully, while she ran her fingers through her hair and stood it wildly on end. "I just want my friends, and I want them whenever I feel like it; but I don't care anything about having a crowd of people round in the way, just because it's fashionable, when I don't, care a snap for them. If I ever grow up and come out, as they call it, I'm going to like my friends for themselves, and not for their clothes and their parties and their good dinners. I can buy those at a hotel, if I get hungry."

"And when hotels fail, there is always the poorhouse," suggested Jean. "But, girls, do you ever want to be very, very rich, just for a little while?"

"I don't think I ever stopped to think much about it," answered Polly; "but I suppose it would be fun."

"'Tisn't so much that I want more things than I have," said Jean; "but, not often, only just once in a while, I do so wish I could go ahead and be real extravagant, spend ever so much money for all sorts of foolish things, have parties and fine clothes, and travel everywhere I wanted. I know perfectly well that I shouldn't enjoy myself half so much as I do now, when I have to work for all I get; but still, I'd like to try the other, just for a change."

"And then, after a little while, you'd be longing to get back again," returned Polly. "I don't believe life is all fun, even to people that are very rich. I never saw anybody yet that I wanted to change places with."

"Let's all tell what we would do, if we were very rich and could have just what we wanted," suggested Alan, from the step.

"All right, only do come in under cover, child," said Polly, in a maternal tone; "or else you'll be so stiff to-morrow that you can't move." And she tucked up the skirt of her best gown, to make room for the lad, who obediently settled himself between her and Katharine.

"Go it, Jean," he said; "you started us to wishing, so it's only fair you should speak first. What would you do, if you could have your choice?"

"Study, till I knew everything there was to be known," returned Jean, without hesitation. "I'd go to college here, and then I'd go to Europe, to one city after another, and learn all I could in each."

"You'd be a perfect valley of dry bones, then," commented Polly. "People that know everything are very stupid."

"I wouldn't be," said Jean. "I'd found colleges with my money, and go round lecturing to them, till they knew just as much as I did."

"H'm!" said Alan. "What will you do, Poll?" Polly laughed.

"It would be hard to choose, but I think I'd begin by adopting about twenty small boys. Then, if I had any time left, I'd— I'd—oh, I think perhaps I'd like to write a book of poems."

"Good for you, Poll! How I envy the boys, only you'd make them all into doctors. Molly?"

"I would travel, all over the whole world, and down into Australia," returned Molly. "I'd go to Russia and Spain and China and the Nile, and stay everywhere just as long as I wanted to."

"Who wouldn't like to do that?" said Jean. "Katharine, what will you do?"

"I'd have a lovely house somewhere in Europe, Venice, perhaps, or else Paris, and it should be full of magnificent pictures. And then I'd have my friends come and stay with me for a year at a time; and I'd have young artists come and live there, and give them lessons,—not teach them, you know, but pay for them, to give them a start, when they couldn't afford it. And when they had learned to paint and were ready to go home, I'd pay their expenses for a year, till they were able to support themselves. And then I'd help poor students through college, and do ever so many things like that."

"Katharine, you are modest in your plans!" said Molly, laughing. "How much of an income do you expect to have?"

"I didn't know we were limited," Katharine answered. "I thought we could have whatever we wished."

"That was the idea," said Alan. "Go on, Jessie; what would you do if you had all the money in the world?"

"Just what I intend to do now," she replied coolly, "be a doctor."

"What!" And Molly stared at her cousin with wide-open eyes.

"Yes, I think that's what I mean to do," answered Jessie. "I believe I should rather like it, and if I can tease mamma into letting me try, I'm coming East again, in a few years, to study."

"Well, you must be in want of something to do," said Molly, "if you have any idea of patching up broken bones and getting yourself exposed to small-pox and all sorts of fevers. But go on, Alan; it's your turn."

"Let's see," said Alan reflectively; "first of all, I'd get over my rheumatism, and then, for a few years, I'd be the very best base-ball player in the world. Then, after I was too old for that, I'd travel round a little while, and then I'd settle down and be—"

Polly listened breathlessly for the decision.

"Be what?" she asked eagerly.

"An undertaker."

"Oh, Alan, how mean of you!" protested Jessie. "Here we've all been and told our wishes as truly as we could, and now you are just making fun of us. That isn't fair."

"Isn't it?" And Alan laughed teasingly. "How do you know I haven't told truly? But, to be honest, I think I'd go into partnership with either Polly or you. I'd like to be a first-class doctor, or else a great author."

"Poems?" inquired Polly sympathetically.

"Poems! No; nor novels either, nor any such trash as that," returned the boy scornfully. "I'd write great, long books with real solid work in them, history, or else some kind of science, books that wouldn't be forgotten just as soon as they were read, but ones that would help the world along by making people know more and more, the more they studied them."

"I wonder if we shall any of us ever get what we want," said Jean thoughtfully." Jessie stands the best chance."

"You wouldn't say so, if you knew mamma as well as Kit and I do," returned Jessie, laughing. "I shan't have an easy time, when I try to persuade her to let me carry out my plan. She wouldn't be any more horrified if I wanted to be a farmer and plant my own potatoes."

"What will Florence be, I wonder," said Polly. "It would have to be something very pretty and dainty, or it would never suit her."

"Florence? Her future is all cut out," said Jean. "Didn't Mrs. Hapgood tell it, last Hallowe'en, a devoted husband and a beautiful home? She'll have everything she can possibly want, and she'll keep it all in apple pie order, and she and her husband will do nothing but bill and coo all day long."

"I don't believe it," said Molly, laughing at the sentimental picture which Jean had called up. "I think Florence has more to her than all that."

"What more can she want?" asked Katharine. "If she is a perfect wife in a happy home, there isn't anything much better for any woman."

"But it's getting dark, and I must go," said Polly, as she rose. "Come, Jean; mamma will think I am lost. Good night, girls."

In spite of their assurances that they were not at all timid, Alan insisted on going with the girls; so they stopped to speak to Mrs. Adams, then walked on together as far as Jean's gate, where they lingered, talking, for a minute or two.

"Come in now, Alan," said Polly, as they reached her house again; "it's early, really, and Jerusalem's out there on the piazza, all alone. You know she always likes to see you."

Alan hesitated for a moment, but the last fading light of the warm June day was too tempting, and he went in. Mrs. Adams rose from her piazza chair to meet them, and stepped forward into the faint light which shone out through the closely drawn shade of the parlor window.

"Yes, it is pleasant out here," she answered Polly; "but if you children are going to sit outside, you must have some wraps, for it is quite cool. Polly dear, just run in to get a shawl to put on, and bring the afghan to tuck around Alan. It's on the parlor sofa."

Polly vanished through the open door. When she came back, she was laughing.

"Why didn't you tell me they were in there, Jerusalem?" she asked, as she tossed the afghan to Alan, and then settled herself on a sweet-grass mat at her mother's feet. "Aunt Jane is reading aloud a report of something or other, and Mr. Baxter looks so bored. He yawned like a chasm when I went in."

"Perhaps you disturbed him in the middle of a nap," suggested Alan.

"Maybe I did. I don't blame him for getting sleepy," responded Polly pityingly. "It all seemed to be about convict labor and penal servitude and such things. I shouldn't wonder if something was the matter in Russia."

Then they were silent, watching the lazy shadows from the full moon creep over the lawn, till there came a footstep on the walk and a voice called,—

"So you are all making the most of the moonlight, are you?"

"Oh, Papa Adams!" exclaimed Polly joyfully. "Home so early?"

"Yes," answered the doctor, as he dropped into the chair next Alan; "and I'm going to play all the rest of the evening. How comes on our future doctor?"

"Doctor!" echoed Polly. "He said to-night that he'd rather be an undertaker than anything else."

"Why, how's that?" said the doctor, laughing. "It isn't a week since Polly told me you were going to follow in my footsteps."

"Oh, Polly has doctor on the brain, just now," answered the boy. "She's started up Jessie on the subject, and they do nothing but talk of pills and skeletons. To-night we were discussing what we'd like best to do, and the girls had such wild plans that I thought I'd bring them down to earth again."

"If you can't make better puns than that, don't try to make any, Alan," said Polly severely. "But our plans weren't wild a bit; we only said just what we would do, if we had all the money in the world."

"And what was the decision," asked the doctor; "cooking and sewing, or society belles?"

"Neither," Polly was beginning earnestly, when Alan broke in,—

"I'll tell you, Dr. Adams, and you can see for yourself if they weren't a little extra. Jean was going to know everything; Molly was going to travel everywhere; Polly was going to found an orphan asylum in her house, and write poetry, besides; and Katharine wanted to support poor but honest young men by the dozen. I think that's all but Jessie. She's going to study medicine."

"Such aspiring young people!" said the doctor. "You'll need all the treasures of the earth at your disposal, if you have such magnificent plans. If you are going to undertake so much, then good-by to bread-making and Bridget. And that reminds me to tell you, children, Bridget is going home, the last of next week."

"Next week?" said Mrs. Adams. "What is that for? Her year isn't over."

"No, but she has gained faster than we thought she could, and she is now almost as well as ever. If she hadn't been taken in time, it would have been much harder to cure her; but now we think that, if she is careful, she can go home to her family again. We told her so to-night, and she was half wild for a moment; but then she began to cry, because she must leave her 'dear young ladies,' as she called you."

"Oh, dear, what shall we ever do without her?" sighed Polly. "I was really getting quite fond of her. Now I'll have to devote myself to Dicky and the other babies."

"Bridget has improved in your hands," said the doctor. "You girls, without knowing it, have been doing the best kind of mission work, and the Bridget who goes home will be a much more attractive Bridget than the one who came here, for she has learned that there is something a little beyond her old life of drudgery that she can hope for and, in the end, gain."

"Hark! What's that?" exclaimed Mrs. Adams abruptly.

There was a sudden commotion in the parlor, the sound of excited voices, mingled with inarticulate cries; then Aunt Jane called, in a tone of agony,—

"Isabel! Polly! John! Quick, quick!"

Springing up, the doctor and his wife, followed by Polly and
Alan, ran to the parlor door where they looked in upon a
strange scene, for a full understanding of which it is
necessary to go back a little, to see what had been passing
inside the room, while the others had been talking on the
piazza.

For the past two or three months, it had been Mr. Baxter's
regular habit to spend every Wednesday evening with the
woman of his choice, when he either talked of his children
and their peculiarities, or his servants and their vices, or, on
the other hand, Miss Roberts attempted to form his mind, as
she called it, by improving and instructive conversation.
Their interviews, it must be confessed, were never of the
nature of a duet. Either Mr. Baxter prattled about trifles, and
Aunt Jane was politely indifferent; or else Miss Roberts
conversed learnedly, and Mr. Baxter dozed off into little
"cat-naps," waked again with an apologetic start, and
immediately assumed a look of owlish wisdom, as if to
convey the idea that he listened to the best advantage with
his eyes shut. Such a beginning, when they spent but one
evening a week together, did not hold out very brilliant
prospects of enlivening domestic intercourse; but the parties
most nearly concerned appeared to be satisfied, so no one
else needed to complain.

On this particular Wednesday evening, Mr. Baxter was
unusually drowsy. His youngest child, he fretfully explained,
had been ill all the night before, and his own rest had been
badly broken. But in spite of this warning. Miss Roberts had
taken up from the table a pamphlet on prison reform, and
announced her intention of reading it aloud. In vain Mr.
Baxter looked about for some way of escape. Seeing none,
he seated himself in the darkest corner of the room, with a

lingering hope that his lapses into dreamland might pass unnoticed. He was not disappointed. In a few moments, Aunt Jane had become so absorbed in her subject that she read on and on, quite unconscious of the fact that her guest, from yawning behind his hand, and nodding now forward, now backward, and now sideways, had passed on into a quiet slumber, unbroken by dreams of restless children and hardened criminals.

But Polly's sudden entrance had roused him, and he propped himself up anew, with a manful resolve to hold his eyes open, or die. Unfortunately it was by no means so easy for Mr. Baxter to hold his mouth shut, and yawn followed yawn, wider and still more wide, until his hand could no longer cover the opening. And yet Miss Roberts read on endlessly, remorselessly. Suddenly she was interrupted by Mr. Baxter who sprang up wildly and, with his body bent forward, his eyes distended and his mouth wide open, began plunging distractedly about the room, with both hands to his face, as if in mortal anguish.

"Oh, Solomon! What is it?" And Miss Roberts sprang up, in her turn.

But Mr. Solomon Baxter only paused to clasp his face more closely and groan, and then resumed his former antics. Miss Roberts was seriously alarmed. Had the man suddenly gone mad? Was he dying?

"Solomon! Solomon!" she implored him. "Tell me, only speak to me and tell me what is the matter!"

"'Y 'ou'," replied Mr. Baxter vehemently, but not very intelligibly.

"What?" Miss Roberts hurried to his side and, bending,

gazed up into his face which was still turned floorward.

"'Y 'ou'; I 'aw' 'uh' 'y 'ou'," answered Mr. Baxter again, this time pointing down his throat.

Miss Roberts saw that there was some trouble with his mouth. It was a relief to find that her lover was of sound mind. From his broken speech, she was beginning to fear some new, strange form of paralysis, but his wild lunges about the room relieved those apprehensions. It was only his mouth, then. She smiled sympathetically.

"I understand," she said; "it is the toothache. It is very painful, while it lasts, but I have something that will stop it. Just shut your mouth and make yourself as comfortable as you can, and I will get it."

But Mr. Baxter shook his head sadly.

"I 'aw' 'uh' 'ih," he answered.

Then Aunt Jane's courage began to fail.

"Can't shut it! Oh, Solomon, Solomon! What is it?"

"I 'o '*oo*'," he replied testily. Then, clasping his jaw in both hands, he began to walk the floor again, groaning dismally. Miss Roberts's tears were flowing. She felt sure that Mr. Baxter's hours were' numbered, and that she would soon be forced to look on at his funeral. Could she be a mother to his little ones, thus doubly bereaved? These thoughts passed in rapid succession through her brain; then, raising her voice to the utmost, she called for aid. That done, for the first and only time in the course of her life, Aunt Jane Roberts, the strong-minded, the firm, sank down on the sofa and quietly fainted away. This was the state of affairs which met the doctor's gaze, as he entered the room.

To his practised eye there was no ground for doubt. He recognized the disease and the remedy. It only needed one pull with his strong hands, one roar of anguish from Mr. Baxter, and the dislocated jaw was slipped back into place once more. Then the doctor turned to help his wife who was trying to restore Aunt Jane to consciousness. At length she gasped, opened one eye, gasped again, opened both and faintly whispered,—

"Is he dead? Tell me gently. Was it lock-jaw?"

Then the doctor's professional dignity gave way. Dropping into the nearest chair, he laughed, and laughed, and laughed again, while Mr. Baxter grew more and more shamefaced, and Miss Roberts more and more exasperated at his unseemly merriment. When he could speak again, he answered,—

"Lockjaw; no. This was all your fault, Jane. You read till the poor man was so sleepy that he fairly yawned his jaw out of joint."

And this time the doctor's shout was echoed by his wife and the two children.

CHAPTER XIX

KATHARINE'S CALL

The next afternoon Katharine and Florence sat on the side piazza of the Hapgood house, Florence in the hammock, Katharine curled up among the cushions of a bamboo lounge, idly stroking the back of Scott, Molly's plump tiger kitten.

"Well, Scotty," she was saying caressingly, as she held up the little creature and gazed straight into its yellow eyes, "are you feeling happy in your mind to-day? Well, so am I."

"What a queer name I" said Florence. "Where did Molly ever get it?"

Katharine laughed.

"I should think you might know," she answered. "Alan was responsible for it, of course. Don't you know how he is always saying '*Great Scott*'?"

"That is it, is it?" said Florence. Then she returned to the subject of which they had just been speaking. "When do you think you will go, Katharine?"

Anna Chapin Ray

"In about two weeks, I think," Katharine replied, as she rolled the cat over on its back and tickled it under its furry chin. "Papa wrote, some time ago, that he wanted us to be at home before July, for then he is going to start on a trip to Alaska, and we are both to go with. him. He hasn't mentioned it for a month, now, but I suppose of course he means to go. I hope so, I am sure, for I love to travel, and Jessie has never taken a real long journey, except to come here."

"To Alaska? How I envy you!" said Florence longingly.

"I wish you could go with us," answered Katharine. "It will be a lovely journey, I know, for it is so different from anything else we have seen. I'll tell you, Florence, you must come out to see us, some day, and then we'll go again. If it were not for this Alaska plan, I should hate to go home, for I have had such a pleasant year, here in New England. Sometimes I feel as if I had never known what it was to really live, till I came here; and Jessie dreads going worse than I do."

"You'll probably forget us, before you've been away a month," said Florenge lightly.

Katharine moved among her cushions until she was facing her friend.

"Do you think I am so fickle as that, Florence?" she asked, and her tone was a little hurt. "If that is all my friendship amounts to, it isn't worth the having."

"I didn't mean that," said Florence; "but it wouldn't be strange if you did forget us, Kit, when you are back again among your other friends."

"What an absurd idea, Florence! Do you think I shall ever forget Bridget and Job and the cooking club, and all the rest of our good times? I shan't be nearly as likely to, just because we don't have anything like it in Omaha. And if I do come out next winter, I know that, right in the middle of all the parties and things, I shall have little homesick twinges for our frolics in the attic, and the cosy talks around Mrs. Adams's open fire."

"It must be so exciting to come out," sighed Florence. "We can't do it in this little place, for we're never in, very much. I should be sorry to leave the girls, Kit, but I almost wish I lived in a city, the way you do."

"You wouldn't, if you had tried it," said Katharine decidedly. "I used to long for the time when I could be in society, as mamma is. Why, only last year I felt as if I couldn't wait; but since I have been here, I don't care half so much about it. It will probably be fun for just a little while, and then I shall get tired of it and wish I could stop, and be cross and pale and headache-y, the way mamma used to be. But, at least, I've had this one year, and I can think about it over and over again, and remember just what we have all done and said. Perhaps sometime we can all be together at our house."

"I do wish you didn't have to go away," said Florence a little forlornly. "We feel as if you belonged to us, Katharine, and we four girls don't seem half so many as we did before you and Jessie came."

"What an idea! And, besides, you have Alan, and he is equal to all the rest of us put together. Dear fellow, how I shall miss him! I wish I had a brother. But, Florence, it isn't as if we weren't likely to drop in on you again, before long. It takes such a little while to go back and forth, now; and I mean to go to Europe in a year or two, and then I shall stop here on the way. It isn't as bad as it would be if papa couldn't afford to let us travel."

But Florence shook her head.

"No," said she, "I know how it will be. You think now that you'll come, but you'll go out there and get so interested in society that you will forget all about New England, and all about us. Or, if you do remember us, it will be when you are dancing all night, and you'll stop a minute to pity us because we go to bed and to sleep like civilized beings." And Florence laughed, in spite of herself, at the idea.

"Now, Florence, that isn't fair to me. I really don't mean to be just a silly girl who thinks of nothing but her clothes. I shall have to go into society, but I believe I can be good for a little something besides that. If I find I can't do both, why, then I'll give up the society part of it; but I won't be a do-nothing all my days. I know there are always more chances for a woman to do good than there are women to do it, and I mean to keep my eyes open to look for my own especial chance. I don't believe that all the helpful ideas auntie and Mrs. Adams have given me this year were intended to be thrown away, and I think the time will come when I can use them. If not, why were they given me? Wait a few years, Florence, and see if I am just a butterfly. It is only fair to give me the chance to win my spurs." Katharine spoke earnestly, for her whole soul was in her words. The past year had been a revelation to her, and her rapid development towards womanhood had been in the line of all that was truest and noblest in her character. She had come to New England an unformed girl whose nature was one of endless possibilities, only waiting for the word which should make them actual and turn her in one way or the other. The word was spoken and, thanks to her aunt's influence and to her association with the simple, natural girls about her, the impulse given was in the right direction. It was as if Katharine had suddenly been born into a new life. No drifting, idle maturity could satisfy her now; her womanhood must be one of purpose and of action. The time for it had come much nearer than she thought.

But now her little outburst was followed by a hearty,—

"Good for you, Kit!"

Both the girls started and looked up, to see Alan's head stretched out from his window, with a look of perfect approval on his boyish face.

"I didn't mean to listen," he said penitently. "I was up here reading and, honestly, I didn't hear a thing but Kit's last speech. That was such a good one that I did just want to pat her on the back. I'm going to stop up my ears now."

"Come down, and stay with us, Alan," his cousin, said.

"No, thanks; not even you can bribe me to leave this book. I want to know what they found in the bottom of the cave." And Alan returned to his reading.

However, the unexpected interruption had put an end to all serious talk, and the girls were chatting idly, now of this matter, now of that, when a boy stepped up on the piazza. He had a telegram in his hand.

"Miss Katharine W. Shepard?" he asked, referring to his address book.

Katharine rose, dropping the kitten on the floor.

"I am Miss Shepard," she said, taking the envelope from his hand and signing the receipt.

"I hope nothing is wrong," said Florence, eyeing the yellow paper with a true feminine dislike of a telegram.

"Wrong? Oh, no; it is probably from papa. He often telegraphs us," said Katharine carelessly, as she tore open the end of the envelope.

She glanced at the paper in her hand, then looked a little surprised.

"It's from mamma," she said. "Papa has probably changed his plans. Listen: 'Start for home first of next week. Have written.'"

"The first of next week! That is so soon, Katharine; we can't let you go." And Florence sat up in the hammock and stared at her friend in bewilderment.

"It is very sudden," said Katharine slowly. "It doesn't seem as if I could go. But isn't it strange? Papa must have decided, all at once, to go to Alaska sooner than he planned, for this is such a little bit of a warning. Let me see, this is Thursday, and we can't get a letter before Monday. We must start on Tuesday. How I do hate to go!" And Katharine choked down a sudden lump that had risen in her throat. "Come in," she added. "I must tell auntie."

"No, I must go home," said Florence. "Oh, dear! Only four days more, Katharine!"

"Don't cry, dear," said Katharine protectingly. "Remember it isn't for always, for I shall come East often."

She stood and watched her guest until she was out of sight, then ran into the house in search of her aunt, to whom she showed the telegram. In spite of herself, Mrs. Hapgood was very uneasy over the sudden summons to the girls. It certainly did seem strange that the message should come from their mother; but for Katharine's sake, her aunt hid her fears as best she could, and only tried to make the girls' last days as pleasant as possible, while she waited with a burning impatience for the letter which should explain everything. However, the girls, accustomed as they were to their father's rapid changes in his plans, were not at all disturbed, but quietly made their arrangements for the journey, sure that Mr. Shepard would either come for them, or else meet them on the way.

Friday and Saturday passed only too quickly for the young people, who were dreading the approaching separation, and Sunday afternoon found them all assembled at Mrs. Hapgood's for a farewell dinner together. But it was rather a silent, subdued party that gathered about the table; the conversation was fitful and broken by long pauses, and the jokes were rather forced and feeble; while Molly's red eyes and Florence's white cheeks showed that something was wrong. If it was bad at the table, it was worse when they all sat in the front porch after dinner, with nothing to do but watch the darkness settle slowly down over the valley, and listen, to the last sleepy twitterings of the birds. They talked little as they sat there. Now and then Alan would attempt a jest, or Katharine would try to start some fresh subject; but soon the voices would die away, and another silence follow the momentary interruption. So they lingered until long past the time for separation. At length Polly started up.

"Come, girls," said she; "I can't stand this any longer. We may as well say good night now, for it won't be any easier by and by."

"Oh, why did you girls ever come here and make us so fond of you, and then have to go and leave us!" wailed Jean. "I wish you hadn't come in the first place."

"I don't," said Polly steadily; "I'm glad I've had just this one year of knowing you. It's ever so much better than nothing, and I'm thankful even for this. Besides," she added, valiantly brushing away the tears, "I don't mean to cry yet, for we have all day to-morrow, and Tuesday morning; and then, you'll come back again some day. When you are gone is time enough to do the crying." And smiling resolutely, she bade them good night, then went away up the street, with the tears running down her cheeks.

"Come, Alan," said Katharine, early the next morning; "come down to the post-office with me. My letter from home must be here by this time, and I'm in a hurry to get it, to see if papa is going to come for us. It takes Jessie so long to get ready, that we won't wait for her."

They walked away together, laughing and talking as they went, determined to forget the morrow, and only enjoy the bright, beautiful morning and their pleasure in each other's society. At the post-office, Alan ran inside, leaving his cousin to wait for him at the door.

"Here it is, sure enough, Kit," he said, as he joined her again.

"What a little thin one, and from mamma, too!" said Katharine, as she deliberately tore it open. "Papa must be away on one of his business trips, I suppose."

Alan made no reply, but left her to read her letter while he walked along at her side, whistling softly to himself. All at once he heard a low exclamation, like a half-smothered cry of pain. Turning quickly, he saw his cousin's face was ashy white, and her breath was coming in short, quick gasps.

"Katharine! What is it?" he cried, in terror at the change in her face.

For answer, she held out the letter to him. "Oh, Alan, what does it mean?"

He thought she was going to fall, and threw his arm around her to support her, but she rallied quickly.

"Read it, Alan," she begged. "I can't seem to understand it."

Alan read it. But before he was half through it, his face was as white as hers had been. "Oh, Kit!" he began; then he paused, not daring to offer one word of pity.

The short letter was the bitter outcry of a selfish woman who forgot her children's suffering in her own, for it bore its sad message abruptly and with no word to soften the blow. Mr. Shepard had proved to be a defaulter and, after he had for years been using money from the bank of which he was president, he had saved himself, on the eve of exposure, by hastily quitting the country, leaving his wife and children to bear the burden of his guilt as best they could.

"Papa has taken money that didn't belong to him; is that it, Alan?" said Katharine slowly, as if dazed by the sudden shock. "I can't believe it. How can mamma say such a cruel thing?" she added indignantly.

Alan made no reply, beyond drawing the girl's limp hand through his arm. Katharine felt the unspoken sympathy of his gesture and pressed closer to him.

"Do say you don't believe it, Alan," she urged. "You must know that papa couldn't do such a thing."

"Oh, Kit, I wish I knew what to say!" the boy burst out. "I am so awfully sorry for you, dear." But Katharine stopped him with a motion of her hand.

"Don't pity me, Alan, or I shall begin to cry; and I mustn't do that here. We must hurry home to tell auntie." And she quickened her pace, almost to a run.

Alan kept by her side, watching the white, set face, and marvelling that she did not give way to her sorrow. His own eyes were full of tears, and his throat was aching with a dull, dry pain; but his cousin, after her first exclamations, was perfectly quiet. So they went up the long, sunny street, deaf to the gay bird-songs, blind to the sunlight that slanted down through the arching elms and set the dewdrops to twinkling, only anxious to reach the safe refuge of the old house, and the motherly woman within it.

They found her on the piazza watching for them, eager for the news the letter must bring.

Even then, Katharine's self-control did not leave her. Pausing before her aunt, she said quietly, as she held out the letter,—

"Do you remember our talk last fall, auntie? My call has come, and I must answer: 'ready.'"

"Katharine!"

Mrs. Hapgood snatched the note, read it, and turned impulsively to the young girl before her.

"You poor child!" she began; but Katharine interrupted her, as she had done Alan.

"Don't worry about me, auntie. But can you tell Jessie now,

please? I am afraid I can't." And she turned away and went into the house.

When Mrs. Hapgood came down-stairs, an hour later, it seemed as if a shadow had always rested on the house, the sorrow it contained had so soon become a part of their lives. Up-stairs, Jessie had cried until she was tired, stopped to listen vaguely to her aunt's comforting words, then cried again, but all without any real understanding of the trouble which had come upon her. Down-stairs, Alan and Molly were walking the room, arm in arm, with a settled look of sadness which was strangely out of place on their young faces. Alan had told his sister the news as gently as he could, and she could only cling to him and cry, as she took in all the meaning of the shame and disgrace, all the consequences of the father's sin upon the coming life of his children.

"But where is Katharine?" asked Mrs. Hapgood anxiously.

"Isn't she up-stairs?" said Molly.

"I haven't seen her," answered her mother.

"Why, we supposed she was with you!" And Alan hurried away to look for his cousin.

At last he found her. Up in the familiar old garret that she had loved so well, close by the great gray chimney which seemed to be shielding her with its giant strength, there lay Katharine on the shabby old sofa, sobbing as if her heart must break. To the young lad, these unrestrained tears were much more alarming than her former quiet, and he dared not speak, as he sat down on the floor by her side, and put his brown hand against her cheek.

"Oh, Alan!"

"Yes, Kit; I know."

"Let me have my cry out now," she said brokenly. "It must come sometime; then I can be brave for mamma and Jessie."

Alan stole away to tell his mother where Katharine was, and then went back to her side. All the morning he remained there, saying little, but keeping near her with a simple, boyish devotion of which, in after years, she never lost the memory.

When Katharine went down-stairs again, she appeared to have grown years older during that one morning. It was not that she was less beautiful than she had been; but she seemed to have gained a new, gentle dignity which suddenly changed her from a child into a woman. As she entered the room, with her hand on Alan's shoulder, she met them with a perfect composure which gave no hint of her trouble; but they all felt instinctively that it was as she had said to her aunt, her call had come, and she had answered "ready."

The day wore slowly away. They were to start on their journey, late the next afternoon, accompanied by Mrs. Hapgood, who had made up her mind to go to her sister for a few weeks, to help her through the sad changes which must inevitably follow. Late in the day, Mrs. Adams and Polly came in, for Molly had told them of the letter. Mrs. Adams took both the girls into her motherly arms, and her few whispered words were very tender, while Polly threw her arms around Katharine, as she said,—

"Alan has told me what you said, Kit, about your call's coming, and I think it was grand; but it isn't one bit more so than we expected, only it makes us proud to be your friends."

At length it was bedtime, and for the last time the girls went up to their pleasant room in the old Hapgood house. The whole place was in confusion, and trunks stood in the middle of the floor, with piles of clothing, books, and pictures heaped about them, just as they had been left in the morning. At sight of them, Jessie threw herself down on the bed.

"Oh, Kit!" she cried; "what are we going to do?" "Please don't cry so, Jessie," said Katharine wearily. "We must try not to be babyish about it."

"Babyish!" And Jessie turned on her petulantly. "I do believe you don't care, Katharine. Oh, poor papa!" Then, as she saw the pain in her sister's face, she added, "Forgive me, Kit! I know you do care; but how can you keep so quiet? It's all so dreadful, and we shall be poor and alone, and nobody will care for us."

"Hush, Jessie!"

Her sister spoke almost sharply, for she felt her own courage fast giving way. Then, sitting down on the side of the bed, with her beautiful brown hair waving loose about her shoulders, she took her sister's hand in hers.

"Jessie dear," she said gently; "listen to me, please. You and I mustn't give up so and cry about this; we must be brave and cheerful for mamma's sake. Poor mamma is out there all alone, and we must go to her and help her to bear it all. We are stronger than she is, and we have each other, so we must help each other and help her. We've had a great many good times already, and nothing can take those away; but now comes the chance to show what we are, and whether we have any courage. There will be a great deal to do when we get home, so we have no right to give up and make ourselves ill with crying. Now we must go to bed and try to sleep, so we can be ready for to-morrow; and—Oh, Jessie, if we only

Anna Chapin Ray

knew where papa was to-night! He was always so good and kind that I know he has never done anything wicked."

Katharine's head went down on the pillow beside Jessie's, and the two daughters sobbed together over their father's guilt.

They were all at the station to see them off the next night. The sun was just setting as the train moved away, and the little group of three on the rear platform looked back to see its golden light fall upon the friends they were leaving: the girls, Alan, Dr. and Mrs. Adams, and even patient old Job, who stood quietly in the background, watching the scene about him with a half wondering air of sympathy.

Jessie turned to enter the car.

"Wait just a minute more," said Katharine wistfully.

A sudden opening between the buildings gave her one more glimpse of the figures still standing there as they had left them, and Katharine strained her eyes to catch the parting wave of Alan's cap, while her lips quivered. Then she exclaimed excitedly,—

"See, Jessie! See!"

They were just passing within sight of the hospital and, from a well-known window, a hand was waving a farewell to them. It was Bridget, who had begged to be moved to the window, that she might be the one to say the final good by, before the train went rushing away into the gathering twilight.

"I feel as if I had just been to a funeral," sighed Molly, as she walked home with Polly; for she and Alan were to stay with

Mrs. Adams during their mother's absence.

"It was just like one," said Jean sorrowfully. But Polly objected.

"No, girls," she said; "no funeral was ever like this, for a funeral is all sad, and this isn't. I'm sorry for them, more so than I can tell; but, after all, it has given Katharine a chance to show how glorious she is. It just makes me glad to know such a magnificent girl."

And Alan added,—

"Yes, you may talk all day about your heroines; but I've just seen one of them, and it's a sight I shan't forget soon, either."

CHAPTER XX

ONE LAST GLIMPSE

Indian summer had come once more, and the same soft haze which, only last year, the girls had seen over the blue Connecticut with its meadows and mountains, now rested quite as lovingly upon the dull waters of the Missouri, as they wound along between their low bluffs and level prairies. There, there had been the restful quiet of the old town, peacefully living on the reputation of its two centuries of strong, honorable life, justly proud of the famous names it had given to its state and country; here, there was the ceaseless, unwearying bustle of a new civilization, the restless activity of a city whose glory was yet to be and whose present ambition was only to grow and to accumulate riches. All the contrast between the two places, all the change from the surroundings of a year ago to the life of to-day were keenly felt by the young girl who was sitting on the piazza of a little house in Omaha, one morning, idly enjoying the late autumn sunshine.

"Come out here a minute, Jessie," she called suddenly, as she heard some one coming down the stairs behind her. "We shan't have many more days like this, and do let's take a few minutes to enjoy this one."

"But Aunt Jane would say it was sinful to waste the golden moments," said Jessie, laughing, as, duster in hand, she came out on the steps.

"Not a bit of it," said the other. "I haven't sat down before this since my breakfast, and I know that lunch will be all the better, if I take a few minutes to rest and breathe this lovely air. Where's mamma?"

"She's lying down; she said her head ached. Oh, Kit, doesn't this make you homesick for last year and all the girls?"

"And Alan, too," added Katharine. "Yes, it does, Jessie, whenever I stop to think of it. We did have a perfect year at auntie's, and once in a while I wish we were back there. Do you remember the day Job was loose, and they couldn't catch him?"

"'I feel it in my bones,' as Miss Bean would say," said Jessie; "that the time will come when we shall all be together again. At least, we made the very most of our time."

"True," said Katharine thoughtfully; "and I don't know what we should have done this summer, Jessie, if we hadn't had those lessons in cooking. I had no idea then that we shouldn't always have servants, and if we'd stayed here, we never should have known anything about housekeeping. And the worst of it is, I like it. I always knew I had plebeian tastes and, now I am used to it, I fairly revel in washing dishes."

"I'm not half so homesick for the old house as I thought I should be," said Jessie, while she meditatively folded a series of tucks in her gingham apron. "It was dreadful at first, having to leave the old place and the servants and the furniture; but, after all, we haven't had such a bad time. I don't know as I want to do housework for a living, I prefer medicine; but I don't mind it a bit, for a while. If I'm to keep old maid's hall, I want to know how to do it."

"Yes; but we can't go on like this much longer, Jessie," her sister replied. "I was talking about it to mamma, only a few days ago. We must try to get a young girl to help about the house, for it is settled that you are to go back into school after Christmas."

"' Sufficient unto the day,'" said Jessie, laughing. "You know I'd much rather stay at home and help you than go back to school. Why must I go, any more than you?"

"I was supposed to be finished last year, ready to come out," answered Katharine; "and so I ought to be finished enough to stay in. But when we get settled down for the winter, I mean to go on and do a little studying by myself, history or something. I don't know yet just what it will be. You've had a hard summer and fall, Jessie," she added, surveying her sister with a motherly air; "but you've gone through it splendidly, and I'm proud of you."

"It's no harder for me than for you," responded Jessie sturdily; "and it hasn't made half the difference in my plans. But there are times, Kit, when I do feel as if I must see papa again."

"I don't dare let myself think about him much," said Katharine slowly. "It is one of the things we can't undo, and must take as they come." She was silent for a few moments, then added, with an evident effort to turn the conversation, "Here comes the postman. I don't suppose he has anything for us, though."

"Maybe he has," answered Jessie hopefully. "It is ever and ever so long since we heard from any of the girls."

The sisters sat watching the man as he came slowly down the street, stopping here and there to leave a part of his precious burden.

"Don't you ever wish you could know just what is in all those letters?" asked Jessie, as she rested her chin in her hands.

"No, I don't know as I do," replied Katharine. "If it were all funny or interesting, it would be well enough; but think of all the letters that have sad or ugly things to tell. I do wish he would bring us one, though."

"Perhaps he will. Yes, he's going to!" And Jessie sprang down the steps to meet the man, who paused long enough to hand her a thick envelope, and then went on out of sight, quite disregarded by the girls who were all-absorbed in their mail.

"It's yours," said Jessie, as she deliberately mounted the steps once more; "but I can't make out whose writing it is. Part of it looks like Alan's, and part like Polly's. It's from some of them, anyway. Do see if you can make it out." And she tossed the envelope into her sister's lap.

No true woman ever opens a letter to find out from whom it comes. Katharine carefully and minutely studied the one in her hand, without attempting to resort to the most natural method of obtaining an answer to the question. At length she raised her head with a laugh.

"It's from them all," she said. "Polly wrote my name, Molly the city, and Alan the state. This is one of that boy's pranks."

"Do hurry to open it," said Jessie impatiently.

Katharine recklessly tore it open and' drew out four separate sheets.

"I told you so," she said triumphantly. "And one from Mrs. Adams, too! Which shall I take first? None of them are very long."

"Begin with Molly," said Jessie, settling herself comfortably to listen while her sister read,-

"DEAR KATHARINE AND JESSIE,—I haven't any idea who owes the other a letter, but I am getting so homesick for you that I shall write to you anyway. It isn't that I have much to say, for it does seem as if nothing had happened since you left here. I wrote you, didn't I, that the Langs have all gone abroad for a year? Only half of us left here, now! I miss Florence, and I rather envy her; but, after all, my first journey is going to be to Omaha. Jean and Polly and I are here, just the same as ever, only Jean is getting dignified and doesn't walk fences, any longer. But you have no idea how proud we are of Polly. She had the dearest little poem in the school paper last month; and this month she is to be editor, the first time a girl has ever done it. She and Alan are writing, too. They came in and found out what I was doing, so they said they were each going to put in a note. I don't think it is quite fair, for I know they will tell you all the news.

"You ought to have seen the new clothes Florence had, before she went away. I went there once to see them, and it was like a whole dry-goods store. She sent for Bridget, one day, and gave her ever so many of her old things, to be made over for the children; and Bridget went off hugging the great bundle and crying because she was 'afraid Miss Florence would get drownded on the way.'"

"Polly has just showed me what she has been writing about Aunt Jane. I do wish you could be here for the wedding. I think Job almost ought to march in the bridal party, for he helped Mr. Baxter to get ready for a second marriage.

"Mrs. Adams has just come in, and wants my pen to write a little note while she waits for mamma to get ready to go out with her, so I'm not going to write another single word till I hear from you. Answer this soon, like dear girls. Mamma would send love, if she knew I was writing.

"Your loving cousin,

"MOLLY HAPGOOD."

"That's short enough, I should think," said Jessie ungratefully. "My last letter to her was two whole sheets long."

"Nevermind," answered Katharine; "let's see what Mrs. Adams says. Isn't it good of her to write?"

"My DEAR GIRLS,—This is only a little note to tuck inside Molly's letter; but I did just want to say how glad I am to hear of the way my two girls are doing the work that has come to them. I am proud of them and happy in them, for they both seem almost like my own daughters.

"And this brings me to my new plan. It occurred to me, the other day, that we shall be a very lonely, forlorn pair of old people, when Polly goes off to college. Why wouldn't it be a good idea for Jessie to plan to come back to us then, and take Polly's place for the four years, bring a little young life into the home, and study medicine with the doctor while she does it. It is too soon, of course, to decide; but I want you both to be thinking about it, for it seems to me an

Anna Chapin Ray

excellent idea.

"And now I must run away and make a call with Aunt Ruth.

"With a great deal of love from

"'AUNT ISABEL.'"

"Oh-h-h!" And Jessie gave a sigh of rapture.

"Yes, it is lovely of her, and just like her," said Katharine; "and I don't see why you can't go. But now let's take Alan's letter. It will be sure to be a good one, even if it is short. Listen I"

"DEAR KIT,—Is it six months or six years since you went home? We are all in the dumps without you, and don't have anybody to pull us out. How comes on your housekeeping? Molly made some biscuits, last night, that were so hard we had to get hammers to crack them open, before we could put on any butter. I told her she'd better send one to you girls, for a curiosity, but she said they were so heavy that she couldn't afford to pay postage on them.

"Did you know Poll and I are taking Latin lessons together of Professor Smythe? We go to him twice a week, and have been at it a month, now. We're racing each other as hard as we can. First she asks for a longer lesson, just to tease me, then I return the compliment, and neither of us will give in, so it keeps us studying all the time, mostly. We don't care much, for nothing seems to be happening, this year. We must have used up all the fun, last winter. You and Jessie are gone, Florence is gone, Bridget is gone, Aunt Jane is going, and the rest of us will follow her pretty soon, unless Molly gives up trying to cook.

"By the way, Miss Bean—Polly says I shan't tell, but I'm going to—asked Mrs. Adams, the other day, how she made that oyster broth she had for first course, the day Polly gave her dinner. She thought the lumps were oysters.

"That's all for this time.

"ALAN O. HAPGOOD."

"P.S. I entirely forgot to send my love to Jessie."

"Saucy boy!" exclaimed Jessie, laughing.

"Isn't he an imp?" said Katharine, as she folded the letter. "He made up all that about Miss Bean, I know, for she didn't take any soup that day. I remember her refusing it. Do you remember—"

"Do you remember?" echoed Jessie mockingly. "I wonder how many times we have said that, Kit. As if we didn't both of us remember every single thing that happened through all the year we were East! What does Polly say?"

"Hers is longer," said Katharine, as she opened it. "She is the best of them all to write, and her letters sound just like her funny, topsy-turvy self."

"DEAR GIRLS,—First of all, I must tell you the one grand item of news. Aunt Jane is going to be married on Thanksgiving Day. The Baxter children have all been exposed to chicken-pox, and Aunt Jane has made up her mind to be married at once, so she can take care of them when they come down with it. Isn't it good of her, really? I don't think she minds much, though, for she acts fond of them. *Uncle Sol*, as I call him behind his back, brought the youngest here, one day early in the fall; and when I went

Anna Chapin Ray

into the room, there,—fancy it!—there sat Aunt Jane with the baby in her lap, playing pat-a-cake with it, just as nice as could be. I was so surprised that I almost dropped down on the floor. But she insists on being married in black silk, she says it will be so serviceable. I think it will look just as if she were in mourning for the first Mrs. Baxter. Alan says that if the children all have chicken-pox, they won't need to buy a turkey for Thanksgiving.

"Papa wants me to tell you that Bridget keeps just as well and strong as can be. He drove up there to see her, two or three weeks ago, and she asked all about yon both. I go to the hospital once in a while, to see the small boys, and I make Alan go with me whenever I can. He has cut me all out with Dicky, and the child won't have anything to say to me, when he can get Alan. You would hardly know Alan, he has grown so tall; and we think he is getting quite good-looking, too. Of course, he is always a duck.

"Molly and I are growing good. We haven't had a squabble since Florence went away. I suppose, now she can't get anybody else, she has to put up with me. She has just three ideas in her head at present: cooking, some singing lessons she is going to begin next month, and her new gown. I suppose she would say I'm envious, for my new gown this winter is one of mamma's made over.

"Miss Bean came to spend the day, last week. She appeared early, for she said she wanted time to look over all Aunt Jane's new things, 'seeing's how' she made the match. She did look them over, too, and asked what everything cost, and why she didn't have something else, and then she gave her any quantity of advice about how to bring up the children.

"I almost forgot to tell you anything about Job. He ran

away, the other day, going up a hill. A bee lighted on the side of his neck and stung him, and it astonished him so that he just started off and ran. for almost a quarter of a mile. Then, all of a sudden, he sat down with all four legs at once, and that stopped him. Poor fellow, he is getting so old!

"What a long letter I am writing! The others are through, and waiting for me to carry this to the mail. Alan is making such a noise that I can't hear myself write. He is singing:

"Do the work that's nearest,
Though it's dull at whiles,
Helping, when we meet them,
Lame dogs over stiles."

"I don't know whether he means us with Job, or Aunt Jane with the Baxter babies, or you with the housekeeping. Perhaps it is for all three. Anyway, it is good advice."

"Now I must stop. Oh, you dear girls, how I do want to see you! Papa and Jerusalem always send love. I could go on for ever so much longer, but at last I must say good by."

"Your friend,

"POLLY ADAMS."

Choose from Thousands of 1stWorldLibrary Classics By

A. M. Barnard
Ada Leverson
Adolphus William Ward
Aesop
Agatha Christie
Alexander Aaronsohn
Alexander Kielland
Alexandre Dumas
Alfred Gatty
Alfred Ollivant
Alice Duer Miller
Alice Turner Curtis
Alice Dunbar
Allen Chapman
Alleyne Ireland
Ambrose Bierce
Amelia E. Barr
Amory H. Bradford
Andrew Lang
Andrew McFarland Davis
Andy Adams
Angela Brazil
Anna Alice Chapin
Anna Sewell
Annie Besant
Annie Hamilton Donnell
Annie Payson Call
Annie Roe Carr
Annonaymous
Anton Chekhov
Archibald Lee Fletcher
Arnold Bennett
Arthur C. Benson
Arthur Conan Doyle
Arthur M. Winfield
Arthur Ransome
Arthur Schnitzler
Arthur Train
Atticus
B.H. Baden-Powell
B. M. Bower
B. C. Chatterjee
Baroness Emmuska Orczy
Baroness Orczy
Basil King
Bayard Taylor
Ben Macomber
Bertha Muzzy Bower
Bjornstjerne Bjornson

Booth Tarkington
Boyd Cable
Bram Stoker
C. Collodi
C. E. Orr
C. M. Ingleby
Carolyn Wells
Catherine Parr Traill
Charles A. Eastman
Charles Amory Beach
Charles Dickens
Charles Dudley Warner
Charles Farrar Browne
Charles Ives
Charles Kingsley
Charles Klein
Charles Hanson Towne
Charles Lathrop Pack
Charles Romyn Dake
Charles Whibley
Charles Willing Beale
Charlotte M. Braeme
Charlotte M. Yonge
Charlotte Perkins Stetson
Clair W. Hayes
Clarence Day Jr.
Clarence E. Mulford
Clemence Housman
Confucius
Coningsby Dawson
Cornelis DeWitt Wilcox
Cyril Burleigh
D. H. Lawrence
Daniel Defoe
David Garnett
Dinah Craik
Don Carlos Janes
Donald Keyhoe
Dorothy Kilner
Dougan Clark
Douglas Fairbanks
E. Nesbit
E. P. Roe
E. Phillips Oppenheim
E. S. Brooks
Earl Barnes
Edgar Rice Burroughs
Edith Van Dyne
Edith Wharton

Edward Everett Hale
Edward J. O'Biren
Edward S. Ellis
Edwin L. Arnold
Eleanor Atkins
Eleanor Hallowell Abbott
Eliot Gregory
Elizabeth Gaskell
Elizabeth McCracken
Elizabeth Von Arnim
Ellem Key
Emerson Hough
Emilie F. Carlen
Emily Bronte
Emily Dickinson
Enid Bagnold
Enilor Macartney Lane
Erasmus W. Jones
Ernie Howard Pie
Ethel May Dell
Ethel Turner
Ethel Watts Mumford
Eugene Sue
Eugenie Foa
Eugene Wood
Eustace Hale Ball
Evelyn Everett-green
Everard Cotes
F. H. Cheley
F. J. Cross
F. Marion Crawford
Fannie E. Newberry
Federick Austin Ogg
Ferdinand Ossendowski
Fergus Hume
Florence A. Kilpatrick
Fremont B. Deering
Francis Bacon
Francis Darwin
Frances Hodgson Burnett
Frances Parkinson Keyes
Frank Gee Patchin
Frank Harris
Frank Jewett Mather
Frank L. Packard
Frank V. Webster
Frederic Stewart Isham
Frederick Trevor Hill
Frederick Winslow Taylor

Friedrich Kerst
Friedrich Nietzsche
Fyodor Dostoyevsky
G.A. Henty
G.K. Chesterton
Gabrielle E. Jackson
Garrett P. Serviss
Gaston Leroux
George A. Warren
George Ade
Geroge Bernard Shaw
George Cary Eggleston
George Durston
George Ebers
George Eliot
George Gissing
George MacDonald
George Meredith
George Orwell
George Sylvester Viereck
George Tucker
George W. Cable
George Wharton James
Gertrude Atherton
Gordon Casserly
Grace E. King
Grace Gallatin
Grace Greenwood
Grant Allen
Guillermo A. Sherwell
Gulielma Zollinger
Gustav Flaubert
H. A. Cody
H. B. Irving
H. C. Bailey
H. G. Wells
H. H. Munro
H. Irving Hancock
H. R. Naylor
H. Rider Haggard
H. W. C. Davis
Haldeman Julius
Hall Caine
Hamilton Wright Mabie
Hans Christian Andersen
Harold Avery
Harold McGrath
Harriet Beecher Stowe
Harry Castlemon
Harry Coghill
Harry Houidini

Hayden Carruth
Helent Hunt Jackson
Helen Nicolay
Hendrik Conscience
Hendy David Thoreau
Henri Barbusse
Henrik Ibsen
Henry Adams
Henry Ford
Henry Frost
Henry James
Henry Jones Ford
Henry Seton Merriman
Henry W Longfellow
Herbert A. Giles
Herbert Carter
Herbert N. Casson
Herman Hesse
Hildegard G. Frey
Homer
Honore De Balzac
Horace B. Day
Horace Walpole
Horatio Alger Jr.
Howard Pyle
Howard R. Garis
Hugh Lofting
Hugh Walpole
Humphry Ward
Ian Maclaren
Inez Haynes Gillmore
Irving Bacheller
Isabel Cecilia Williams
Isabel Hornibrook
Israel Abrahams
Ivan Turgenev
J. G.Austin
J. Henri Fabre
J. M. Barrie
J. M. Walsh
J. Macdonald Oxley
J. R. Miller
J. S. Fletcher
J. S. Knowles
J. Storer Clouston
J. W. Duffield
Jack London
Jacob Abbott
James Allen
James Andrews
James Baldwin

James Branch Cabell
James DeMille
James Joyce
James Lane Allen
James Lane Allen
James Oliver Curwood
James Oppenheim
James Otis
James R. Driscoll
Jane Abbott
Jane Austen
Jane L. Stewart
Janet Aldridge
Jens Peter Jacobsen
Jerome K. Jerome
Jessie Graham Flower
John Buchan
John Burroughs
John Cournos
John F. Kennedy
John Gay
John Glasworthy
John Habberton
John Joy Bell
John Kendrick Bangs
John Milton
John Philip Sousa
John Taintor Foote
Jonas Lauritz Idemil Lie
Jonathan Swift
Joseph A. Altsheler
Joseph Carey
Joseph Conrad
Joseph E. Badger Jr
Joseph Hergesheimer
Joseph Jacobs
Jules Vernes
Julian Hawthrone
Julie A Lippmann
Justin Huntly McCarthy
Kakuzo Okakura
Karle Wilson Baker
Kate Chopin
Kenneth Grahame
Kenneth McGaffey
Kate Langley Bosher
Kate Langley Bosher
Katherine Cecil Thurston
Katherine Stokes
L. A. Abbot
L. T. Meade

L. Frank Baum
Latta Griswold
Laura Dent Crane
Laura Lee Hope
Laurence Housman
Lawrence Beasley
Leo Tolstoy
Leonid Andreyev
Lewis Carroll
Lewis Sperry Chafer
Lilian Bell
Lloyd Osbourne
Louis Hughes
Louis Joseph Vance
Louis Tracy
Louisa May Alcott
Lucy Fitch Perkins
Lucy Maud Montgomery
Luther Benson
Lydia Miller Middleton
Lyndon Orr
M. Corvus
M. H. Adams
Margaret E. Sangster
Margret Howth
Margaret Vandercook
Margaret W. Hungerford
Margret Penrose
Maria Edgeworth
Maria Thompson Daviess
Mariano Azuela
Marion Polk Angellotti
Mark Overton
Mark Twain
Mary Austin
Mary Catherine Crowley
Mary Cole
Mary Hastings Bradley
Mary Roberts Rinehart
Mary Rowlandson
M. Wollstonecraft Shelley
Maud Lindsay
Max Beerbohm
Myra Kelly
Nathaniel Hawthrone
Nicolo Machiavelli
O. F. Walton
Oscar Wilde

Owen Johnson
P.G. Wodehouse
Paul and Mabel Thorne
Paul G. Tomlinson
Paul Severing
Percy Brebner
Percy Keese Fitzhugh
Peter B. Kyne
Plato
Quincy Allen
R. Derby Holmes
R. L. Stevenson
R. S. Ball
Rabindranath Tagore
Rahul Alvares
Ralph Bonehill
Ralph Henry Barbour
Ralph Victor
Ralph Waldo Emmerson
Rene Descartes
Ray Cummings
Rex Beach
Rex E. Beach
Richard Harding Davis
Richard Jefferies
Richard Le Gallienne
Robert Barr
Robert Frost
Robert Gordon Anderson
Robert L. Drake
Robert Lansing
Robert Lynd
Robert Michael Ballantyne
Robert W. Chambers
Rosa Nouchette Carey
Rudyard Kipling
Saint Augustine
Samuel B. Allison
Samuel Hopkins Adams
Sarah Bernhardt
Sarah C. Hallowell
Selma Lagerlof
Sherwood Anderson
Sigmund Freud
Standish O'Grady
Stanley Weyman
Stella Benson
Stella M. Francis

Stephen Crane
Stewart Edward White
Stijn Streuvels
Swami Abhedananda
Swami Parmananda
T. S. Ackland
T. S. Arthur
The Princess Der Ling
Thomas A. Janvier
Thomas A Kempis
Thomas Anderton
Thomas Bailey Aldrich
Thomas Bulfinch
Thomas De Quincey
Thomas Dixon
Thomas H. Huxley
Thomas Hardy
Thomas More
Thornton W. Burgess
U. S. Grant
Upton Sinclair
Valentine Williams
Various Authors
Vaughan Kester
Victor Appleton
Victor G. Durham
Victoria Cross
Virginia Woolf
Wadsworth Camp
Walter Camp
Walter Scott
Washington Irving
Wilbur Lawton
Wilkie Collins
Willa Cather
Willard F. Baker
William Dean Howells
William le Queux
W. Makepeace Thackeray
William W. Walter
William Shakespeare
Winston Churchill
Yei Theodora Ozaki
Yogi Ramacharaka
Young E. Allison
Zane Grey